Callum

The Craigdon Family Dynasty

Book One

CHRIS TAYLOR

LCT Productions Pty Ltd
18364 Kamilaroi Highway, Narrabri NSW 2390

ISBN. 978-1-925119-74-9 (Paperback)

Callum is a work of fiction. Names, characters, places, brands, media and incidents either are the product of the author's imagination or are used fictitiously. Any resemblance to actual persons, living or dead, events, or locales, is entirely coincidental.

Published in the United States of America.

Books by Chris Taylor

THE MUNRO FAMILY SERIES
The Profiler
The Investigator
The Predator
The Betrayal
The Deception
The Negotiator
The Christmas Vigil
The Ransom
The Defendant
The Shooting
The Maker
(Available in Audio)

THE SYDNEY HARBOUR HOSPITAL SERIES
The Perfect Husband
The Body Thief
The Baby Snatchers
The Final Bullet
The Debt Collector
The Lab Test
The Stolen Identity
The Cliff-top Killer
The Likeable Fraudster

THE SYDNEY LEGAL SERIES
An Accidental Murderer
At the Hand of Her Father
A Woman Scorned
Lies and Deception
Ordinary Evil
The Ties That Bind
The Perfect Crime
A Toxic Inheritance
Malicious Love

THE CRAIGDON FAMILY SERIES
Callum
Joel
Isabella
Nicholas
Sophia
Flynn
Noah
Logan
Elizabeth

THE BARRINGTON FAMILY SERIES
Broken Lives
Broken Promises
Broken Bonds
Broken Spirits
Broken Vows
Broken Minds
Broken Dreams
Broken Hearts
Broken Homes

Chris Taylor writing as
BELLA CHRISTIAN

THIS IS WHERE IT ENDS SERIES
(in order)
Jessie's Story
Ryan's Story
Holly's Story
Sarah's Story
Veronica's Story

Get a FREE book when you sign up for Chris Taylor's
newsletter at: www.christaylorauthor.com.au

Love Audiobooks? Check out Chris Taylor Books on audio on Audible.com, Amazon.com and Apple Books.

Join Chris Taylor's Facebook reader group/fan page and be among the first to receive news of book releases, read and review books prior to release and other amazing offers. Join Now at: www.facebook.com/groups/1758023621144744/

Find out more about all of Chris Taylor's books, by visiting her website at: www.christaylorauthor.com.au

Dedication

This book is dedicated to my wonderful and supportive friends, Sue Ricardo and Ally Thomson and my big sister, Nic Guihot. Thank you for always being there for me and for your help in making Callum the hero we all knew he could be.

And as always, to my husband, Linden. My best friend, my soul mate. I love you to the moon and back.

Acknowledgments

As usual, no book comes into being without a lot of help and support by my friends and family. A world of thanks must go to my wonderful editor, Pat Thomas. Thank you for everything that you do to make my stories even more amazing than I could ever dare to dream. To former Detective Superintendent Michael Kilfoyle, thank you for lending my story credibility. Any mistakes are wholly my own.

To Mary and all of the team at Miblart, thank you for the fantastic book cover. To my sister, Nicole Guihot and to my friends, Ally Thomson and Sue Ricardo, thank you for your excellent editorial comments, proof reading skills and suggestions. I hope you like the final result.

To Amy Atwell, Kirby and the dedicated team at Author E.M.S. who are so much more than book formatters. Amy, once again, thank you for your magic.

To the fantastic writer organizations such as Romance Writers of Australia, Romance Writers of America and Romance Writers of New Zealand for all the help, support and encouragement they offer new and aspiring writers, including me.

To my readers, thank you for your support and love for my stories. Your encouragement and enjoyment make this journey all worthwhile.

And lastly, to my friends and family, especially my husband and children. Thank you for putting up with late dinners and even later conversations as I've emerged day after day from the sometimes scary but always enthralling world I've created on my computer.

Chapter One

In keeping with the somber occasion, the mood inside the late Henry Craigdon's study was dark and solemn. Late afternoon sunlight filtered through the closed curtains and cast gloomy shadows across the room. The air was faintly stuffy, as if the windows had been closed against the fresh air for too long. Given Henry had been dead for the better part of a week, it was highly likely they had been.

Callum Craigdon helped his mother into one of the studded, dark leather, high-backed chairs favored by his late father.

"Are you comfortable, Mom?" he murmured in an effort to distract himself.

"I'm fine, Callum."

"Can I get you anything? A coffee?" He smiled slightly. "Something stronger?"

She shook her head. "No, thanks. I just want to get this over with."

Despite the fact Elizabeth Craigdon had buried her husband of thirty-three years only hours earlier, her expression was calm and controlled, if not a little grim. She sat dry-eyed, ramrod straight with her hands folded in her lap and her gaze fixed on the family lawyer who'd taken residence behind Henry's carved cedar desk.

The attorney, John Edgerton Junior, looked out of place there. Small of stature, balding and with none of the air of authority Henry had exuded in life, Callum had always been curious about how the wiry, unassuming attorney had landed the prestigious position of Craigdon family lawyer. Now that his father was dead, Callum supposed he'd never know.

With his mother settled, he took the empty seat beside her. He glanced over his shoulder at the rest of his family who'd gathered *en masse* for the reading of Henry's will. The Craigdon women, in their expensive designer dresses with carefully selected, matching accessories, were black from head to toe. The men, his brothers and cousins and uncle, were dressed in equally expensive, dark and somber suits.

Additional chairs had been borrowed from the formal dining room and hastily placed in preparation for the reading of the will. The air was filled with sadness, expectation and an undeniable tension. In life, Henry Craigdon had been unpredictable. No one quite knew what to expect upon his death.

Callum's oldest brother, Jett, sat stiffly beside his wife. Danielle patted at a few tears that slid down her cheeks. In the three years since they'd been married, Danielle had gotten to know her father-in-law a little and was saddened by his untimely death. Or perhaps the funeral had merely brought back unhappy memories of the day she'd buried her sister a few years earlier. She wasn't the only one who appeared upset, although not all of Henry's family were distraught at his parting. The knowledge filled Callum with a sudden rush of nerves.

At twenty-eight, Joel was two years younger than Callum and was Henry and Elizabeth's third-born child. He'd defied Henry's expectations to follow his maternal grandfather into law and had opted for police service instead. Now a detective, he was well on the way to a prestigious career in a job he loved and Callum was pleased for him. He also admired him. It wasn't easy to stand up to their father at any time, let alone for something as important as a career decision. Callum ought to know.

A soft sniffle behind him snagged his attention. He turned and gave his sister, Isabella, a comforting glance. Of all of Henry's six children, Isabella had been closest to their father. Hours after the funeral, she still hid behind an oversized pair of black Versace sunglasses, occasionally dabbing at her cheeks with a white lace handkerchief. She clung to their brother, Nicholas, who stared straight ahead, stony faced.

The lawyer cleared his throat and shuffled a sheaf of papers. "Are we all here?" he asked politely.

As the self-appointed spokesman, Callum opened his mouth to respond in the affirmative, but before he could do so a slight disturbance issued from the other side of the closed door. A moment later, the long-serving family butler, Gregory, entered the room looking harried.

"I'm sorry, Mrs Craigdon. I tried to tell Mr Barrington this was a private meeting for family only, but he insisted."

Before Callum's mother could reply, Christopher Barrington pushed into the room, forcing Gregory to step aside.

"And I tried to tell him I was just as much family to the dear departed Henry Craigdon as the rest of you. After all, I *am* his first born. That gives me more claim to the word 'family' than some of you." Christopher's voice dripped with sarcasm. He looked pointedly around the room at each in turn, as if daring them to disagree.

Callum swallowed a groan. Behind him, two of his brothers muttered oaths. It was just like Christopher to leave out the bit about his illegitimacy.

"I went looking for you and couldn't find you," Jett explained.

Christopher sneered. "You couldn't have looked too hard. I was in the bathroom. Now you've decided to start without me. How convenient."

His half-brother's eyes were red, but Callum knew it wasn't from crying. Christopher's cheeks were flushed and as he moved further into the room, he stumbled. When he came level with Callum, it was all Callum could do not to turn away from the overpowering fumes of alcohol.

Callum glanced at his mother, gaging her reaction. He was relieved but not surprised to discover she remained calm, her expression placid. The meds their family doctor had prescribed for her earlier had taken effect. She offered Christopher a gracious smile.

"Of course, Christopher. Come in. Take a seat. You're just in time."

The lawyer cleared his throat again. "I'd like to thank everyone for coming. Henry was very clear that he wanted his whole family present, including his extended family."

Edgerton looked around the room, acknowledging various family members, including Callum's cousin Flynn, who was also a lawyer, cousins Noah and Logan, as well as Callum's Uncle Archie and Callum's youngest sibling, Sophia.

"Right. Let's get started." With that, Edgerton unfolded an official-looking document and began to read.

"The last Will and Testament of Henry Francis John Craigdon. The will is dated 18 November, 2019." Edgerton glanced up a little nervously. "Just so you know, Henry attended my office three months ago and instructed me to make a few alterations to his will. This is that document."

A ripple of shock rolled through the room, sweeping over all of the occupants. Callum's mother tensed beside him. Callum stilled momentarily and then let the wave of disquiet pass over him. He was more than halfway through his studies at the Catholic seminary, having already completed a theology degree.

In a few more years, he'd be ordained a priest. One of his vows, when he took them, would be a vow of poverty. The truth was, he didn't care one way or the other about the outcome of his father's will. He was only there to support his mother and the rest of the Craigdon clan. Still, the knowledge that Henry had changed his will such a short time ago was troubling.

Why would Dad do such a thing? What had happened to precipitate the visit to his attorney? Was it a good sign or a bad one that changes had been made? Had his mother known?

Callum glanced around at the assembled family members and saw the very same questions playing across their faces. He swallowed a sigh and reached for his mother's hand. He gave it a reassuring squeeze and prayed there weren't too many more surprises.

"I appoint my son Callum Henry Craigdon and my nephew Flynn Archibald Craigdon joint executors and administrators of my estate." The lawyer looked up briefly and then continued.

"To my oldest son, Jett Francis Craigdon, I leave the sum of ten million dollars."

Christopher immediately jumped to his feet, his face flushed with anger. "This is an outrage! That son of a bitch! How dare he? *I'm* the oldest son!"

Through his horn-rimmed glasses, Edgerton gave Christopher a steely eyed glare. For all of the lawyer's pint-sized presence, it was obvious he was a man who brooked no disobedience. *Perhaps that's why Dad had him on the payroll?*

"Mr Barrington, would you please sit down. If you're hell bent on uncontrollable outbursts, I'm afraid I'm going to have to ask you to leave. There's a lot to get through. I can't have you interrupting every time I say something that displeases you. Do you understand?"

Christopher's breath came fast. Color continued to heighten

his cheeks, but with a show of reluctance, he regained his seat.

"Right. Let's continue." Edgerton once again looked down at the papers in his hand. "To my son, Callum Henry Craigdon I leave the sum of ten million dollars."

Callum gasped in shock, his thoughts in turmoil. *Ten million dollars? What would a priest need with ten million dollars?* His father had been raised a strict Catholic. He knew better than anyone that a priest wouldn't be able to accept such a gift. Okay, so Callum hadn't gotten to the point where he'd made his final vows, but that was in his future. *Wasn't it?* That's what his father had always wanted. In fact, Henry had wanted his ordination more than Callum…

Callum shied away from the thought. Somehow, only hours after his father's funeral, it felt disloyal. Over the years, Callum had let his dreams of becoming a police officer fade and had embraced the life of the clergy. He'd finished his theology degree with honors and was excelling in his coursework at the seminary. If occasionally he thought wistfully of his earlier dreams, they were swiftly forced aside. This was the life he wanted. This was the life his father had promised God.

The lawyer continued reading and Callum forced himself to concentrate.

"To my son, Joel Fitzwilliam Craigdon I leave the sum of ten million dollars."

Callum glanced toward his brother and noted Joel's nod of satisfaction. So far, their father had been more than generous and completely fair. A little of Callum's tension eased.

"To my daughter, Isabella Louise Craigdon I leave the sum of twenty million dollars."

There was a collective gasp from those gathered in the study. Callum swiveled his head toward Isabella. She'd removed her sunglasses and her red-rimmed eyes were wide with shock and confusion. She looked as stunned as the rest of them.

So much for Dad being fair…

Of course, they all knew Isabella had been Henry's favorite. No one could work out why. After all, she wasn't his only daughter. It had always remained a mystery to Callum, but no one could deny it was true. Not even Isabella.

The closeness between Isabella and their father had been apparent for as long as Callum could remember. Growing up, she'd been his shadow. He'd showered her with love and affection. Such obvious favoritism might have caused resentment among her siblings, but as far as Callum was aware, none of them saw it that way. The fact their father doted on Isabella wasn't her fault. If anything, it said more about his character than hers. It was just one of those unexplained shortcomings their father possessed. To be wondered about, but never questioned.

As if oblivious to the mood that now permeated the room, the lawyer kept reading.

"To my son, Nicholas James Craigdon I leave the sum of one million dollars."

Another shocked gasp filled the room, followed by a murmur of angry voices. Callum blinked.

What the hell were you thinking, Dad? Twenty million to Isabella and a paltry one million to her brother? And yet a generous ten million to your other three sons?

It was even worse than he'd thought. He glanced over his shoulder toward Sophia. Her face looked like it was carved from granite. It was no secret among them that Sophia had been Henry's least favorite. While their father thought Isabella had hung the moon and stars, it had always seemed Sophia could do nothing right.

And it wasn't like she didn't try hard to impress him. In Callum's opinion, she probably tried too hard. Like the time she'd designed, printed and then hand-delivered thousands of glossy flyers to all the letterboxes within a five-mile radius of their father's latest development—a block of apartments with a minimum asking price of two million dollars for the most modest one. Too young to hold a driver's license, Sophia had walked an accumulation of more than thirty miles to get the job done.

She'd returned to the offices of Craigdon Enterprises, tired and sore but proud of her efforts only to be met by Henry who couldn't have shown less interest in her achievement. Callum had been in the office the day Sophia had returned from her massive enterprise and had watched their father's reaction. Dismissing his daughter's efforts with a few disparaging words had made Callum heartsick for her, at the sadness and disappointment that flooded her young face. She'd been all of thirteen. *Couldn't he have acknowledged what she'd done? Thanked her?* Apparently not. Callum could only hope he'd treated Sophia better in his final will and testament. They were about to find out.

"To Sophia Elizabeth Craigdon I leave the sum of one hundred thousand dollars."

Sophia's gasp was audible in the suddenly silent room. If they'd been shocked at the way Henry had treated Nicholas, they were stunned speechless by what had been done to Sophia.

Callum bowed his head in despair and sent up a silent prayer for his father's soul. *Oh, Dad. Oh, no. How could you? How could you be so hurtful?*

Of course, to those who knew him, Henry's cruelty toward his youngest daughter wasn't surprising. He'd been hurtful toward her all her life. Sometimes one or another of them would try and intervene, to diffuse the anger Henry seemed to feel toward her, but they rarely succeeded. Just as they tried to understand his adoration of Isabella, none of the family could work out any reason for his antagonism toward Sophia.

Of course, a hundred thousand dollars was a large sum of money and one most people would have been grateful to receive. But when compared to the millions already gifted to other members of the family, it was an insult and Callum was certain Sophia would regard it as such. It seemed she'd irritated him right to the very end.

He stole another glance in her direction. She stared blindly toward the wall of books that lined one side of their father's study. Her beautiful brown eyes were filled with pain. Silent tears slid down her cheeks. Callum's veins throbbed with anger. It was wrong to wish ill of the dead, but right then he could have happily throttled Henry Craigdon.

And then he was flooded with guilt. He bowed his head and silently prayed for forgiveness. Callum's father was far from perfect, but each and every one of them had flaws. It wasn't Callum's job to pass judgment. He'd leave that to a higher power.

Ignoring the muffled conversation and anger that swirled around the room, Edgerton continued in the same measured tone.

"In the event Sophia Elizabeth Craigdon chooses to marry and remains married for a minimum period of twelve months and convinces her mother, Elizabeth Georgina Louise Craigdon and her brother, Callum Henry Craigdon the marriage is real in every sense, she will receive an additional five million dollars."

Callum's gut clenched. *So it wasn't as bad as it first appeared. But still, to tie the gift to such a condition… It was barbaric. Poor Sophia.*

He glanced at his mother. Her mouth was tight with tension and anger smoldered in her eyes. Callum reached for her hand again.

"To my wife, Elizabeth Georgina Louise Craigdon I leave a life interest in the family estate situated at 22 Richmond Valley Way, Richmond. Upon her death, this property will revert to my daughter, Isabella Louise Craigdon."

Once again, a ripple of shock went through the occupants of the room. Callum felt his mother tense beside him and saw her jaw tighten at the affront. His father owned a billion-dollar company. To be left only a life interest in her home was an insult. Surely there must be more for her in the will. Callum tightened his hold on his mother's hand and stared straight ahead, once again willing his anger away.

"To my nephews, Flynn Archibald Craigdon and Noah Duncan Craigdon, I give the sum of one million dollars each."

Callum's eyebrows lifted in surprise. He hadn't expected his father to leave his cousins anything. There had always been a rivalry between his father and his brother, their Uncle Archie, and that rivalry had often been unpleasant. As far as Callum knew, his father hadn't been particularly close to his brother's sons either. Still, it was nice of him to leave them something. And though it wasn't overly generous in the scheme of things, it was more than he'd left Sophia.

His gaze cut to Flynn and Noah, seated in the back row beside their brother, Logan. The men murmured among themselves in low voices, but they appeared pleased at the unexpected gift. And then Callum realized Logan had been left out.

For heaven's sake, Dad. What were you thinking? How can you give two of your nephews a million dollars each and leave the third one out in the cold? How could you be so mean? I should have pulled you up for your bad behavior more often. We all should have. Callum couldn't bear to turn around to face his cousin.

After adjusting his glasses on his nose, the lawyer continued to read aloud. "I bequeath the sum of fifteen million dollars to the Stella Taunton House for Widows and Orphans."

Callum glanced at his mother and frowned. She gave a brief shake of her head, looking as confused as he felt. He'd never heard of the Stella Taunton House for Widows and Orphans. He didn't know such charitable institutions still existed. Even more surprising was that his father had bequeathed to it such a generous sum of money. For all his incredible wealth and purported belief in Catholic teachings, Henry Craigdon hadn't been known for his altruism and philanthropy. The bequest was completely baffling.

Once again, Callum looked over his shoulder toward the rest of his family. Jett shrugged. Joel shook his head. Isabella's gaze remained fixed on the floor. Nicholas looked perplexed and Sophia continued to look stony-faced. It appeared his brothers and sisters were as clueless as he was about the unexpected gift. Callum turned back to face the lawyer.

Edgerton moved the sheaf of papers around in his hand and shifted in his seat. He glanced at the gathering and then just as quickly looked away.

"Is that all?" Callum asked politely.

The lawyer shook his head. "Not quite." Once again, his gaze darted away.

Callum frowned, wondering what had sparked the man's sudden bout of nervousness. *Surely there can't be another bombshell?* As the attorney began once again to read aloud, Callum braced himself for the worst.

"Lastly, to Logan Henry Craigdon I give, devise and bequeath the rest and residue of my estate including but not limited to my company, Craigdon Enterprises, my bank accounts, my motor vehicles, my super yacht and any other property owned by me or by Craigdon Enterprises at the time of my death."

"What?"

The cry of disbelief came from Logan himself. Callum

swiveled in his chair and stared at his cousin. He thought he must have misheard the lawyer until he started to take in the identical looks of shock and confusion that painted the faces of his family. Callum turned back to the lawyer, seeking clarification.

"Did you just say Dad left the balance of his estate, including Craigdon Enterprises, to Logan?"

The attorney nodded briskly. "Yes."

"But…" Logan said weakly from the back row. "How could that be? I'm his nephew. What about Nicholas? This doesn't make sense. There must be some mistake. Craigdon Enterprises is worth a fortune."

Edgerton packed up the papers, shuffling them into a neat pile before setting them inside his leather briefcase.

"You're right, Mr Craigdon. At the time of the last estimate, it was guessed Craigdon Enterprises was worth just over a billion dollars. And please be assured, there's been no mistake. Your uncle was very clear that you were to receive the bulk of his estate."

"What about *me*?" Christopher cried. He jumped to his feet, knocking over his chair as he did so. His eyes were wild. His face was suffused with anger. "*I'm* his firstborn child. The fucking prick didn't even mention me! It's like I don't exist!"

Seated on the other side of Elizabeth, Callum's Uncle Archie leaned toward her, a sad and rueful smile turning up his lips. "He didn't mention me, either and I'm his only brother. You don't see me getting upset," he murmured. Elizabeth's expression was strained, but she patted his hand gently.

Christopher stormed his way to the front of the room. "I don't give a shit about you, old man," he sneered. "Your brother was a prick. You know what, I'm *glad* he's dead. Good riddance to bad rubbish."

Isabella gasped, her face pale. Her eyes sparkled with anger. "Christopher! How dare you! Show some respect! That's our father you're talking about."

"It's all right for you, little Miss Goody Two Shoes. Daddy saw fit to leave you millions."

Callum got to his feet. He held up his hands for a show of calm and spoke in a placating tone. "Christopher, mate. Take a breather. This isn't the time or place. Everyone's hurting; everyone's stressed. Dad's fresh in the ground. Can't we at least be civil to one another, today of all days?"

Christopher's eyes flashed with anger. "Civil? You heard what he did! That mean old bastard didn't even mention me! He named Jett his oldest son! What an insult! He—"

"You're right," Callum interrupted, maintaining his calm tone. "It was unforgivable. But today is his funeral. Let's give him this day, at least."

Christopher stared Callum down, his chest still heaving with the force of his anger. But gradually, the fury in his eyes subsided to a dull glow.

Callum slowly released a breath. "How about you call it a day, mate? We've all had a rough time of it, Mom included."

Christopher cut his eyes to Elizabeth, who remained seated, her expression revealing her sadness that even in death, Henry had pitted his children against each other, causing anguish. Christopher's shoulders slumped in defeat. As if coming to a decision, he compressed his lips and nodded, his expression grim.

"Okay, I'll leave. But only out of respect for you, Elizabeth." He glared at the other members of the family, now gathering close, as if circling the wagons. "As for the rest of you, this isn't the end of this. I have just as much right as you do to a piece of my father's estate. You'll be hearing from my lawyer." With that, Christopher spun on his heel and stalked out of the room, slamming the door behind him.

Chapter Two

The sound of the slamming door echoed through the room. Elizabeth stood and brushed out the skirt of her Calvin Klein black linen dress and offered Callum a wan smile.

"Well, I guess that's that. Thank you, son, for dealing with Christopher. I feel for him, I really do. He's been treated appallingly by your father, but I'm afraid I've had about all I can take for one day."

Callum kissed her. At sixty, with a slim, athletic figure, keen intelligence and a headful of thick, immaculately coiffed white hair, she was still a force to be reckoned with, but he saw the weariness in her gaze and the wrinkles that had deepened into lines across her forehead and at the corners of her eyes. It had been a long day for all of them. In fact, it had been a long week.

Ever since they'd been given the news that Henry had dropped dead of a heart attack, sleep for Callum had been fitful. He'd barely managed a few hours each night and woke to face each morning with eyes that were dry and gritty. He could only imagine how difficult it was for his mother.

He'd been the first she'd called when the police gave her the news. He wasn't the oldest in the family, but as a priest in training, his mother seemed to gravitate toward him whenever she was troubled or in need of advice. They'd always been close.

It had been up to Callum to notify his brothers and sisters about their father's death. Henry Craigdon had been sixty-five and though he'd been carrying a few extra pounds, he'd never been sick in his life. His death had come as a shock to everyone. And now they were here.

The day had faded fast, along with the remaining members of his family. Fatigue was etched into their faces, along with varying degrees of sadness, resignation and anger. Shadows had lengthened outside the study window. A gentle summer breeze lifted the leaves of an ancient Moreton Bay fig tree, reminding Callum of the perfect weather they'd been blessed with on the day they buried their father.

Edgerton packed up his papers and dropped them into his briefcase. He offered his quiet sympathies to Callum's mother and bid farewell l to the rest of the family before Gregory was asked to see him out. Callum sighed wearily and rubbed at his eyes. He hoped now that the funeral and the other formalities were over, he might finally be able to find some oblivion in sleep. No doubt the family would want to discuss the terms of the will, but right at that moment, he didn't think he could summon the energy required to reassure those who needed reassurance, pacify those who were angry and sympathize with those who were still locked in their grief.

Then Sophia pushed her way to the front and came to a stop before him, her eyes flashing fire. Callum swallowed a groan and braced himself for her outburst.

"I don't believe it! I just don't believe it! How *could* he?" she cried.

Callum regarded her wearily. "It's been a long day, Soph. Everyone's had enough. I understand your disappointment, but can we leave this discussion for another time? I'm beat and so is Mom. She needs to rest."

Sophia turned her angry gaze upon their mother. "Rest?

Really, Mom? How can you think about rest at a time like this! Daddy did you over almost as good as he did me! How can you stand there so calmly, as if it doesn't *matter*?"

"Of course it matters," Elizabeth replied in a moderate tone. "But what do you want me to do about it, honey? The only way to change it is to challenge the terms of the will. We could be tied up in the courts for years, airing our dirty laundry and there's no guarantee the result would be any more to our liking. Is that what you want?"

"She's right," Flynn replied, coming up beside them. "Supreme Court matters can take years."

Sophia appeared unconvinced, her face still flushed with anger. "So, you're just going to sit back and accept it? Is that what you're planning to do?" She turned to encompass the whole group. There were shrugs and mutterings, but no one seemed brave enough to come right out in support of her. Once again, Callum tried to pacify her.

"Soph, do you really think this is the time for that discussion? Let's just try and get through the rest of this day. Tomorrow will be soon enough for other conversations. You're not the only one with questions about why Dad left his estate the way he did."

Most of Callum's siblings turned to look at Logan. A couple of them looked at Isabella. On a surge of impatience, Callum shook his head.

"I'm not talking about anyone in particular and I surely don't begrudge anyone their inheritance. I'm just as confused about what Dad left me as anyone. I mean, I'm going to become a priest. He knew that. He also knew I couldn't accept his gift."

"Maybe it's his way of releasing you from his promise." The quiet comment came from Isabella.

Callum looked at her, his mouth gaping in shock. "What did you say?"

Isabella's gaze skittered away from his. When she spoke again, she sounded far less sure of herself.

"We all know that when you were a newborn Daddy promised God He could have you for a priest if He saved your life, right?"

Callum nodded cautiously, still uncertain about where this was headed. He glanced at his mother.

"Isabella's right," Elizabeth replied. "You were born eight weeks premature. The doctors told us there was a good chance you might not live. We were told to prepare ourselves for the fact you wouldn't pull through. Your father spent the night on his knees in the chapel. He made a bargain with God. If He saved you, your father would see to it that you became a priest."

"It's an old, familiar story, Mom," Callum said tiredly. He glanced back at Isabella. "What does it have to do with Dad leaving me ten million dollars?"

"It's like you said," Isabella continued. "Dad knew better than most the deal he'd made. You grew up knowing it was expected that you enter the priesthood." She shrugged. "We all did."

"For a while there, I wanted to be a police officer," Callum said quietly.

Isabella grimaced. "Yeah. Well, Dad had other plans."

"And God," Callum added. "I'd like to think our Almighty approves of me becoming a priest."

"Yeah, whatever," Isabella replied. "Anyway, we all know it was more what Dad wanted than your desire to spend your life serving God. As you said, at one stage you wanted to join the police force, like Joel and Jett."

Callum cut his gaze toward his oldest brother. Jett stood with his arm around his wife, holding her close. Callum had always admired his older brother. It was the main reason he'd wanted to follow him into policing. God and his father had other plans.

Now his father had left him ten million dollars. Callum was sure it had been a deliberate decision. Henry Craigdon was a shrewd and intelligent man. He didn't create a billion-dollar business by not being smart. He'd left Callum a massive amount of money. Money he had no need of, nor could he accept.

What does it all mean?

Isabella continued. "The more I think about it, the more I believe this is Dad's way of releasing you from his promise. He knew it wasn't your first career choice. He also knew you'd agreed more to appease him than because it was what you felt called to do. Being a priest is a vocation. It's not something you can force yourself into. Don't you agree, Mom?"

"Yes," she concurred.

"But you were behind Dad all the way!" Callum protested. "You encouraged me to take up the vocation."

"I encouraged you to pray and ask God for guidance during your journey. And yes, I supported your father in his quest to see you become a priest." She wrung her hands together. "You need to understand how worried we were that you wouldn't survive those first few weeks of life. We both prayed endlessly. Your father made his promise and I supported him in it. When you pulled through and grew into a strong and healthy child, I thought honoring your father's bargain with God was the least we could do."

Callum shook his head slowly back and forth. "But it doesn't work like that, Mom. You can't force yourself to embrace a career or a lifestyle just because someone wants you to. Nicholas can't stand the sight of blood." He turned to where Nicholas stood beside Joel. "He would never have made a doctor, no matter how much you or Dad might have wished it."

"It's not quite the same, Callum," Elizabeth remonstrated.

A wave of irritation washed over him. "Of course it is,

Mom. The only difference is some bargain Dad made with God. Okay, so I understand when you have a sick child you'll do anything to see them well, even making ridiculous promises to God you might or might not keep, but I got better Mom. I grew into a man. I had hopes and dreams of my own that didn't necessarily align with Dad's. Or yours."

His words held a faint note of accusation.

A stain of embarrassment, or maybe shame, stole across his mother's cheeks. The sight of it brought an end to Callum's rising anger. This wasn't his mother's fault and the last thing he wanted was to hurt her. He should have stood up to his father, found the same kind of courage Joel had.

As the years went on, it was easier to go along with his father's plans and if Callum were honest, he'd come to embrace the life of a seminarian, even if it hadn't been his first choice.

But now he'd been thrust into a tailspin. His head whirled with confusion. He glanced at his mother. She looked distressed.

"I'm sorry, Mom," he muttered and pulled her in for a brief hug. "I didn't mean to upset you. You and Dad did what you thought best." He grimaced. "I think I've even convinced myself that being a priest is the best thing for me. That it's not only the fulfillment of a promise. It's God's will."

His mother looked stricken. "Oh, Callum! I'm so sorry! You shouldn't need to convince yourself of anything and especially not about something as life changing as becoming a priest! Why didn't you say something sooner?"

Callum regarded her grimly. "You're right. I should have. I guess I wanted to make Dad proud of me. Becoming a priest was something he wanted me to do." He shrugged. "I didn't want to let anyone down."

"Oh, son!" Elizabeth cried, looking even more distressed. "We've always been proud of the good and decent man you've become. You don't need to become a priest to be that."

"That's not how it felt, Mom," Callum mumbled.

There was an uncomfortable silence. His brothers and sisters stared at the floor. No one knew what to say. They didn't want to come out against their mother, especially on the day of their father's funeral, but all of them had grown up knowing the truth.

"How about we go and find something to eat?" Joel finally suggested. "I'm sure there are plenty of leftovers."

A murmur of agreement quickly followed and people began to head for the door, grateful for the distraction. The wake had been catered by a premium catering company. A buffet lunch had been set up on the long sideboard in the formal dining room. Many of the platters were still laden with food.

Among murmured conversations, Callum's family set about filling their plates. Even with a number of the dining room chairs remaining in the study, there was plenty of room for everyone to be seated around the impressive Tasmanian oak table.

The mansion his mother had just inherited wasn't where Callum had spent the early years of his childhood, but the family had lived there long enough for it to feel like home. The suburb of Richmond was about an hour's drive from the city of Sydney, perched at the base of the Blue Mountains. Privately nestled in one of Richmond's most prestigious dress-circles, the Craigdon family sanctuary showcased magnificent proportions and rich historical significance.

Erected *circa* 1927, Craigdon Manor displayed all the hallmarks of its impressive Art Deco architectural period, including rounded corners and stylized geometric detailing. The three-story house was set across an expansive six hectares, with stately grounds that incorporated a full-size tennis court, golf course, heated pool and spa. It even had an elevator.

There was no doubt it was a grand place to live, but that didn't mean the halls had always rung freely with laughter.

Callum stared down at the empty plate in his hand. He hadn't eaten all day, but the thought of food right now didn't appeal. His mind still spun with confusion and the questions that would likely never be answered.

What does it all mean? What did Dad want me to do? What do I *want to do?*

"So, what are you planning to do with your inheritance, Callum?"

The question came from Flynn. Callum blinked in an effort to clear his head. He shrugged. "I don't know what I'm going to do yet," he admitted truthfully.

"Fair enough, but back there it sounded like you'd already made up your mind about the priesthood."

Irritated, Callum stared at his cousin. "I haven't made up my mind about anything."

Flynn held his hands up in a sign of surrender. "Hey, that's cool. I'm just curious." He shot Callum a rueful grin. "I'm just saying, for all Uncle Henry's faults and failings, he never struck me as stupid. For what it's worth, I agree with Isabella. I think your father knew exactly what he was doing when he left you that money."

Could it be true? Had his father really orchestrated such an overwhelming and unexpected act of kindness? Callum had loved his father and had much admiration for what he'd achieved, but he wasn't blind to the fact Henry didn't always act honorably. And he wasn't always nice.

During the years after high school and before Callum finally bit the bullet and began his theology degree, he'd worked for Craigdon Enterprises. Mainly in an administrative capacity rather than on construction sites, but he'd managed to see quite a lot of his father in Henry's own environment. It hadn't always been pretty.

Callum lost count of the number of young, attractive secretaries who spent inordinate amounts of time in his father's office with the blinds drawn. More often than not they came out still adjusting their clothing, some of them with secretive, self-satisfied smiles on their faces.

There were other character weaknesses, too. Henry was hot-tempered and quick to assign blame. Anyone who fell short of his expectations or didn't perform to the level of excellence he expected was publicly roasted, humiliated and forced to resign, with or without proof of any wrong-doing. It was a gross abuse of power and quite frankly, illegal, but it happened time and time again. All these years later, it still weighed heavily on Callum's conscience that he'd failed to stand up to his father and call out such abhorrent behavior.

And yet, now it seemed Henry had finally attempted to redeem himself, at least with Callum, and had offered his son a precious gift that had nothing to do with the money. The question was, did Callum want to avail himself of it?

Once again, he was overcome with a wall of confusion. His head thumped from lack of sleep and the stress that he'd been burdened with all day. He'd been strong for his mother and his siblings, but the cracks were beginning to show. The turmoil caused by his father's will had only exacerbated things.

Setting aside his empty plate, he mumbled an apology toward the rest of his family and headed for the exit.

"Callum? Where are you going?" his mother asked, her tone one of concern.

"I need some fresh air," he managed and kept going.

Once outside, he gulped in huge lungfuls of air. A profusion of flowers that bordered the paved walkway that led to the turning circle filled the air with their heavy perfume. His nose twitched and his eyes watered. He let out an almighty sneeze.

Locating his mother's SUV, parked outside one of the three-car garages, he slipped inside the vehicle and switched on the ignition. She'd offered him the use of the car whenever he wanted and right now he had to get away. The pressure of the past week had gotten to him. He needed to clear his head before he said or did something unforgivable. He needed to regain the control he was famous for, the same control his family relied upon. And he needed to do it now.

Chapter Three

Callum squinted through the darkness at the oncoming traffic. Though rush hour was over, there were still plenty of people out and about in their vehicles. The bright headlights hurt his eyes and intensified the pain in his head. He was so tired. He longed for a soft, warm place to curl up, to hide away from the world until he had a chance to think through the implications of the past couple of hours and what it might mean for his future.

He couldn't deny the appeal of leaving the seminary and forging a path of his own choosing. On the other hand, he'd already spent eight years studying—with the end goal of becoming a priest.

Do I really want to throw all that time and effort and sacrifice away?

There had definitely been plenty of sacrifice. Though he was naturally quiet and reserved and had always looked out for others, it had taken a strength of will and countless prayers to not only accept, but to embrace the priestly way of life. There had been many times when he didn't think he'd make it. Many times when he'd approached his tutors and suggested it might be best for him to quit, but each time he'd been gently persuaded to pray about it and leave it in the hands of God.

Now it appeared his father had given him another way out.

The knowledge still made his head spin. He wished he had the smallest clue what to do about it.

The traffic lights changed to green and he hit the accelerator. The car leaped forward. With no clear destination, Callum sped up and slowed down and changed lanes at will. He left the traffic behind him as he made his way deeper into the suburbs. A long straight stretch of road lay ahead of him. It bordered a park that was often frequented by drug dealers and people looking to score. Most of the streetlights were broken and the place was filled with shadows. It made the perfect setting for an illicit meeting.

Every now and then there was a murder there when a drug deal went awfully wrong. It usually made the six o'clock news and served as a reminder to the rest of the community that the park wasn't the kind of place anyone should choose to hang around. He had no business being there and he sure as heck didn't want to find himself in the middle of any trouble. He'd had more than enough excitement for one day.

Depressing the accelerator, he sped up in an effort to clear the park. A man appeared from nowhere, stumbling into his path. Before he could brake the car collided with the man, sending him flying onto the hood of the car. The sickening thump of the man's body as he bounced off the windscreen then slid back across the hood was horrifying. As if in slow motion, the man slid to the ground.

Callum cried out in shock. Acting on autopilot, he brought the vehicle to a stop, his heart thumping. He stared blindly at the steering wheel. Nausea churned in his gut. His chest was tight with barely restrained panic as he tried to get a handle on what had happened.

I think I just hit somebody…a man… I didn't even see him… Oh, God…

The confusion of thoughts whirled through his mind and all the time he fought against the urge to vomit. The migraine that had threatened all day now hit him with a vengeance. He squeezed his eyes shut tightly in an effort to ward off the pain, but there was nothing he could do to stop it.

I need to get out… He's hurt… I need to see if I can help him…

He tried to open the door, but his fingers wouldn't obey his command. It was like they were frozen in place, frozen with fear like the rest of him. And then his stomach revolted. With barely enough time to open the window, he stuck out his head and vomited all down the side.

With his throat raw and filled with sourness, he wiped his mouth with the back of his hand and stared through the broken windscreen in shock. He shook so hard his teeth chattered. Goosebumps pebbled his skin.

What the heck am I doing? I just ran into a man… I need to help him… I need to call an ambulance…

The jumble of thoughts crashed through his head until the noise of them nearly sent him mad. With shaking hands, he reached for his phone and dialed the emergency number. The operator answered in no time at all and in halting sentences he managed to tell her what happened.

"Stay calm, sir. The ambulance is on its way. Is there only one person injured?"

"Yes."

"Okay, stay with him and let him know help will be there in a few minutes."

Callum couldn't remember if he thanked her, but he ended the call and dropped the phone back into his pocket. Trying hard to pull himself together, he climbed out of his vehicle and hurried to where the injured man lay.

Please, God, Please let him be okay… Please, God. Please help him…

The man was covered in blood. One side of his face was caved in. There was a vacant look in his eyes. Frantic now, Callum felt for a pulse, praying all the while.

There was nothing.

The faint sound of sirens came to him in the distance. Overwhelmed with guilt and horror, he reached for the man's hand and prayed over him in quiet desperation. There was nothing else he could do but wait.

It had been three days since his father's funeral, a difficult day that had culminated in an innocent man's death. The police had questioned him at length and after testing him for the presence of both drugs and alcohol, they eventually released him. The next day, they'd called him to tell him the autopsy showed high amounts of methamphetamine and cocaine in the dead man's body.

The fact the man was high on drugs and probably hadn't realized he'd stepped out into the path of an oncoming vehicle brought Callum little comfort. It didn't change the fact he'd hit and killed a man. On top of all his questions and his shame and sadness for the victim, there was the upheaval caused by the terms of his father's will.

The only person Callum had told about the accident was his mother. She'd been understandably shocked and horrified and expressed her sympathy for both him and the man who'd died.

"Do you have any idea who he was?"

"No. They didn't know at the time. No ID."

"Well, I guess it doesn't matter. I feel badly for his family."

"Yes. So do I. I guess I could ask the police for his name again. Perhaps I can visit his family, offer them my condolences."

His mother nodded. "That might be nice. Talk to the police about it. See if they think it's a good idea."

"I will." He paused and then added. "Do you mind keeping this between us for now? The family's in enough turmoil as it is. They don't need worrying about me to add to their shock and grief. Besides, there's nothing anyone can do about what happened to the man I hit."

"I think that's a good idea."

The police had told him they'd conduct a thorough investigation. Apparently there were at least a couple witnesses—motorists who happened to drive past around the same time Callum collided with the victim. Callum could only hope they supported his version of events.

Yes, on the night in question his mind had definitely been on other things and yes, he'd been tired and overwrought, but the man had stepped out from nowhere. It had all happened in a split second. There hadn't been time for Callum to react.

He put his faith in the legal system. He was sure the police would do their job. He tried not to worry about it. In the meantime, what he could do was pray for the victim and his family and give more thought to making a decision about his future. It was with that in mind he found himself heading for the Good Shepherd Seminary located in the inner west suburb of Homebush.

Surrounded by traffic, he swallowed a sigh and rubbed at his temple where another headache had made itself known. The lights finally turned green and he made the turn into the driveway of the seminary. This was where he'd lived and worked and studied for the last four years. He'd had fun, made many strong friendships, engaged in much learning and had grown to admire his tutors for their dedication, intelligence and patience. It had begun to feel like home. But now he was returning with a troubled heart, unsure of where his future lay.

He hoped this meeting with his mentor would provide some guidance. Father Danny had been a priest for more than forty years and with his years of wisdom and gentle intuitive ways he was perfect as spiritual advisor to the seminarians.

Callum had warmed to him from the beginning and valued his insight and advice.

He entered the seminary carpark and parked the hire car his mother's insurance company had provided while her SUV was repaired. Walking across the wide expanse of lawn and gardens, he felt a familiar calmness and serenity descend upon him. Small birds flew in and out of a bottlebrush tree that was in full bloom, its crimson flowers a bright contrast against the olive-green foliage.

From somewhere in the vicinity of the chapel came the sound of an organist playing a slow and soulful hymn. The notes were haunting and beautiful. After the events of the past week, just being back there in the grounds of the seminary were a balm to his troubled spirit. He looked up and saw Father Danny waiting for him at the end of the path.

The old priest came toward him with both hands extended in greeting. As Callum clasped them, some more of the turmoil inside him receded.

"Father. Thank you for seeing me."

"Callum, my son. It's good to see you. Please accept my condolences for the death of your father."

"Thank you. It was unexpected. Our family is still in shock. My father was…a force to be reckoned with. He kept us all anchored. He'll be greatly missed."

"Yes, indeed. I knew your father well. He was a loyal servant to our Lord. He was also very generous. He donated a sizeable sum toward the building fund of this seminary. Did you know that?"

"No, Father. But he thought very highly of the Church and especially those who were called to help in the formation of priests."

"Your father encouraged you to make your life here." It was a statement more than a question.

Callum had confessed to the older man only a few months

into his formation that he was there at the request of his father. Father Danny had listened, but he hadn't dissuaded Callum from entering the priesthood. Instead, Callum had been advised to pray continually and to listen to what God had to say. Father Danny was confident God would tell Callum what He wanted him to do. Callum sighed inwardly at the memory and then pushed it aside. This was about his future, not his past.

Together, the two of them turned toward the chapel. Father Danny's office was located in a room opposite. They walked the long corridor in silence. The priest scratched at the stubble on his chin.

Callum shot him a sideways glance. "You trying out a new look?"

Father Danny chuckled. "No. I gave up shaving for Lent. It's beginning to itch already."

Callum shook his head in sympathy and grinned, his troubles momentarily forgotten. "It's going to be a long six weeks."

The corridor was cool and dim and quiet. Even the music had ceased. This time of day, most of the seminarians were studying—either in the library or in their rooms. They followed a very strict schedule that never changed. Discipline in thoughts and deeds every moment of their day was considered an important part of their formation.

Father Danny opened the door to his office and stood back to allow Callum to enter. The small room comprised nothing more than a modest desk and two chairs and piles of books everywhere; Father Danny was an avid reader. The curtains were open on a large window that flooded the room with late summer sunlight.

"Take a seat," the priest offered and made his way to the chair behind his desk.

Callum sat opposite him and thought about all the other

times he'd found himself in the same position over the past four years. It comforted him to know that he always left Father Danny's office feeling less burdened than when he walked in.

The priest adjusted the glasses on his nose and then leaned forward with his elbows on his desk. "So, Callum. What troubles you?"

Callum gave a half-hearted chuckle. "Is it that obvious?"

The priest regarded him with affection. "It is to me."

Callum hesitated. He'd arranged the meeting with Father Danny for the sole purpose of obtaining advice. But this was such a big thing. He was seriously considering leaving the seminary. Was he really willing to throw away the past eight years? Would Father Danny be disappointed? Callum cared a great deal about what his mentor might think. *And then there was the accident…*

"What's troubling you, son?"

The question was asked quietly, calmly, with no inflection or judgment. Only kindness and concern glinted in the old priest's eyes. Callum's shoulders slumped on a heavy sigh.

"I'm not sure where to begin," he admitted.

"Does this have something to do with your father's death?"

"Yes. Partly."

The priest's eyebrows rose momentarily, but his tone remained calm. "Are you questioning God's decision? Why He took your father so soon?"

Callum waved away the questions. "No, no. Nothing like that."

"Then what?"

"My father left me some money. In his will."

"Yes?"

"A substantial sum. Ten million dollars."

The usually unflappable priest gasped. Behind his glasses, his eyes widened in shock. "Ten million dollars?"

"Yes."

"You're right. That's certainly a substantial sum."

"Yes. The thing is, I don't know what he meant by it. As you know, my father's the reason I went into the priesthood. I was honoring a promise he made to God."

"Yes, I remember you telling me about that not long after you arrived here. You were born very ill, not expected to live. Your father made a deal with God to save your life." The priest offered him a small smile. "He's not the first one to do something like that."

"No. But most people bind *themselves* to something or another. They don't bind their son."

"And yet you felt the need to fulfill the obligation?"

Callum nodded. "Yes. My father was very…persuasive."

"Have you benefited from your studies and enjoyed your time here?"

"Yes. It hasn't always been easy, but recently I'd started to feel like I belonged." Callum gave a half-chuckle. "You've done an exceptional job, Father."

Father Danny waved away the compliment. "It has nothing to do with me, son. Only God can take the credit for that."

"Well, anyway. That's what makes everything so confusing. My father left me all this money. He knew what it would mean if I were to take my final vows. A would-be priest is not someone in the position to accept a monetary gift. And yet he left it to me anyway."

"Are you sure your father knew about your vow of poverty?"

"Yes."

"Then you're right. It does seem like a calculated move on his part. What do *you* think he meant by it?"

Callum made a sound of exasperation in the back of his throat. "That's why I'm here, Father Danny! I need your advice."

"I don't think you need me to tell you what it means, Callum."

Callum bit his lip and slowly nodded. "Yeah. You're right. I think it was his way of releasing me from his promise. Letting me know that he was okay if I choose not to go through with my final vows."

"That's a pretty big deal," the priest murmured.

"Yeah."

Silence fell between them. Finally, Father Danny broke it. "So have you given any thought to what you might do?"

"No. Not really. Every time I let myself think about what it might be like to leave the seminary and do something else with my life, I get nervous. It seems impossible."

"What would you like to do?"

"I don't know. I used to think I wanted to be a police officer."

"Really? A very noble profession."

"Yeah. A couple of my brothers are detectives and so is one cousin."

"Are you still interested in policing?"

Callum gave the question some thought. "I don't think so. As much as I admire my brothers and my cousin for their dedication to keeping us safe, I don't think that's for me."

"Did you have anything else in mind?"

"It's hard to say. Up until three days ago, I was kind of convinced my future lay with the Church. Then I was given ten million reasons to reconsider." He paused. "There's something else," he added somberly, unable to meet his mentor's eye.

"What is it?'

Callum drew in a deep breath and eased it out on a heavy sigh. "The night of my father's funeral, I had a car accident."

"Okay. I take it you're all right?"

Callum waved away the concern in Father Danny's eyes.

"Yes. I'm fine. The thing is, I… I hit a pedestrian and…killed him."

Father Danny gasped. Shock filled his expression, but to Callum's relief there was no judgment. He hastened to continue, feeling the need to explain.

"It was dark. He came from nowhere. Stepped onto the road. I didn't see him until it was too late. There was nothing I could do."

"Callum, it's okay. I'm sure you didn't hit him intentionally, that you did all you could. Had you been drinking?"

"No, of course not!"

"What did the police say?"

"I talked to them at length. I told them exactly what I told you. They're interviewing a couple of other witnesses and then they'll let me know what they intend to do."

"Is there a chance you might be charged with this man's death?"

Callum blew out his breath and shook his head slowly back and forth. His gut filled with dread. "I don't know," he admitted. His voice cracked with emotion, but he forced himself to continue. "Maybe. It was an accident, but who knows how the police might see it. And of course I replay it all the time, wondering if there had been some way I could have avoided him."

"Oh, Callum! How awful for you! This is a terrible, terrible tragedy, but accidents happen. I know in my heart you did everything you could. Let's hope and pray the police come to that conclusion too."

"Thank you, Father. I appreciate your support." He paused. "I just wish I knew how to keep myself busy in the meantime. With all that's going on with my father's will and now this… My head's in turmoil."

The old priest looked thoughtful. "This has all come as a bit of a shock. You have so much going on. And at this time, you can't possibly devote the attention needed to excel in your studies. I think you owe it to yourself to take a break, to think things through. Why don't you take some time off, away from this place, and try and deal with events in your life and clear your thoughts. There's nothing you can do to hasten the police investigation. It will run its course. So let's talk about your father's will. The thing is, you've been presented with an opportunity you never thought you'd have. There are so many possibilities. All of them are life changing. You owe it to yourself not to rush your decision."

"But what will I do in the meantime? I can't just sit around with my thoughts. I'll go crazy."

The old priest thought for a moment. "I have an idea."

Callum sat forward in anticipation. "Tell me."

Father Danny regarded him steadily. "I have a friend who runs a soup kitchen in the city. Jennifer's Kitchen. It was named after a wealthy benefactress who was instrumental in setting it up and getting it running. They serve up to a hundred meals a day. It comes under the auspices of the Little Sisters of the Poor and is mainly staffed by nuns and a few lay people. They're always looking for volunteers. You'd be doing some good and at the same time you'd have plenty of time to think about your future. Is that something you'd consider?"

Callum's heart skipped a beat. The fact he might be part of something so important felt good. Father Danny was right. Working at the soup kitchen would be something worthwhile. It would also give him plenty of time to think about his inheritance, was a way to give back, and working would keep his mind off the tragic accident that had resulted in a man's death.

He smiled slowly. "Yes. It's absolutely something I'd consider."

The priest nodded. "I thought you might."

"When could I start?"

"They serve meals there seven days a week. There's no reason you can't start straight away. I'm sure they'd welcome the extra help."

A surge of excitement went through him at the opportunity opening up before him.

"Do I need a letter of introduction?"

Father Danny waved his question away. "No, nothing as formal as that. I know the administrator in charge of the kitchen. Ron Marchant. He works for the Catholic Archdiocese of Sydney. The soup kitchen is under their umbrella. I'll call him and let him know you're coming. In the meantime, here's the address."

Father Danny scribbled something then handed over the piece of paper. Callum murmured his thanks and slipped it into the pocket of his pants. Once again, he felt a little frisson of anticipation. It was the best he'd felt since the day he'd been told about his father's untimely death.

Where it might lead, he didn't know but right now it was a good option and he owed it to himself and the memory of his father to take the time to sort himself out.

Chapter Four

Grace Gunning tucked a strand of sweaty dark hair behind her ear and adjusted her hair net. There was no air conditioning inside the old building and despite the fact it was mid-February and summer was almost over, the heat coming through the small window over the sink in the kitchen was uncomfortable. To make matters worse, she'd spent all morning bent over the stove, preparing the midday meal. Today it was mashed potato, green beans and rissoles.

The lunch hour was almost upon them. Jennifer's Kitchen had already begun to fill with their regulars, as well as a few new faces. Every day, there seemed to be a couple more. Thanks to many generous donations, she was nearly always able to ensure there was enough food to go round, but the soup kitchen only supplied one meal a day. Enough for a person to survive on, but nowhere near enough to thrive, especially for the children. She also worried about where patrons slept at night. The kind of people who ate at the soup kitchen were the same people who usually had nowhere to live. She knew that firsthand.

"You ready to start serving, Grace?"

Grace blinked to clear her thoughts and turned away from the stove to look at her co-worker and friend. She gave Sister Mary-Catherine a grin.

"Absolutely. I'll just finish filling the bain-marie and we're good to go."

Mary-Catherine nodded. She peered through the large opening above the kitchen counter and out into the main room. "They've started lining up. We have a fair crowd, as usual."

Grace looked out and saw a line of people already snaking from the serving area all the way to the front door. With quiet efficiency, she finished ladling rissoles and vegetables into the food warmer and after depositing the dirty pots and pans in the sink, returned to the service post. Sister Mary-Catherine was already there, serving spoon in hand.

As the line inched from the rissoles to the vegetables, Grace smiled warmly and greeted their first patron. "Hello, Jack. How are you today?"

"Not too bad, Miss Grace. My rheumatism is playing up a bit, but no complaints."

"Good to hear." She heaped mashed potato and a serving of green beans onto his plate. He murmured his thanks and shuffled away, heading toward the row of tables and chairs that lined the main part of the dining hall.

A frail-looking woman with snow white hair and pockmarked cheeks was next in line. Once again, Grace offered a friendly smile. "How are you, Dorothy? How's that cough?"

"Not good, Grace. Feel like I'm hacking up a lung most days."

"Did you get to that clinic I mentioned last week?"

"Yeah. They were good. Told me what medicine to take. Problem is, I can't afford it."

Grace's heart filled with compassion. She reached into her pocket and pulled out a twenty dollar note. She'd been saving every spare penny of her modest salary in the hope of finding someplace better to live, but Dorothy's cough sounded awful. She needed the money more than Grace.

"Here. Will this cover the cost?'

Dorothy's eyes widened in surprise. "I can't take your money, Grace."

"Of course you can. Please, Dorothy. Take it. Buy the medicine," Grace insisted.

Dorothy's expression filled with reluctance, but she slowly reached out for the money. "Thanks, Grace. You're an angel."

Grace served her beans and mashed potato in between Dorothy's nasty coughing bouts. "Just make sure you get that medicine. You take care, Dorothy. And stay warm."

"Yes, Grace." The elderly woman turned away with her laden plate and slowly made her way to a table.

Next in line was Ralph. He'd been coming to the soup kitchen for almost as long as Grace had been working there. He never missed his mid-day meal there. She gave him a fond smile.

"Ralph! How has the day been treating you?"

The dark-skinned Aboriginal man with the wiry gray hair gave her a wink. "All the better for seeing you, Grace. I love what you've done with your hair."

She smiled and self-consciously touched the hairnet the health department required them to wear. "Always the charmer. Enjoy your meal, Ralph."

"Oh, I always enjoy eating here, Grace. Hot food, hot women." He cut his glance toward Mary-Catherine. "What's not to like?"

He chuckled at his own joke. Grace smiled. "Get on with you."

He grinned, nodded his thanks then turned away with his meal.

"Oh, it looks like Ron Marchant has arrived. I wonder what he's doing here today," Sister Mary-Catherine mused.

Grace looked up and spied the soup kitchen's church-appointed administrator walking toward them. Ron's cherubic face was framed by a soft cloud of white hair. Small of stature, kind of heart and quietly spoken, he looked like an angel. He was a distant nephew of Jennifer Rawlings, the original benefactress of the soup kitchen, and he put his heart and soul and more importantly, his money into keeping the kitchen operational. Everyone who knew him loved and admired him.

In addition to the time Ron put in helping out at the soup kitchen, he spent many hours building relationships in the community with philanthropic-minded businessmen in the hope they could be persuaded to lend the charity some financial muscle. As a not-for-profit organization, the soup kitchen relied heavily on the generosity of donors. Sometimes it was in the form of monetary donations, but just as important were the donations of food. Grace's menu often depended upon what they had in stock.

Her gaze slid to the unfamiliar man who stood beside Ron. He had shoulders as broad as a footballer's and short, dark-blond hair. Tall and muscular, he was about her age and had an air of authority that was in keeping with his designer clothes. The black T-shirt and jeans might appear plain and inconspicuous to the casual observer, but she knew enough about expensive clothing to know this was no ordinary volunteer.

Perhaps he's a potential donor?

Hope flooded through her. They sure could do with an injection of cash. Only that morning she and Sister Mary-Catherine had added a heartfelt request to their daily prayers for God to send them a generous donor. The situation was getting dire.

Ron and the stranger headed toward them. Ron stopped to greet some familiar faces along the way. Finally they reached the serving area where Grace and Mary-Catherine stood.

Ron beamed at the two of them. "Good afternoon Mary-Catherine. Hello, Grace. How are you doing today?"

Grace smiled. "Great, thanks, Ron. How about you?"

"Wonderful. Just wonderful." He turned to the stranger beside him. "Ladies, I'd like to introduce you to Callum Craigdon. He's our newest volunteer. Please make him feel welcome."

Grace nodded politely, but her mind went into a spin. There was no way a man who dressed the way he did was just another volunteer. The newcomer carried that air of confidence that came from never having to worry where your next meal came from. There was something going on. No doubt Ron was oblivious to it. That man didn't have a deceptive bone in his body. But it was possible he'd been hoodwinked by the good-looking stranger and Grace would have none of that.

She'd learned the hard way not to trust anyone at face value. Grace had seen donors like him before. They thought that because they were paying the soup kitchen's bills, they could dictate how things were to be run. That kind of men and women didn't last long. They usually lost interest in their charity project long before the money ran out. Still, it was a pain in the neck to have to deal with them while they were in full stride.

Grace's livelihood depended upon her work at the soup kitchen. She drew a modest wage that covered her basic needs and she lived in the small apartment off the kitchen and paid only a nominal rent. Having a stable place to live and secure employment, even in a soup kitchen, was necessary if she wanted to regain custody of her kids. It was all she'd been working toward these past twelve months. She couldn't afford to have her efforts jeopardized now and she couldn't afford to live anywhere else.

The man who'd been introduced as Callum regarded her keenly. Frank curiosity shone out of his ocean-blue eyes. And something else she couldn't define… His smile was friendly and charming and open. She blushed under his regard, unable to help herself, and was immediately annoyed by her response.

What do I care if the man's sinfully good-looking? She'd been taken in by a good-looking man once before. That hadn't turned out well.

"It's nice to meet you, Callum," Sister Mary-Catherine was saying. "We can always do with an extra set of hands, can't we Grace?"

"Y-yes, of course," Grace stammered. Another rush of heat spread across her cheeks.

Callum continued to regard her closely. "Do you mind if I spend some time with your patrons, Mary-Catherine?" He directed the question to Grace's colleague, but his gaze never left Grace's face.

"No, of course not. Grace and I have this under control. Go and talk to our guests. They get as much sustenance from the social interaction as they do the food."

Ron clapped a hand on Callum's shoulder. "Come on, let me introduce you. They're going to love you."

The two men walked away, leaving Grace to stare after them. The jury was still out as to whether the arrival of this handsome stranger boded ill or well for all of them.

Callum felt poleaxed. The woman who'd been introduced as Grace wasn't merely beautiful. She had the kind of face you saw on movie posters. The hairnet framed her face so that the perfection of her flawless skin and her big brown eyes was magnified. Unable to drag his gaze away, he'd stared at her longer than had been polite. And she'd noticed.

Never before had he felt like that around a woman. He'd always held himself aloof from women, even when he was young. His father's promise to God had always been there, sometimes at the back of his mind, sometimes at the fore, but it never went away. He supposed that was the main reason he hadn't allowed himself to think of women as anything other than helpmates, colleagues, friends.

Her reaction to him was mystifying too. She didn't even know him and yet her posture had been stiff and defensive. He wondered who she thought he was and why she seemed threatened by him.

Father Danny had told him the charity was run by nuns from the Little Sisters of the Poor. He wondered if she was one of them and immediately felt a wave of disappointment. The first woman who stirred something inside him since he'd allowed himself to think of a future outside of the Church and she might already have promised her life to God. He didn't see any humor in that irony.

He wandered down the rows of tables that overflowed with patrons. The simple meal of rissoles and vegetables smelled good and from the number of empty plates around him, it tasted good, too. He came to a halt beside an elderly Aboriginal gentleman who was mopping up the last of his gravy with a roll. There was a vacant seat beside him. Callum sat down.

"Hi. I'm Callum. I'm new here."

The man glanced up and then returned his attention to his food.

Not one to be put off easily, Callum tried again. "Do you come here often?"

The man shrugged. "Often enough."

"The food's good?"

"Yeah. The food's always good."

"Who does all the cooking?"

"Grace, mostly."

Callum looked over to where Grace now stacked dirty plates on the counter. She turned to someone behind her and said something, then smiled. In that moment, the beauty of her expression lit up her face and snatched his breath away. He had to force himself to look away.

"Has she worked here long?"

"Not sure."

"Does she have any family?"

"Don't know."

"Is she one of the sisters?"

"Nup."

Callum felt a measure of relief. He did his best to conceal it, but he couldn't prevent the grin that spread his lips wide. His gaze was drawn once again to where Grace stood surrounded by a pile of dirty plates and all he could do was stare.

His reaction to the woman was still profoundly confusing. He'd met beautiful women before. What was it about her that was so compelling? Or was it simpler than that? Was it merely because he'd temporarily stepped away from being a seminarian and could be just plain, ordinary Callum Craigdon.

Becoming a priest was no longer an inevitable part of his future. All of a sudden, he was free to choose how and where and with whom he would spend the rest of his life. The knowledge was both nerve wracking and exhilarating.

From the corner of her eye, Grace watched the newcomer while loading plates into the kitchen's three industrial dishwashers. He talked and laughed with their patrons, moving from table to table, shaking hands, sharing conversation. He seemed so at ease with the people, it surprised her.

Maybe she was overthinking this, reacting to the air of wealth and privilege that surrounded him rather than accepting Ron's words at face value.

Perhaps he's a volunteer, after all? Perhaps he has no intention of becoming a donor and throwing his weight around. He certainly didn't appear arrogant now.

And there was no denying the way he charmed the clientele. She saw Dorothy smile up at him when he spoke to her. The old woman even primped her hair. Jack was involved in an animated conversation that ended in him thumping Callum good-naturedly on the back. Even Ralph was grinning. Ordinarily, she'd be thrilled to have a volunteer who fit so easily and so well into their kitchen. But there was nothing ordinary about the newcomer and she remained suspicious of his motives.

Her late husband had also been a good-looking charmer. She'd discovered much too late that looks and charm often concealed a darker personality. The memory caused a shiver of disquiet. The last months of her marriage to Daniel Gunning had been the worst months of her life.

Now she was thirty years of age, far from young and innocent, but she honestly didn't know if she could trust her judgment when it came to men. She only had to look to her recent past to see she hadn't done so well thus far.

Chapter Five

Callum climbed into the rented car and joined the stream of traffic heading in a north-westerly direction out of Sydney. He felt a nervousness when he drove now. Almost skittish, he over-thought each lane change and each pressure he applied to the pedal. He stuck to the slow lane, keeping out of the way of the passing traffic. He knew it would take time to build up his confidence as a driver again.

It had been a week since he'd made the decision to put his studies at the seminary on hold. He'd also decided to move back in with his mother until such time as he made a decision on his future. His sister, Isabella, who'd recently broken up with her long-term boyfriend, had also moved home.

Richmond was about an hour's drive out of the city, depending on traffic. It was only mid-afternoon. With a bit of luck, he'd get a head start on the rush hour. As he nervously merged with the traffic, his thoughts turned to the matters causing him the most concern.

He'd put in a call to the lead detective investigating the accident and had asked the man for the victim's details. The officer had explained that, despite what he might have seen on TV, the police didn't normally give out that kind of information and until the coronial enquiry was over, it would be inappropriate for Callum to have contact with the victim's family.

When Callum asked the detective how much longer the enquiry might take before a decision was handed down, he was given a vague answer that really told him nothing. He'd casually put the question to Jett about how long the average police investigation took and was told it was usually at least a few weeks, but it could take a lot longer depending upon the complexity of the case. Jett had given him a probing look, but Callum hadn't elaborated any further.

He was also concerned about the fallout from his father's will. Nicholas remained devastated their father had handed over Craigdon Enterprises to Logan. Sophia still fumed over the fact she'd been left a pittance unless she chose to marry. The knowledge Henry was controlling her life from the grave set her blood boiling. Callum couldn't even guess how long it might take for her to cool down. And he understood her response.

He was just thankful he wasn't in that situation, although his father could have been a little more transparent about intent. Still, after talking it over with Father Danny, Callum was convinced he needed to try new things and see if life as a priest was really meant for him.

Unbidden, an image of the woman at the soup kitchen filled his mind. She was more than beautiful. There was something ethereal about her. She looked as fragile as glass with her petite figure, big brown, doe-like eyes that dominated her face and her pale, alabaster skin. Her smile lit up her face, but didn't quite conceal the sadness in her gaze.

She drew him like he'd wanted to be drawn to Christ. He burned with the desire to know more about her. Her name was Grace, but who was she? If the man at the kitchen could be believed, she wasn't one of the nuns, but what was her story? She might be married. A mother. Have a life completely separate from the soup kitchen.

He wished he'd had the foresight to ask Ron a few more questions. The truth was, Callum had been side-swiped by his reaction to her, and his mind had been muddled for most of the time he was there. But for the first time in his life, one complication had been removed. Now he could make decisions on his own, not ones based on an old promise made by his father. That knowledge was liberating.

Glancing over his shoulder, he flicked on his indicator and carefully made the turn toward Richmond. His thoughts switched to his mother. He was still shocked she'd been dealt with so harshly under her husband's will. Leaving her the family home was a no brainer. They'd lived there for most of their married life. It was the fact she'd been left nothing *else* that had Callum shaking his head.

Dad, what were you thinking?

According to the lawyer, the will had been written only a few months earlier. It was inconceivable that Henry didn't leave a substantial part of his fortune to his wife. He'd left fifteen million dollars to a charity, for goodness sake! All of them were baffled by that.

An incoming call registered on the screen in front of him. *Joel.*

Damn. He hoped Jett hadn't told Joel about Callum's odd question. He didn't feel like evading another curious brother. Swallowing a sigh, he pressed the button to accept the call.

"Joel. What's up?"

"Nothing, bro. Just thought I'd call and say hello, see how you're doing. I haven't spoken to you since the funeral."

Callum eased out his breath. "Yeah. I'm fine. How 'bout you?"

"Good. Trying to get my head around the fact Dad's gone. It happened so suddenly."

"Yeah. I think we're all struggling with that."

"So, how's it going being a civilian? Isabella told me you've taken a leave of absence from the seminary. You made any decisions about your future?"

"It's going fine," Callum replied carefully. "And no, it's way too early to make any decisions."

"How's Mom?"

"She seems to be holding up all right, at least in public. I keep encouraging her to grieve properly, but she insists she's fine."

"Maybe she's grieving when no one can see her?"

"Maybe. She does spend a lot of time in her room. I'm not sure what she does behind closed doors."

"Well, I'm glad you're staying with her. Isabella, too. It's good that Mom has family around her at this time."

"*Mmm.*"

"You don't sound too enthusiastic," Joel commented dryly.

"Don't get me wrong, I love Mom as much as any of us and I want to be there for her if she needs me. But… It would be nice to have some time alone. Dad's thrown me a curve ball. I've put my future as a priest on hold and I'm supposed to be taking the time to look deeply into myself to ascertain exactly what it is I want. My mentor assures me it's the only way I'll know for sure what God has in store for me."

"So what's the problem?"

Callum sighed. "This is going to sound really selfish."

Joel's laughter was filled with disbelief. "You're joking, right? You're the first one to volunteer to do anything. You're always there when one of us needs someone and that's the way it's been my whole life. Callum Craigdon, you're the least selfish person I know."

Callum swallowed against the lump of emotion that suddenly clogged his throat. His voice was gruff when he spoke.

"Thanks, Joel. That means a lot to me."

"It's true," Joel replied.

"Yeah, well. The thing is, I need some time to process all of this. I need time alone to pray, to think, to live. I don't want to make the wrong decision. I've been left a helluva lot of money. More than I could ever spend. And that's if I decide to leave the priesthood. If I stay, well…I won't need any of it."

"You should go for it, Callum. Live life to the fullest. You've spent your entire life with the knowledge of Dad's promise hanging over your head, directing your path. It's time to set that aside to find out what *you* want, how *you* want to live your life. If that's as a priest, then so be it; I wish you all the best. If it's as a civilian living a different life entirely, then that's okay, too. With his bequest, Dad gave you permission to make up your own mind. I really admire him for that and I think you should honor his gift by taking full advantage."

"Do you really believe that's why he did it?"

"Yeah, I do."

Callum felt a wave of relief wash over him. Joel was the fourth family member who'd expressed such feelings. It filled Callum with a new determination to make the right decision about his future and live his life as the very best person he could be. If he decided he was being called in a different direction, living a good life as a civilian—maybe even as a husband, a father—then that was okay, too.

"You still there, Callum?"

Callum blinked away his thoughts. "Yeah, mate."

"I'm going away for a while."

"Going away?"

"Yeah. It's been hectic at work for so long I can't remember the last time I had a chance to unwind. I need to get away, learn to relax again. I have banked a lot of unused vacation and now that I'm cashed up with a very generous inheritance, I thought I'd take some time off and go overseas."

"Good on you. Where to?"

"Europe."

"Nice. How long will you be gone?"

"Three months."

"Wow. That's one heck of a holiday."

"Hey, ten million dollars is one heck of an inheritance."

Callum chuckled. "You're right about that. What about Mary-Jane? Is she going with you?"

"Nup. We…ah… We split up."

Callum blinked in surprise. "But you've been together for years! What happened?"

"Nothing. We just wanted different things. She was angling to settle down, get married. I'm not ready for that. Maybe I'll never be ready for that."

"Fair enough. Well, good luck overseas. Don't do anything I wouldn't do."

"Oh, Callum! You're such a sap. The French Riviera is calling my name and I'm going to make the most of it."

"Who's looking after your place?"

"I'm not sure. I haven't given that much thought."

An idea germinated in Callum's mind. "I guess I could housesit for you," he slowly offered.

"Hey, that's a great idea!"

"Any pets or potted plants I need to know about?"

"No, mate. All good. Just don't go having any wild parties. Any damage, you pay for."

The two of them joined in good-natured laughter. "Are you sure you're okay with me staying there?" Callum asked.

"Yes, of course. You need some peace and quiet to be able to think about the direction your life's going to take and I need someone to look after my place. It's a win for both of us."

"You're right. It sounds like it could work out. When do you leave?"

"The day after tomorrow."

"Wow."

"Yep. I don't see any reason to hang around. My boss approved my leave this morning. I've already booked my ticket."

Callum laughed, his admiration evident. Joel had always been decisive. He'd had his heart set on being a police officer and he allowed nothing to get in the way of his dream. Not even their father.

After providing Callum with some information on the security code and the location of the spare keys to his apartment, Joel finally ended the call. Cautiously Callum moved into the turning lane and pulled up at the traffic lights. He'd made good time and would arrive at his mother's place in the next few minutes.

The lights changed and as he turned and moved through the majestic, wrought iron gates that guarded the entrance to Craigdon Manor, his thoughts once again returned to Grace. His reaction to her had blindsided him. Even now, with all he had going on in his life, she was all he could think about. The fact she worked at a soup kitchen told him she had a kind heart, a few spare hours each day and a sense she wanted to give back to her community. It didn't tell him anything about her private life. It made him want to go right back there the next day and the next day after that, until he knew all there was to know about Grace, the angel he'd crossed paths with at Jennifer's Kitchen. And luckily that's where he'd volunteered to be for the foreseeable future.

He found his mother in the kitchen, toiling over the eight-burner, industrial-sized gas stove. Though her housekeeper and cook came in every day, his mother found relaxation in preparing food. Callum remembered mouth-watering chocolate chip cookies, shortbread, pastries, homemade ice cream and any number of other treats waiting for them when they arrived home from school. He usually ended up eating most of his lunch by recess and was always starving at the end of the day. Today was no different.

He'd spent his time over the lunch break at the soup kitchen and though they'd been serving a meal, he'd been too busy talking to the patrons and sneaking glances at Grace to eat. Right on cue, his belly grumbled.

His mother turned and smiled. "Sounds like you're just in time."

Callum moved closer and kissed her on the cheek. He poked a spoon in the pot of simmering sauce on the stove and tasted it.

"*Mmm*, tastes great, Mom. What are you cooking?"

"Meatballs."

"My favorite."

"And Isabella's."

"Is she joining us for dinner?"

His mother grimaced. "She was, but she was called to an emergency. A shooting."

Callum frowned. "Really? That's not good."

"No. As the hospital's expert on bullet wounds they have to call her. Anyway, that means it'll be just the two of us."

"I feel sorry for Issy missing your famous spaghetti and meatballs, but I guess that means there's more for me." He grinned.

"Don't get too excited. I'll put some aside for her. She'll be hungry when she gets home." His mother eyed him quizzically, picking up on his good mood. "What have you been up to?"

"Remember I told you about the soup kitchen where Father Danny suggested I volunteer?"

"Yes."

"Well, I went there today. They serve lunch every day. Close to a hundred people turned up over the course of a few hours. They were all very orderly and polite and talked highly of the soup kitchen and the people who run it."

"It's run by the Little Sisters of the Poor, isn't it?"

"Yes. And some lay staff and a few volunteers."

"So are you going to become a volunteer there?"

He nodded. "Yes. I think I will."

"Good on you."

Untying her apron, his mother washed and dried her hands and then reached for a couple of pasta bowls.

"Will you set the table for me, Callum? Seeing it's just the two of us, I thought we might eat in the morning room."

"Sure Mom."

Callum moved to the small room off the kitchen. A rectangular-shaped table and eight chairs and a hand-carved wooden sideboard were the only pieces of furniture. Even though it was early evening, this time of year the large windows on both the western and southern walls flooded the room with dappled sunlight.

Callum went to the sideboard and pulled out a white linen tablecloth and two place settings. His mother came in a short time later with a bowl of steaming food in each hand.

"Yum, I'm starving," he said.

She placed the bowls on the table and he waited for her to sit before he drew out his chair and sat.

"So, tell me more about this soup kitchen."

Callum twirled some spaghetti on his fork and took his first mouthful before responding. "Really good, Mom." He dabbed his mouth with a dinner napkin then began. "I wasn't quite sure how it would go, but I was taken there by the administrator and he introduced me to the staff. I spent time talking to them and the patrons and…it was good. I enjoyed myself and it felt good to be in that space with them. Certainly different from hours of seclusion and study at the seminary."

"You've always been good with people, Callum, regardless where you meet them. And you care for everyone. It's instinctive. You've never been judgmental. I always thought you'd make a wonderful priest."

Callum grimaced. "I guess that's because that path was laid out for me from my birth. We all assumed that's the way things would be."

Elizabeth stared down at her bowl. "Even though I supported your father's decision, I was never happy about the way he directed you into the priesthood," she said slowly.

Callum reared back in surprise. "Really? You never hinted you didn't support him one hundred percent."

She shrugged. "I guess that's because in the early years, I did. I was so grateful that you'd survived your rocky start that I was also happy to help keep up that end of the bargain. It was something that became accepted, settled. Even in *your* mind."

"Because I never believed I had a choice, Mom. I'd been told about the "promise" all of my life. I knew what was expected of me."

His mother looked distressed. "Is that all you were doing? Fulfilling our expectations?"

"Of course, Mom. What else?"

Chapter Six

Callum's mother shook her head. "Oh, honey! I thought you genuinely felt a calling from God. You've spent the last eight years studying to become a priest! How have you remained so committed if you didn't feel it was your vocation?"

Callum's shoulders slumped on a sigh. "It isn't all bad. In fact, over the years there are many aspects of that life I've come to enjoy. And I've learned so much from my studies. Sometimes, when I'm deep in prayer, I even believe that perhaps it *is* my vocation. That's what makes the decision so difficult. Now that I've been given a choice, I don't know what to do."

"Then Father Danny's right. You need to take time off from your studies and do some different things, to clear your mind. And take time to do some deep thinking and pray long and hard to God. He'll guide you in the right direction. He always does."

Callum smiled in gratitude and reached across the table and gave his mother's hand a squeeze.

"Thanks, Mom. Your support means a lot to me."

"You've always had my support, Callum. I love you more than you know."

"I love you too, Mom."

They returned their attention to their meal and ate for a while in silence. Elizabeth was the first to break it.

"Have you heard from any of your brothers and sisters? How are they doing? I think it's time we got together for a family dinner."

"That sounds good Mom. But you'll need to do it soon if you want all of us there. Joel called me on my way home. He's heading to Europe in a couple of days."

His mother's perfectly groomed eyebrows lifted in surprise. "Really? He hasn't said anything to me."

"I'm sure he'll get around to calling you. He's burned out from work and he's just come into a decent amount of money. What better way to spend it than on a long-put-off holiday?"

"Well, I'm glad he's decided to take some time for himself. I was worried about him. He works so hard."

"Yeah." Callum paused. He wasn't sure how his mother would take the news he intended to move out, at least for the time Joel was away, but this seemed as good a time as any to tell her.

"Joel asked me to housesit his apartment."

Okay, so it wasn't exactly the truth and he was immediately filled with guilt, but he didn't want his mother to think the move had been his idea. Or think he was trying to distance himself. She was fragile at the moment, still grieving, even if on the outside she appeared fine.

"Really?" Elizabeth replied, disappointment shadowing her blue eyes.

"Yes. I… I'm thinking about doing it. What do you think?"

"But you've only just moved back home, Callum! It's been wonderful having you here! Especially now your father is gone."

Callum bit his lip. "Yeah, Mom. I know. At least you still have Issy. See, the thing is, Joel's going away for three months. He needs someone to look after his place and I… I need somewhere I can be alone with my thoughts. I have some big decisions to make and I'd like to do it on my own."

"But I'm here for you, darling! I could be your sounding board! I could help you make a decision."

Callum shook his head. "I appreciate your offer, Mom. I really do. But that's the thing, *I* need to make this decision. All my life I've lived with the knowledge my future was decided for me in the hours after my birth. It's time I looked at my choices from all angles and decide how I want to move forward. Please tell me you understand."

Her expression softened. "Of course I do. I love you. I just want to see you happy. I'll support whatever decision you make, no matter what. And it's good of you to housesit for your brother."

"Thanks Mom."

"Anytime. I'm your mother and your decision will be accepted and respected. No guilt from me."

They continued to eat. Callum thought about the countless times they'd sat together as a family. More often than not, their father was absent, busy building his property empire, and it would be just his mom and his brothers and sisters around the table. The seven of them would talk and laugh and tease and annoy—and generally do what families did around the dinner table. He wondered if his father ever regretted missing so many family meals.

"You and Dad had a good marriage, didn't you?"

The question struck him from nowhere. His mother blinked in surprise and then lifted her shoulder in a casual shrug.

"As good as anyone, I guess. It wasn't perfect. But what marriage is?"

Callum frowned. "What kind of answer is that? You guys were married for thirty-three years. You must have learned how to make it work."

"Maybe. Maybe we just learned how to keep out of each other's way."

Callum stared at her in shock. "Mom! What are you saying?"

His mother stared back at him. After a long moment, she looked away and sighed.

"I'm not saying anything, Callum. It's not for me to speak ill of your father, especially now that he's dead."

Callum knew firsthand how selfish and arrogant his father could be. For the first time he wondered what it would be like for her to be married to such a man. Perhaps there had been a lot more tension between his parents than they let on. All of a sudden, his father's lack of generosity toward his wife in his will made a kind of sense.

"Why did Dad leave you nothing more than this house?" he asked softly.

Elizabeth's cheeks lost some of their color. She toyed with her food, looked away, stared at the table and finally raised her eyes to meet Callum's steady gaze. The expression in her eyes was so bleak his heart stuttered with fear and all of a sudden he wished he'd never asked the question.

"It's all right Mom. It's none of my business," he said hurriedly.

She compressed her lips and shook her head. "No, Callum. I… I want to tell you."

"But—"

She held up her hand and cut him off. She picked up her linen napkin and dabbed at her mouth before folding it carefully and setting it aside. Callum's heart hammered against his chest.

"Many years ago, I had an affair. Your father found out about it. He never forgave me."

"*What?*" Callum gaped in shock. The air in his lungs seemed to have dissipated and he gasped for breath.

In contrast, his mother remained calm across from him.

"Your father and I didn't always have a harmonious relationship. I'm sure that doesn't come as any surprise. There was a time when I was very unhappy. I sought… companionship elsewhere. I'm not proud of it, but there's nothing I can do to change it."

"But… But you're a Catholic! You believe in the Catholic teachings! An affair, Mom? Really? I don't believe it!"

"I'm sorry, Callum. I'm sorry for letting you down. Yes, I am a Catholic and I believe in a loving and forgiving God. I made a mistake. I'm guilty of poor judgment and I'll live with my actions for the rest of my life. But I believe God has forgiven me. It's too bad your father couldn't bring himself to do the same thing."

"How long ago did it happen?"

She looked away. "Too long ago for you to remember."

"Then why didn't Dad ever come to terms with it? Why did he stay married?"

"I don't know. I guess it suited him to have a wife on his arm and someone to host his parties. Being married never stopped him from seeing other women."

Callum lowered his gaze and remained silent. His mother looked at him. "I see you know about that."

"Yeah," Callum mumbled. "I never thought it was right."

Elizabeth sighed. "No sense in rehashing it now. It didn't seem to matter to Henry that he hadn't remained faithful. *I* was expected to behave better. Besides, I'm sure he also considered what it would cost him if he were to file for divorce. I wouldn't have gone down without a fight and there was no way on this earth I would give up custody of my kids."

She shrugged and continued. "He liked his life the way it was and he was prepared to overlook my indiscretion, for appearances' sake, but he never let me forget it."

"So that's why he left you nothing but this house."

Elizabeth nodded. "Yes. It was half mine anyway."

"Aren't you angry at him for not leaving you what you deserve? You should have been given the bulk of his estate."

"I have no need of his money. My parents were very wealthy. I was their only child. They left me their entire estate. I have enough to keep me comfortable for the rest of my life."

"Was Dad aware of that?"

"Probably. He never asked how much I'd inherited, but he wasn't stupid."

"Okay, so now I understand why he left you what he did. Still, it was mean. I… I know Dad wasn't the easiest person to live with. I don't know if your affair was payback or not, but I want you to know, I don't judge you. None of us are perfect. We all make mistakes. I'm glad you've found your peace with God."

"It is what it is, Callum, but I appreciate your thoughts on it." She paused and then added, "You're the only one who knows about what happened. I'd be grateful if you kept it that way."

Callum regarded his mother steadily. "Of course, Mom. Your secret's safe with me."

She stood and came around to his side of the table and pressed a kiss on the top of his head. "I feel relieved to have told you. Thank you, son. I knew I could trust you."

They finished their meal in silence and then Callum pushed away from the table. "Thanks for dinner Mom. It was great. I have a few things to do. If you don't mind, I'll see you later."

"Oh, all right. What time will be you be back?"

He shot her a look, but it was accompanied by a smile. "Mom, I'm thirty."

"I know; I know. It's just habit, I guess. It's good to have you back, Callum. Even if it's for a short time."

He leaned over and kissed her. "Thanks, Mom. I love you."

"I love you, too. I'll make some phone calls and see when your brothers and sisters can get together. I'll include Uncle Archie's sons, too. After all, we're all family."

With most of the family unavailable on such short notice, the family dinner was put off until the following week. Callum drove Joel to the airport and waved good-bye with well wishes. He was pleased his brother was off on an exciting adventure and wished him all the best. He'd ditched the hire car for Joel's silver BMW convertible and as he left the airport, he couldn't help a burst of anticipation as he looked forward to spending time in his brother's ritzy inner city apartment. Callum could only imagine how much of Joel's pay went into making the mortgage payments. Of course that was no longer an issue; he *had* just inherited ten million dollars.

In the back of the car were two suitcases and a backpack, the sum total of Callum's belongings. Owning so few items had never worried him in the past. He'd been supplied with a seminary room that came furnished with a bed, a desk and a chair. That had been all he needed.

Now, as he surveyed Joel's fifth-floor apartment with its water views, designer leather sofa in a pale mint color, the plush white rug that felt just as soft as it looked beneath his bare feet and the enormous flat screen TV that boasted more channels than he'd had birthdays, he could see what it might be like to live in comfort and style when money was no problem. *But is that the kind of life I want?*

The very notion of a life of luxury was difficult to comprehend. It was diametrically opposed to the lifestyle he'd led to date. Choosing between them should have been easy: Either he was willing and happy to embrace a simple and useful life devoted to the Lord, or he wanted something different. It wasn't possible to have both.

Then again, even if he chose a life outside the Church, that didn't mean he couldn't serve God. There were plenty of charitable ways he could spend his time—and his money. Take Jennifer's Kitchen.

He'd done some research on the place since his visit. Jennifer Rawlings had been a long-term supporter of the poor and had donated many hours of her time and money to various charities run by the Catholic Church. In 1997, she'd been approached by the bishop with a view to gaining her financial support to set up a soup kitchen. In no time at all, premises had been located and Jennifer's Kitchen was up and running, providing a vital service for those in need. Jennifer had died nine years ago, but the soup kitchen continued to run in her memory, receiving support from much-needed donations and a generous financial gift in Jennifer's will.

Still, like all charities, the kitchen was always in need of help, particularly needing money for equipment, supplies and staff. For days now, he'd mulled over an idea. He'd just inherited ten million dollars. That kind of money could buy a lot of food and other necessities for a soup kitchen.

From what he could tell, a substantial portion of the kitchen's donations was used to cover the monthly rent on the building. He wasn't sure who owned it, but he was very interested to find out. If he could buy the building and lease it back to the charity rent-free, that would be a significant saving for them. Enough that they wouldn't have to worry about running out of money.

His thoughts turned to Grace and immediately warmth flooded through him. He wasn't sure how involved she was in the day-to-day running of the kitchen, but he wanted to help out. He wanted to do something real, something that would make a difference. Acting on the urge to see her, he headed out once again in Joel's car. He squeezed into a parking spot down a narrow street across from the soup kitchen and cut the engine. Climbing out of the vehicle, he ignored the rush of nerves that suddenly centered in his gut.

The last time he'd been there, he'd noticed a hand-painted sign on the door to the building that advised lunch was served between eleven and one each day. It wasn't yet ten. He'd arrived in plenty of time before the lunch rush, hoping to spend some time with Grace before she got busy with patrons. He also wanted a chance to take a good look at the building and see what other opportunities it might afford.

Cheap accommodation was in short supply in the city. The shelters that were available were often overcrowded, with many forced to sleep on the street or in parks, leaving them vulnerable to the elements, robbery and assault. During his university studies, he'd been staggered by the extent of the affordable housing problem in cities worldwide and the inherent challenges helping people escape from dire poverty. The future priest inside him had yearned to be able to do something for people who'd found themselves in such a situation, most often because of circumstances beyond their control.

Now that he'd been released from upholding his father's promise, everything had changed. Maybe the life of a priest was his true vocation, but for the first time he was able to consider a different kind of life.

As he approached the soup kitchen, his gaze moved up and over the building. It was several stories high. The floors above ground level looked vacant. Dull, dirt-stained glass windows, several of them broken, faced out onto the street. Pigeons flew in and out and roosted on the roofline. The paintwork was cracked and peeling, but the concrete structure appeared solid. He reached the front door and noticed it was shut. When he tried the handle, it was locked. Lifting his hand, he rapped his knuckles on the panel, hoping someone was inside.

He'd be disappointed if Grace weren't there, but he still wanted the opportunity to take a better look inside.

The sound of a dog barking behind him drew his attention. He turned in time to see an old blue heeler with a muzzle that was almost completely gray make its way slowly over to him. The dog barked a couple of more times, but there was no malice in its tone.

As the dog came closer, Callum's eyes began to water. Ignoring his allergic reaction, he crouched down and scratched the dog between its ears.

"Hey, boy. There you go. It's all right. What's your name?"

The dog licked Callum's hand in response. Callum chuckled. "You're a nice boy, aren't you? Do you live around here?"

Another bark. Another lick. A sneeze began to build. Callum fought against it, but the sneeze exploded out of him just as the door to the soup kitchen opened. Grace's face appeared. Embarrassed, Callum struggled with his handkerchief and noisily blew his nose.

Grace regard him not unkindly. "I hope Bluey isn't worrying you."

"No, not at all." He gave her a wry grin. "I love dogs. It's just that I'm allergic."

"Oh. Well, that's unfortunate."

Callum glanced down at the dog that had moved to sit at Grace's feet. "Is he yours?"

She nodded. "Yes. I… He belongs to my son. Bluey's been in my family for years." As if uncomfortable with the conversation, she moved to close the door. "You'll have to come back later. We're closed until eleven."

"Oh. Um, Grace, it's me. Callum Craigdon. I-I'm not here to eat. I was here about a week ago, with Ron Marchant. I'd… I'd like to help out again."

At once her expression changed to one of suspicion. She looked him up and down. Under her narrow-eyed scrutiny, he moved uncomfortably from one foot to the other, not sure what it was about him that bothered her. He was dressed similarly to what he'd worn the last time he was there. Jeans and a T-shirt. He'd added a jacket against the light breeze that had blown up from the harbor.

After a long moment, she shrugged and opened the door wider to let him in. "Can you cook?" she asked.

He grinned. "I can. In fact, until recently I lived in the seminary and cooking was one of my jobs."

She blinked in surprise and her demeanor changed almost immediately. Color spread across her cheeks and she ducked her head. Her shoulders relaxed and the tension eased from around her mouth.

"Oh, I beg your pardon, Father. I didn't know you were a priest."

"Well, not quite. I haven't finished my studies yet."

She smiled, her eyes now bright and friendly. Her earlier suspicion seemed to have disappeared. "How far are you into the program?"

"I have another three years to go."

"Wow. Are you enjoying it?"

He shrugged and didn't elaborate. Stepping through the doorway, he was greeted with the mouth-watering smells of meat cooking and pastries baking in the oven.

"*Mmm.* Are you sure you need a cook? It smells like you have everything under control."

She blushed and he could tell she was pleased by the compliment. "Sister Mary-Catherine has a cold," she explained. "She couldn't come in today. Young Alice is here to help with the serving, but she's hopeless as a cook. I've been flat out keeping on schedule all morning."

He gazed in the direction she indicated and saw a girl of

about eighteen or nineteen ladling steaming hot food into the stainless steel trays of the bain-marie. The girl looked up and saw him and offered him a shy smile. He raised a hand in greeting.

"What's on the menu?" he asked, turning back to Grace.

"Beef stroganoff and rice. For dessert we have apple pie and custard."

"Sounds great."

She offered him a wry half-smile. "You haven't tasted it yet, Father."

"Please, call me Callum," he replied gently. "I haven't earned the honor of being called Father, yet."

She smiled and the beauty of it momentarily stole his breath. "All right; Callum it is."

She turned and headed toward the kitchen. He followed behind her, taking note of the solid wooden beams that formed part of the high ceilings. His mind whirred with possibilities.

Grace tossed him an apron, snapping his attention back to her. "Let's see how you are at making custard."

He grinned, eager to take up the challenge. She pulled out custard powder, milk and sugar from the pantry and set them on the counter. He found an enormous pot in a cupboard near the stove. In short order, he'd mixed the ingredients and the pot was on the stove.

"We ran out of gas this morning. Lucky I started in here early. We wouldn't be finished in time otherwise," Grace commented, watching him as she alternated between stirring five large vats of stroganoff.

"You ran out of gas? Did someone forget to pay the bill?"

"No, nothing like that. The church takes care of the utilities. It's just that there isn't any gas piped directly to the premises. Only gas cylinders. We usually keep a pretty close eye on them and replace them before they run out, but I miscalculated. I had to wait over an hour for the hardware shop to deliver a couple more." She grimaced. "Another reason I've been pressed for time."

The custard came to the boil and Callum turned down the heat. "Well, it looks like you have everything under control now."

She smiled gratefully. "Yes, thanks to you." She dipped a spoon into the custard and tasted it. "*Mmm*, this is good. It looks like you were telling the truth."

He winked at her. "Did you doubt me?"

She grinned and his heart turned over. "Only for an instant."

Chapter Seven

The time went swiftly. Grace helped Alice and Callum serve meals to countless hungry people, swapped stories, sympathized, listened and laughed. Many of the patrons were regulars, who'd been coming to the soup kitchen for years. Grace had only been working there for twelve months, but already the regulars felt like family and she enjoyed catching up with them.

It was obvious Callum also felt at ease. He served pie and custard and then moved between the tables, chatting to the patrons, collecting dirty plates. She couldn't believe how easily he fit in. It was like he'd been doing this sort of thing for years. And perhaps he had. He was training to become a priest. That was a pretty specialized occupation that called for a certain kind of person. No one became a priest without feeling a deep need to serve, to protect, to help and support God's people. *All* of God's people, no matter their background, race or gender.

Finally the lunch rush was over and as Grace wiped the last counter clean, Alice closed and locked the front door. Grace filled two cups with coffee and brought them over to where Callum had just sat down at one of the tables. She offered him a cup, along with cream and sugar.

"No, thanks. Black is fine."

She acknowledged his comment with a nod and then added condiments to her cup. She pulled out a seat beside him and sighed.

"Oh, that tastes good. My feet are killing me. We had a few extras today. I was worried there might not be enough to go round."

"There was plenty. Everyone ate their fill. There were a lot of compliments about the stroganoff."

She winked at him. "And the pie and custard, too." She paused and then added, "Thank you for your help today, Callum. It was great."

He looked away, appearing a little uncomfortable with her praise. "It was nothing. I was glad to help."

A thought suddenly occurred to her. "How come you're not at the seminary? Don't you have to study, like…all the time?"

He chuckled. "Yeah, we do. Between our studies and our prayers, there's little time for anything else."

"Except cooking."

"Yes, you're right. Cooking. We all take a turn at that."

She grinned. "If the custard's anything to go by, you've learned your lessons well."

"You, too," he replied. "I had a mouthful of the stroganoff earlier. It's good." He looked at her, his blue eyes wide with interest. "Where did you learn to cook?"

Her smile faded as a mountain of memories besieged her. "My mom was a great cook," she said softly. "We didn't have much money, but she still managed to make something that tasted great."

His voice lowered to an intimate level. "Tell me more about your family."

The kindness and compassion in his gaze drew her in. She opened her mouth to respond and then abruptly closed it again. She didn't speak about her past with anyone. Not even someone as kind and warmhearted as an up-and-coming priest. She stood and put some distance between them.

"I'm sorry, Grace. I didn't mean to pry."

She brushed away his apology. "It's fine."

"Tell me about this place," he said, deftly changing the subject.

"What do you want to know?"

"Well, I'm interested in buying this building. Do you know who owns it?"

All of a sudden, her natural suspicion of strangers returned. She glared at him. "Wow, you are good. I nearly fell for that whole priest-in-training nonsense. What a fool I am! I should have trusted my instincts."

Callum frowned, his expression filled with confusion. "What are you talking about?"

"As if a priest or an almost-priest could afford to buy this building! From the very first moment I saw you I could tell you were trouble. Prancing in here in your designer clothes like you owned the place, pretending to be interested in the people, in *me*," she scoffed, annoyed with herself for being duped.

She shook her head and made a sound of disgust, her temper building. "You're not here to volunteer, or even to become a donor. You're here to sell the place out from underneath us." She crossed her arms over her chest and glared at him as her anger found its head. "Well, you can't. So there. We have a lease. You can't take it away from us."

Oh, God. What if he can? What if I lose my job, my apartment? I'll never get my kids back...

Something of the turmoil and panic that swirled inside her must have shown on her face. He stood and held up his hands in a placating gesture.

"Whoa! Grace! Back up a bit. I don't want to take the place away from you. I want to *help* you."

His attempt to calm her fired her up even more. She glared at him. He continued to regard her steadily, calmly and then his words registered and some of her anger eased. "Help me? What do you mean?"

"I mean, I want to buy the place so I can lease it to Jennifer's Kitchen, rent free. I did a little research. A sizable part of the donations you receive go toward paying the rent. I thought it would be a good thing if I could take that financial burden away."

She shook her head, unconvinced. "Why would you do something like that? No one buys an investment property and then gives away the rent. That makes absolutely no sense. You must believe I'm stupid."

"Grace, I don't think you're stupid. Even though we've barely met, I can tell you're strong and tough and savvy. And generous and sweet."

He moved closer. Sincerity shone from his eyes. "I understand your reaction. It does sound kind of unbelievable, especially since you know I'm studying at a seminary. The thing is, my father died recently and left me a sizable sum of money. I'd like to do something good with it."

Her eyes narrowed on a frown. "But you're on your way to being a priest. You can't inherit money."

He smiled. "You must be a Catholic."

She shrugged, neither confirming nor denying. It was none of his business.

"You're right," he continued. "As a priest, I'll take a vow of poverty. The thing is, I'm not a priest, yet."

She rolled her eyes. "Semantics, surely."

"No. In fact, even though I've completed a degree in theology and four years of study at the seminary already, if I decide not to take my final vows, I'll never be a priest."

She regarded him with skepticism. "Are you trying to tell me you're actually still trying to make up your mind? After all this time?"

Impatience flashed in his eyes, but his tone remained reasonable. "Yes, that's what I'm saying. And regardless of what I decide, I'm very much interested in buying this building and I'd be grateful if you could show me around."

With a nonchalant shrug, she turned away from him and started walking toward the rear of the building. Callum followed her.

"What you see is what you get," she said in a bored tone. "In addition to the dining hall, down at the back are toilets. Separate for male and female. You've already seen the kitchen and walk-in pantry. There's also a storeroom. Unfortunately, the floors above are in a state of disrepair. They're dangerous, not useable. Adjoining the kitchen is a small apartment."

"A studio?"

"Something like that. You can access it from the rear door in the kitchen."

"Is it tenanted?"

Her stomach somersaulted with a sudden flash of fear, but she tried hard to conceal it. With her arms crossed protectively over her chest, she turned to face him.

"Yes. *I* live there and I'm not moving out anytime soon." She stared at him hard, challenging him to contradict her.

He merely shrugged. "That's fine with me."

His easy acceptance of her statement didn't reassure her. She hastened to explain. "The Church leases the personal space to me for nominal rent in return for looking after this place."

His gaze remained steady on hers. "Grace. If I bought the place, I wouldn't evict you. It's a good idea to have someone living on site." He frowned. "I assume there's also a back-to-base security system?"

"Yes, of course. Though we've never had a problem. At least, not since I've been here."

"And how long have you been here?"

"Twelve months, give or take a week or two."

"Where were you before?"

She turned away so he couldn't see her face. The two years she'd spent on the streets following the death of her husband was still too painful to discuss with anyone, let alone a stranger, no matter how kind and compassionate he seemed.

"Grace," he said quietly. "I'm not here to judge you. The thing is, I like you. I'd like to get to know you better."

She shook her head, panicking. She'd come this far by being tough, refusing to let anyone close. It was the only way she survived. She couldn't succumb to kindness now, no matter if it were well-intended and she definitely couldn't let anyone get close. She was barely hanging on as it was. Especially after what had recently happened to her brother.

"That's not a good idea," she said stiffly, keeping her back to him. "I'm nobody. Just a woman who wants to give back to my community. That's all."

She felt his gaze boring into her back, but refused to turn around. Questions swirled in the air between them, but there was no way she'd satisfy his curiosity. She was still concerned about his long-term intentions for the building and until that was clarified once and for all, she'd do well to remain cautious. After all, priest-in-training or not, she barely knew him and she definitely had no basis for trusting him. In accord with her thoughts, Bluey hung back, as if to encourage them to return to the kitchen. To reality.

Grace needed to get things back on an even keel so she fixed a calm expression on her face and slowly turned around.

"So, you've seen all there is to see here. Is there anything else?"

The expression in his eyes told her he saw through her attempt to change the subject and he wasn't buying it, but to her relief, he let it go.

"This room is a great size," he said, "but I think we can use the space a lot more efficiently."

Despite her reservations, he'd piqued her interest. "Really?"

"You see up there?" He pointed toward the ceiling.

"Yes."

"I'm thinking mezzanine." He grinned. "What do you think?"

She tried to remain detached, but a surprised smile tugged at her lips. "Wow. That would be amazing. What would you use it for?"

"I don't know. I'd have to talk to some engineers to see what's possible, but I'm thinking perhaps a proper office space and additional storage. I'd also like to look more closely at the other floors above us. I think they have potential. There's such a shortage of affordable accommodation in the city. I'd like to do something about that."

Her eyes widened in surprise. Almost simultaneously, a jolt of panic went through her. "I agree we could certainly do with more affordable housing options, but is this what you're intending to use this building for? What about the kitchen?"

"Calm down; calm down. Nothing's going to happen to the kitchen. In fact, if anything, I think we could expand it. This building is on a good-sized chunk of land. There's room to add on. We could add another room or two. Put on more paid staff. We could also look at getting gas piped to the premises."

Grace offered him a reluctant grin. "I'd sure like to see that." Bluey plunked himself down at her feet. Almost immediately, he began a tail-wagging that thumped his approval too.

As they walked together companionably, Callum continued to point out features of the soup kitchen that could be improved upon, expanded, used more efficiently. His face was alight with enthusiasm and she couldn't help but be carried along by it. But at the back of her mind, there was a whisper of caution. Though everything he said sounded terrific, she still wasn't convinced about his motives.

She gave him a sideways glance. "You say you'd like to do something to provide affordable accommodation for those who need it. I assume you're talking about people who are currently without work or homeless?"

"Yes. Among others. Whoever is most in need."

"You do realize those people often can't afford to pay anything for housing?"

"Yes, of course. That's exactly the reason I want to help them."

"Are you crazy? Who invests hundreds of thousands of dollars—maybe even millions—in a project with no hope of getting a decent return? Or *any* return for that matter."

"Do you doubt my motives again?"

She stared at him. "Yes. I do. Your grand ideas don't make sense."

"You're right. And my father would turn over in his grave if he had an inkling of what I plan."

She raised an eyebrow in question and he obliged.

"My father was a property developer. A very successful one."

"I see. So he would never have bought a property with the intention of losing money."

"Never," Callum agreed.

"And yet that's exactly what you plan to do?"

He thrust his arms out wide and spun around. "Yes!" He grinned widely and said it with so much conviction she couldn't help but offer him a begrudging smile. Though still concerned about what the changes might mean for her and her job, a tiny frisson of excitement ran through her as, just for a moment, she let herself believe he was sincere.

"Of course, the soup kitchen would have to close during the renovations," he added.

And just like that, her excitement evaporated and she was back to worrying about what his plans would mean for her future and the future she had planned for her children. Oblivious to the concrete block that had lodged itself in her stomach, he turned to her and smiled, his eyes shining with enthusiasm.

"So, what do you think?"

Chapter Eight

Callum pulled away from Jennifer's Kitchen with his heart full of excitement for the future. Talking to Grace about his plans had solidified them in his mind and for a short while he even managed to forget about the accident and what the police might be up to in their investigation. Even if there was nothing further on the legal side, it would take a lifetime to forgive himself, if he ever could. He'd be forever haunted by the possibility that if he hadn't been distracted by events of the day he could have prevented a man's death. A man who was a son and perhaps a brother, even a father to someone.

And prayer hadn't helped. *If only I'd…*

Resolutely, he pushed the thought aside and focused on something good, what he *could* control—the purchase of Grace's building. He didn't even know if the owner was prepared to sell, but that didn't matter. Somehow he knew things would fall into place. What that meant for his future as a priest, he wasn't sure, but he didn't have to make any permanent decisions in that regard just yet. Father Danny had urged him to take all the time he needed.

When thoughts of the accident encroached again, he deliberately set them aside and refocused on how he could help in this world. That meant he could put his plans for the soup kitchen into play. He had the means. He had the opportunity. He also believed in the rightness of it. He could well understand Grace's skepticism. No investor in his right mind would put money into a project that was never going to see a return. But Callum wasn't interested in making money. All he wanted was to do something good.

He was concerned about Grace's response to his plans. She vacillated between enthusiasm and something much less than that. Perhaps she was distracted too. He'd noticed her eyes were red and there were obvious shadows under her eyes…

He could understand her concerns when she'd thought her job was threatened, but he'd reassured her that wasn't the case. He could only assume there was something else behind her strained glances, something she wasn't prepared to share. At least, not with him.

Checking the directions on the GPS, he made a turn at the lights and then cautiously moved into the left lane before making another turn. A few moments later, the GPS announced he'd arrived at his destination. The sign above the glass doors that provided entry to the building told him he had reached the offices of the Catholic Archdiocese of Sydney.

He'd called ahead and made an appointment to meet with Ron Marchant. The administrator of the soup kitchen had been surprised to hear from him, but had been more than willing to meet. Callum gave his name to the receptionist and was asked to take a seat. A few moments later, Ron came forward, his hand outstretched for a handshake.

"Callum. How are you? It's nice to see you again. Please, come in."

They walked down a carpeted corridor until they reached a door with *Ronald Marchant* scripted on a small bronze plate. Ron waved Callum in ahead of him and then offered him a seat.

Ron moved around his cluttered desk and took the seat opposite. After exchanging pleasantries, Callum got straight to the point.

"I'm interested in purchasing the building that houses Jennifer's Kitchen."

Marchant's eyes widened in surprise. "Um, excuse me?"

Taking pity on him, Callum explained. "I understand your confusion, but I've recently come into a substantial sum of money. I'd like to invest it in the soup kitchen. In particular, I'd like to buy the building and then lease it back to them, rent free. I'm also thinking about expanding the services provided. I believe the floors above the soup kitchen are empty, right?"

"Right. They're not in good shape. They were abandoned some years ago."

"That's what I thought. I'm thinking to renovate those floors and providing cheap or even free short-term accommodation for those in need."

Marchant sat back in his chair. He pulled off his glasses and began to clean them. He looked back at Callum and shook his head.

"Wow. Well, it seems like I've missed something. When Father Danny called me and asked if you could volunteer at Jennifer's Kitchen, I had no idea it might lead to this." The man regarded him keenly. "I've learned through experience people who do this type of good deed often are trying to make up for a lapse or disappointment to others."

Callum forced a smile. He pushed away thoughts of the accident and focused on the discussion at hand. "I'll confess. Neither did I. In fact, when I first walked into the kitchen, I had no thought of wanting to own the building. But it's strange how things happen. I like to think God has a hand in my plans. They sort of just came to me and here I am."

"But you're a seminarian. What will you do with the place after you take your final vows?"

Callum stared down at his hands. "I'm not sure about anything, yet. To tell you the truth, I don't know where my future lies. All my life I thought I'd become a priest. Then my father died. Now I'm not so sure."

Marchant regarded him quizzically. "What did your father's death have to do with this?"

Callum waved away his question. "It doesn't matter. Let's just say Father Danny has granted me a leave of absence from the seminary so I can take some time to think about my future and what I want to do. Maybe that future's in the priesthood. Maybe not. I'm hoping God will help me decide. In the meantime, I'd like to buy that building and help out the Little Sisters. If I decide to enter the priesthood, it will go into an enduring trust so Jennifer's Kitchen will still benefit."

"That's mighty generous of you. Even though they're only using the ground floor, the rent on that place is pretty steep. They'd have so much more money to spend on things they need if they didn't have to find rent each month."

"Yes, so I understand. Buying the building and offering them the space free is an easy thing for me to do. Provided the owner is prepared to sell, of course."

"Yes, I guess that needs to be ascertained."

"Do you know who owns the building?" Callum pressed.

"Not off the top of my head, but I have a copy of the lease. It contains those details."

He pushed back from his desk, stood and made his way to a filing cabinet in a corner of the room. After flicking through various folders, he pulled one out.

"Here it is. I'll ask Miranda to make you a copy." With that, he pressed a button on his phone and put in the request. A moment later a gray-haired, pleasant-looking woman opened the door to the office.

"Thanks, Miranda. Here you go," Marchant said, offering her the lease. The woman disappeared as quickly and quietly as she'd arrived. Marchant returned to his chair.

"I understand the kitchen was set up with the generous financial support of a woman by the name of Jennifer Rawlings," Callum said.

Marchant nodded. "Yes. Back in 1997. Before my time here. They originally set up in an old church hall in Haymarket. Over the years, it became necessary to source a larger space. That's when we found the building in Surry Hills. They've been working out of there for the past ten years."

Callum sat back in his chair. "Tell me about Grace."

Marchant took his time answering. "I took over the administration of Jennifer's Kitchen nearly fifteen years ago. We've had a lot of volunteers through there over the years. Some stay a few weeks, others a few months. We've been lucky to have a handful of them for a number of years. They come and go as they're able and we appreciate any time they can give. Grace Gunning arrived at the kitchen about twelve months ago."

Callum nodded. This was consistent with what Grace had told him. "How often does she volunteer there?"

Marchant pursed his lips. "Grace started out as a volunteer and she came in every day to help out. She was happy to roll up her sleeves and give anything a go. Even the cooking. One day our usual cook fell ill and couldn't come back. Grace offered to take over. She's been doing it ever since. That was at least six months ago. She isn't a volunteer in the full sense now. She's our head cook and kitchen manager. She works there every day. She's paid a modest wage and pays a nominal rent on the small apartment attached to the building."

"What about her family? Does she have any?"

"She's a very private person. She never talks about her family. At least, not to me."

Callum compressed his lips. Grace had shut down any of

his questions of a personal nature, too. Guilt stabbed through him. It was obvious she didn't want people knowing her business, but he burned with the need to know more. She intrigued him. He wanted to know more. Much more. But that was proving difficult. Did anyone know the real Grace Gunning?

What was she hiding? Something didn't sit right. She looked about his age. Old enough to have a husband, maybe even some kids. In fact, she'd mentioned a son. She was intelligent and articulate, but didn't speak with the additional polish that came from a private school education. She was competent, kind and compassionate and yet an aura of sadness surrounded her. Especially the last time he'd seen her.

At least he knew her surname now. He'd put her name into an Internet search engine and see what he could find. Most everyone was on social media. He might be able to discover more about her that way. He resolutely ignored the fresh prickle of guilt.

"She seems to have a good rapport with the staff and clientele," he said.

Marchant nodded. "Yes. She's always had a special way about her. Our staff and patrons love her."

"It's funny," Callum continued. "When I mentioned my interest in buying the building and expanding the current services, she was less than enthusiastic"

Marchant's eyes widened in surprise. "Really? If you'd asked me, I would have thought she'd be thrilled by the possibility of expansion. She's totally invested in the soup kitchen. She spends many additional hours working there. Hours she doesn't get paid for. She even door knocks for donations of money and other grocery items when we're short. She's the first person there in the morning and the last to leave in the afternoon. The kitchen and what it represents means a lot to her, even if she doesn't say so."

"So you think she's someone I could rely on in the event I decide to proceed?"

"Absolutely. I think she would champion your cause."

Callum nodded with satisfaction. "That's good to know."

The door to the office opened and Miranda reappeared with the lease. "Here you go." She handed a sheaf of papers to her boss.

"Thank you," Marchant replied, taking them from her. He handed a copy to Callum. "This contains all the terms of the lease. You'll be able to get in contact with the landlord and discuss sale considerations. I wish you luck."

"Thank you," Callum said. "Let's hope we don't need it. The more I think about the possibilities of that place, the more determined I am to make it happen. It just feels right." With that, Callum stood and shook the administrator's hand then quietly took his leave.

Grace stirred the four huge vats of pumpkin soup on the stove, but her thoughts were far away from the meal she'd prepared. Ever since Callum Craigdon had entered her life, he was on her mind.

It wasn't just the fact he was sinfully good-looking and had a smile that could make a woman turn weak at the knees. It wasn't just the fact he appeared genuinely concerned about the people who relied on Jennifer's Kitchen for a hot meal. It wasn't just the kindness and compassion she'd spied in his expression when he thought she wasn't looking. It wasn't just the fact he'd announced his intentions to buy this building. And not just buy it, but turn it into some much-needed affordable accommodation for those who were down on their luck, including an expansion of her precious kitchen.

It all seemed too good to be true. *He* seemed too good to be true. Was he really a priest-in-training, like he claimed?

She had no way to check his story. She didn't know his friends or anyone else who might verify his claim. The only thing she had to go on was his name.

Callum Craigdon.

Craigdon was a familiar name in Sydney high society. An old family name with a long history behind it. It was synonymous with wealth. They made their money through property development. Was Callum from the same family?

Turning down the heat on the stove and setting aside the stirring spoon, she pulled out her phone and plugged the Craigdon name into a search engine. Sure enough, within seconds there was a list of hits. The most recent of them referred to the death of Henry Craigdon, the patriarch of the Craigdon family clan.

She skimmed over a series of articles. Many described the way Henry's father had set up the property development business and, after working for a handful of years as an accountant, Henry had followed in his father's footsteps. In just under a decade, the son had quadrupled his father's business and it had continued to prosper under Henry's guiding hand. His net worth had been estimated at over a billion dollars.

There was the odd article suggesting that some of Henry's millions might have been made through nefarious means, but those articles were fleeting and were overwhelmingly outnumbered by the many positive stories that focused on Henry's significant contribution to the Sydney property market.

Scrolling a little further down, she found a recent article from a reputable newspaper where several prominent business-men offered condolences at Henry's unexpected passing. He'd died from a massive heart attack only a couple of weeks earlier. He'd been pronounced dead at the scene by the paramedics, unable to be revived. He'd only been sixty-five.

Her gaze moved lower and snagged on a family picture. A raft of tall, good-looking men flanked three women. Two of the women were young—maybe in their early twenties—the third was much older with a thick head of wavy white hair. All eight of them were dressed formally in the latest designer gear. Most of them smiled in the direction of the photographer, showing brilliant white teeth.

The article listed the names of Henry's children and his wife of thirty-three years. They were celebrating Henry's sixty-fifth birthday. She saw Callum's name and zoomed in on him. Yes, it was definitely him, although he looked remarkably like some of his brothers.

She set aside her phone with a sigh. Despite her efforts to ascertain the truthfulness of his story, she was none the wiser. There was no mention in any of the articles of Callum's impending entry into the priesthood. Was she being unreasonable not taking him at his word? He'd given her no reason to disbelieve him. He'd been honest with her about his name and his family. Perhaps he'd also been honest about his past. Perhaps he was exactly who he said he was and she should simply accept him for what he was.

If he was really genuine in his desire to own their building and expand their current services, she ought to be celebrating. The plight of the less fortunate was a cause very close to her heart. She knew firsthand what it was like to be hungry and homeless. That was why she was determined to do whatever she could to ease their burden, one hot meal at a time.

But could she trust Callum to follow through with his plans? What if he bought the building and then evicted them? She'd not only be out of a job, she'd also have nowhere to live. The thought filled her with panic.

Every day she spent apart from her children was a day she'd never get back. Her heart broke each time she thought of all the milestones and special occasions she'd missed.

Birthdays, Christmases, special school events... It was imperative she keep her job and the roof over her head.

It wasn't like she had a resumé bursting with qualifications. She'd met Daniel at university. They'd fallen in love at first sight. By the time she was nineteen, she was pregnant with her son. Completing her nursing degree was then no longer an option. She married Daniel a year later. By the time she was twenty-two, her daughter had arrived and it was all she could do to look after her babies and manage the home she'd set up with her husband.

Though Daniel came from old money, his parents weren't inclined to offer financial help. They'd disapproved of her right from the beginning. For a start, she came from a humble background with both her parents being blue collar workers. They were also convinced she'd seen Daniel as a way out of a life of poverty and believed she'd deliberately set out to fall pregnant.

While she'd never given a moment's thought to trapping him, she hadn't been able to convince her in-laws of that truth. Over the months and years of her marriage, their constant disapproval had shredded her self-esteem. They only tolerated her for the sake of Daniel and their two grandchildren.

Daniel's parents adored Seth and Alyssa and the feeling was mutual. Showered with expensive gifts and outings, her children loved every minute they spent around Daniel's parents. Grace had tried more than once to talk to her husband about the way his parents spoiled them, but Daniel waved away her concerns.

Then he was killed in an accident and her life spiraled out of control. Daniel's parents blamed her for his death. Shocked and distraught, she couldn't think straight. She sought refuge in alcohol.

Daniel's parents swooped in. Before she knew what was happening, they'd petitioned the court for custody. Her in-laws even took the stand. They painted a picture of her as an addict, a drunkard, an unfit mother. It had been a nightmare.

The judge found against her and awarded Daniel's parents full custody of her children. That was three years ago. Seth was now ten and Alyssa was eight. Grace saw them for only a few hours one day a week and even that contact was supervised.

Supervised! As if she posed a threat to her children! That broke her heart. It also gave her the incentive to clean up her act and do her best to put her life back together. And that included a steady job, a place to live. Stability and security. She couldn't let all she'd worked for be taken away from her. She had to make sure Callum Craigdon was genuine and that his word could be trusted.

Chapter Nine

Callum pushed open the sliding glass door and stepped onto Joel's balcony. The balmy, late summer evening breeze that blew across the harbor gently lifted his hair. He normally wore it quite short at the seminary, but there was no longer a pressing need to keep it in order. It also had something to do with his newfound freedom and his right to live life as he chose. He still hadn't made up his mind about his long-term future, but there was no rush.

One thing he was certain of was his determination to buy the building in Surry Hills. No matter what the outcome of the police investigation, he wanted to do it. If he was found to be negligent he could face charges and Lord knows what might happen after that. And even if he were totally cleared of wrongdoing, and he eventually returned to the seminary and completed his studies and took his final vows, he'd feel such deep sadness over the unfortunate man's death that owning property wouldn't matter in the grand scheme of things. He'd simply have to sign over ownership to someone else. One of his brothers, or even Grace.

Grace.

Beautiful, mysterious, intriguing, caring Grace. It was obvious how much the soup kitchen meant to her. It was more than just a job. He sensed she really cared about the people who came there and she knew most of them by name.

He'd hoped to gain some insights about her from Ron Marchant, but the man had been less than forthcoming. Or maybe he'd been telling the truth when he'd told Callum he didn't know about Grace's past. Callum had left the meeting dissatisfied.

What was her story? Where was she from? What had motivated her to work at the kitchen and to keep coming back, day after day? Where was her son?

Though he was almost certain she wanted to embrace his plan to buy the building and expand the services they could offer, he sensed she also felt threatened for some reason. Then it became clear: The soup kitchen meant permanent employment and a place for her to live. That security would be turned upside down if his plans got the go ahead. The kitchen would become a building site and no one but the tradesmen and contractors would be allowed to enter. During those renovations, what would happen to the people who relied on the kitchen for a meal? What would happen to Grace?

She had legitimate concerns. Only now did he realize he'd gotten carried away by enthusiasm for his future plans. He had to try harder to reassure her that he would do his best to maintain the status quo, including keeping the staff who were already there and safeguarding Grace's abode. He wasn't sure how he was going to make that work, but he would. There was no way he'd put her out of a job, or even worse, out on the street. The challenge for him was to get her to trust him and make her realize he would ensure she had a place to stay and a steady income, and even more: that his motives were pure.

Seated on a stool at the kitchen counter the next morning, Grace chewed on a fingernail while she tried to put together the lunch menu based on the limited supplies in the pantry. It was still early, not long past seven. It wasn't unusual for her to be in the kitchen that time of day. She was never sure how many volunteers would turn up on a given day and she needed to start early if she wanted to have the meal ready on time.

A whining at the door caught her attention and she smiled and opened it. Bluey stood on the other side. He looked at her with such love and gratitude, her heart melted.

"Hey, boy. Are you hungry? Is that why you're here?"

She patted him on the shoulder and then turned away. He padded in slowly after her. Having him around her brought her comfort. He reminded her of her children. She'd bought him from a shelter as a pet for Seth. Her son had only been a baby at the time, but he'd fallen in love with Bluey right away. And the feeling had been mutual.

Bluey became Seth's shadow. The toddler couldn't go anywhere without his dog trailing behind him. He was like Seth's personal security guard. Friends would warn her that it wasn't safe for her to leave a young child in the company of a blue heeler, but Grace refused to pay them heed. Bluey loved her son without question. He'd never let any harm come to him. Grace knew beyond a shadow of a doubt that her baby was safe with the dog. When Alyssa came along, Bluey embraced her just like he had Seth. He had plenty of love for the two of them.

And then her in-laws had taken her children, only they hadn't wanted their dog. Apparently Bluey wasn't welcome in their mansion, or on the manicured lawns and carefully tended gardens behind it. Seth and Alyssa had been devastated. Their lives had already been torn apart. Not only had they been forcibly removed from their mother but they had lost their precious dog.

Grace was grateful her children hadn't witnessed the awful argument she'd had with her mother-in-law when Nerida made it clear while she couldn't get hold of Grace's babies quick enough, Bluey wouldn't be coming with them.

With a sigh, Grace opened the fridge and pulled out a couple of containers of leftovers from the day before. There wasn't much. A bit of ham. Some mashed potato. She found Bluey's dish and filled it with food. Some weeks she managed to scrape together enough money to buy him some dog food, but he seemed to enjoy the leftovers just the same. As the smell drifted toward him, he whimpered in anticipation. She smiled and gave him a pat.

"There you go, boy. It's all yours." She set the dish on the ground just inside the door and gave him another pat. He threw her a look of gratitude and immediately began to eat.

With another soft sigh, she returned to her task at the kitchen counter. Her mind kept drifting to Callum Craigdon and his promise to improve the lives of the people she now considered her family, the people she cared about, even loved. He'd told her the kitchen would close for the duration of the renovations. That's what concerned her the most. Where would all the people go who relied on the kitchen for a meal? Where would *she* go? Not only would she be out of work, she'd also be out of a home. It might not be forever, but any kind of renovation would take weeks, if not months. Something as substantial as what Callum had mentioned might even take a year.

A *year!* It was too much! She couldn't support his plan. It wasn't fair to the people who needed them and if she lost her job and her apartment, she'd never get her kids. She'd recently lost her only brother and even though she and Ken hadn't been close, his shocking and unexpected death had brought home all too clearly the fragility of life and the importance of making the most of every moment. The time she was allowed to spend with her children was all too short and she was more determined than ever to do whatever it took to get them back.

She made a sound of frustration as fear and resentment

spilled over. Callum's plans for the place seemed like a dream come true if she only considered the end product, but the way she saw it, the downside far outweighed any advantages. So what was the solution? She wished she knew.

Maybe I'm worrying about this for nothing?

She still hadn't decided if Callum was a man of his word. Why would someone put a substantial sum into a charity, with no hope of achieving a positive return? Perhaps his charming, caring demeanor was an act. Perhaps he had no intention to follow through with the plans he'd enthusiastically shared with her. Perhaps that's why it sounded far too good to be true.

A knock at the door interrupted her thoughts. She set down her pen and left the kitchen. Crossing over to the exterior door, she pulled it slowly open, already suspecting who it might be. After all, he'd been there every day this week.

"You again," she said by way of greeting.

Callum spied the distrust in her gaze and offered her his most genuine smile. "Good-morning, Grace. It's nice to see you."

She replied with a huff and turned away, leaving the door open. He followed her into the kitchen where a pad and pen lay on the table. He couldn't read the scrawl that half-filled the top page, but it looked like a list. Bluey stood by the back door, polishing off the last remnants of food in his bowl. Callum felt his eyes water.

"I'm sorry to arrive here so early. I hope I'm not disturbing you," he said, offering her an apologetic grin.

She dismissed him with a wave of her hand and sat down. "It's fine. I'm just trying to come up with something to cook for lunch. We're short of some essential staples. Either we are blessed by a miracle in the form of a last minute donation, or it will have to be a vegetarian pasta and no dessert."

Ignoring his allergic reaction to the dog, he took a seat opposite her. "What do you need?"

"Meat, eggs, flour, milk, sugar. A bit more butter wouldn't go astray."

"I'll duck down to the supermarket and see what I can find. Will that do?"

She blinked at him in surprise and then her gaze narrowed with suspicion. "Who are you, Callum Craigdon? You've appeared out of nowhere, like a fairy godfather, waving a magic wand and making all sorts of promises and yet I know nothing about you. You say you're studying to be a priest, but you've been given a leave of absence. That seems odd in itself. And confounding everything is that you come across as open and honest. I hate myself because I want to believe in you, but I also know what it feels like to get your hopes up and have them dashed. It can be devastating."

She looked at him with such sadness in her eyes, his heart clenched. He wished he could take her pain away, every last drop of it.

"Grace," he said gently. "I don't know what else you want me to say. And I don't know about the trials in your past. The people you met—good and bad. But I'm being as upfront and honest as I can be. I accept you don't know me and as such, I need to work hard to earn your trust. I intend to do that, Grace. I'll work as hard and as long as it takes. I never make promises I can't keep. I'll never let you down."

He kept his gaze locked on hers and hoped the sincerity in his heart showed on his face. She continued to regard him with uncertainty, but some of the suspicion eased from her eyes. Without thinking, he reached for her hand and squeezed it. A tingling warmth spread up his arm. Caught off guard by his reaction, he dropped her hand and stared at the floor, heat suffusing his cheeks.

"Um, I-I... I was thinking about you, I mean the soup

kitchen and my plans and everything last night. I realized I might not have reassured you properly about the security of your position here in the event my plans come to fruition."

He paused, gaging her reaction before continuing. "The thing is, I know how much this place means to you and having the kitchen closed for renovations could affect you big time. I want you to know I'll come up with a solution. The renovations I have in mind are substantial and it would mean access to the building would be limited while they're going on, but it won't mean the closure of the kitchen and it definitely won't mean you'll be asked to move on."

He offered her an encouraging smile. "I haven't figured out all the details and heaven knows, I haven't even bought the place yet, but I just want to reassure you. Everything will be fine. For you, for Mary-Catherine and for all of the people who rely on this place."

She stared at him, wide-eyed with surprise. Hope warred with confusion on her face and noticing, he flushed again.

"I'm sorry. I'm rambling, completely out of my depth. You do that to me, Grace. You invade my thoughts and muddle my thinking until I don't know where I am. But what I do know is I won't ever hurt you or the things you hold dear."

Before she had a chance to respond, his eyes watered again, his nose tingled and a moment later, he let out an explosive sneeze. He flushed in embarrassment. "I-I'm sorry."

She giggled. "It must be Bluey. He stopped by for something to eat." She indicated behind him and he turned and saw the old blue heeler licking the sides of his now-empty bowl.

"Yeah, I noticed him when I came in," he managed before getting caught up in another sneeze.

Once again, Grace laughed. "I'm sorry. I'll put him outside."

"No, don't do that. I'll be fine. It's not his fault."

Still, he was grateful when she stood and gently coaxed the dog outside before closing the door between them. She made her way back to her seat and regarded him steadily.

"What you said back then… Wow! I… I don't know what to say. It's like you read my mind. It's true, I vacillate between wanting to believe in you and your plans and wondering if I can trust you and questioning who are you and why you would be willing to do this for us. It's very confusing and to be frank, it's driving me crazy!"

Callum laughed. "I'm glad I'm not the only one feeling topsy-turvy. Don't ask me how I know this is going to happen. I just do. I have the money and I definitely have the determination. I don't want you to go anywhere else. In fact, I want you to be a part of it. Given your wide range of experience here, I welcome your input."

She frowned and he immediately knew he'd said the wrong thing. He swallowed a curse. *What is it she's taken offense to?*

"What do you mean, my wide range of experience? Who have you been talking too?" She'd crossed her arms over her chest and her chin jutted out defensively.

Callum suddenly realized where he'd overstepped. She was a private person. He knew that. She wouldn't appreciate that he'd spoken to her boss about her.

"Grace, I'm sorry. I…" There was nothing for it. He had to come clean. "I met with Ron Marchant yesterday. I wanted to gage his reaction to my proposal to buy this building and my expansion plans. I… I also asked him about you."

Anger flared in the depths of her dark eyes. "You asked Ron about me? You went behind my back for information on my private life? How dare you!"

Callum held up his hands in an effort to placate her. "I'm sorry. I couldn't help it! I wanted to know more about you. It was obvious you weren't keen to share anything of yourself with me. You gave me no choice."

She pushed away from the table, her eyes now blazing with fury. "So this is now my fault! How dare you think you can come in here and take over without so much as a by your leave? My private life is none of your business! I thought I made that clear." She pointed toward the door. "I think you should leave!"

"Grace! Please!"

Her expression remained cold and unrelenting. "I said, get out!"

Callum stumbled to his feet and after attempting a few more apologies, he left. Once outside, he let out a vicious curse, disgusted with himself. It was immediately followed by a mumbled apology to God. He knew better than to let out his frustrations like that. Swearing was unbecoming of a seminarian, but oh, it felt good.

Climbing into Joel's convertible, he left the kitchen and headed down the street. Large shopping malls with supermarkets were in short supply in the city, but he finally spied a Woolworths near Town Hall. It took forever to find a parking spot and he had to walk some distance back to the store, but it didn't matter. He was on a mission to help. That's all that was important. On his way inside, he collected a trolley and started down the first aisle.

Grace had mentioned meat and eggs, flour, milk, sugar and butter. He couldn't imagine the quantities he needed to feed the number of people who regularly turned up at the kitchen, but he'd do his best. He threw packets of steak and sausages and raw chicken into the trolley. Twelve dozen eggs, five large bags of flour, the same for sugar and tubs of butter. He shopped until he couldn't fit another item in his overflowing trolley and then he went and got another. All the time he could think of nothing but the fight he'd had with the woman who ran the kitchen.

What was I thinking when I pried into her past?

She'd made it clear it was none of his business, but he hadn't been able to help himself. He'd posed his questions to Marchant and the man, respecting Grace's privacy, had told him very little.

And now she hated him for it.

Grace heard rustling noises outside the door to the kitchen and ignored them. Bluey sat by her side. He cocked his head and looked at her. She gave him a pat.

"It's all right, Bluey. He can stay out there for all I care." She was still fuming over Callum's gross breach of her privacy. There was no way she was letting him in again.

How dare he? He had no right to quiz her boss about her history. That was nobody's business but hers. Thank God she'd given Ron only the bare details. The truth was, he had no real information to hand on. That knowledge was little comfort. Callum should never have poked his nose into her business.

After a while, the noises outside the door ceased and the kitchen fell silent once again. Looking over her list, she sighed. It would have to be the vegetarian pasta. They were out of meat and sugar. No dessert today.

She glanced at the clock on the wall of the kitchen. It was already half-past eight. She needed to get the meal started if it was to be served on time. Another noise at the front door caught her attention. She looked across. The frown that had been forming dissolved as Sister Mary-Catherine filled the opening.

"Sister! It's good to see you! You're just in time to help me with the vegetables."

The affable nun smiled. "Ah, peeling vegetables! Exactly what I had in mind!"

They shared a chuckle and Grace turned away to begin gathering the ingredients she needed for the meal.

"What are all those grocery bags doing out on the front step?"

Sister Mary-Catherine's question pulled Grace up short. "Excuse me?"

"Someone's left a delivery on our doorstep. I wasn't sure if you knew."

Grace frowned. "No. They didn't knock. I had no idea." As she walked toward the front door, she had a sneaking suspicion Callum had come through on his promise to provide them with some much-needed supplies. A peek in some of the bags convinced her.

Not only had he purchased the items she'd requested, there was also tea and coffee, biscuits, bread rolls, apples. Chicken, sausages, meat. There was so much food they would be set for a week or two at least. And he'd done it even after they'd argued. After she'd thrown him out. He'd promised he wouldn't let her down and he hadn't. She was immediately contrite.

Perhaps I shouldn't have been so harsh with him. After all, he'd told her he'd only been curious about her because he liked her. He'd already confessed that. *Why am I so worked up about it? Why do I care so much?*

She knew why. She was ashamed of her past and went to great lengths to conceal it. She'd done nothing illegal, but the memory of her actions after her husband's death still had the power to humiliate her. The thing was, she'd worked hard since then and was no longer that weak person. She wanted people to judge her by who she was now, not by what she'd been then. And even though she struggled every day with her addiction, for the past twelve months she'd not once fallen off the wagon and she had no intention of doing so now.

With a heavy sigh, she carried in the bags of groceries and deposited them on the counters in the kitchen. When Sister Mary-Catherine asked her about the identity of the generous benefactor, she told her the truth.

The old nun beamed. "I liked that Callum Craigdon from the very first moment I met him. There's something very special about that young man."

Grace murmured something unintelligible and continued to unpack the food.

The kitchen teemed with people eating and sharing stories. Grace ladled a serving of pasta into the bowl of one of her regulars and smiled. Thanks to Callum's generosity, the vegetarian dish she'd planned now contained generous chunks of chicken.

"How are you today, Dorothy? Your cough seems better."

"Yes, thanks Grace. It is. I bought that medicine with the money you gave me. It worked a treat. Thanks so much again. You're an angel, Grace."

Grace forced a strained smile. "I'm glad I could help."

The old woman shot her a look of concern. "How are you doing?" she asked. "You seemed a bit down last week."

Grace was flooded with warmth at the caring in the other woman's eyes. "I'm good," she managed past the lump that had lodged itself in her throat. Dorothy eyed her for a moment longer and then nodded, as if satisfied with what she saw.

Ralph, Patricia and Jack all waited patiently in line to be served. Grace greeted each familiar face with a smile and a few words of comfort or encouragement.

Ralph leaned over his bowl and breathed in the fragrant steam. "Smells great, Grace. Thank you."

"Oh, pasta! My favorite! Thanks, Grace," Patricia said, giving her a wide, toothless grin.

"A little more noodles, if you wouldn't mind; thanks Grace. It looks good." This from Jack who'd eat pasta at every meal if he could.

This was what Grace loved about being there. It might

only be preparing and serving a hot meal, but the connection she made with the people who frequented Jennifer's Kitchen made her feel like she was making a difference.

After the unexpected death of her husband, which was then compounded by the loss of her kids, she'd floundered in a world of pain and confusion. Even now, three years later, life was a struggle. During those hard times, Bluey had been there to protect and comfort her.

Through the window over the sink, she saw him patiently waiting on the steps and beyond him, the liquor store, where the siren call of alcohol beckoned. Some days it took all her strength to resist the temptation. Especially after the devastating news about her brother.

Even now, she couldn't believe Ken was dead. It saddened her to admit he'd suffered from a drug addiction for years and had been in and out of jail most of his life. It had been years since she'd seen him. Until the police had contacted her and told her about his death, she hadn't even known where he was. Still, she knew what it was like to suffer from an addiction. She had to continually remind herself of what she'd lose if she spiraled down into that blackness again. It saddened her that Ken hadn't found the strength to turn his life around.

As she let Bluey in, she recalled the morning the police had come to her door with the news. They'd told her Ken had been high on meth and cocaine when he'd walked onto the roadway and been struck by an oncoming car. The driver had called the ambulance, but it had been too late.

Since she'd been given the news she alternated between remembering the tender times they had as happy children… and what she'd imagined his life had been like as an addict on the streets for so long. She missed the brother of her childhood and remembering the good times had her in tears as easily as the imaginings of the accident that killed him.

The police were still carrying out their investigations, but no doubt they'd rule it an accident and the perpetrator would get off scot-free. The police had already indicated that was a strong possibility. Grace was only grateful she had her work to keep her sane in all the madness.

So, more than ever, the people who turned up to the soup kitchen were her lifeline. They distracted her from her struggles and accepted her for what and who she was. They didn't poke into her background or ask uncomfortable questions. They were uncomplicated honest people and she clung to them. None of them had the faintest clue she needed them more than they needed her. She'd be adrift without their constant and predictable presence in her life. The friendship she had with them far surpassed any effort she put forth to fill their stomachs. The truth was they were a sort of family for her. That knowledge filled her with both warmth and sadness and reminded her even more keenly of her brother's death.

The main door to the dining hall opened. Grace looked up and saw Callum weaving his way through the tables. He was dressed as he had been earlier, in casual black slacks and a blue polo shirt. His thick hair was mussed, like it had been blown by the wind, or maybe he'd been running his hands through it. Either way, he looked as devastatingly handsome as he had the first time she'd seen him and she steeled herself against her inevitable reaction to him.

Chapter Ten

As surreptitiously as she could, Grace followed Callum's progress around the dining hall. She wished she was still mad at him. Of all the nerve—asking her boss personal questions about her! That still didn't sit well. But his overly generous donation of food and other essential items had gone a long way to alleviating her anger. She supposed she could accept his curiosity about her. After all, she'd done some research and was curious about him, too.

As he made his way through the rows of tables, he stopped every now and then to greet someone or to comment on the food. There was plenty of laughter between him and the patrons and she could tell they were all at ease. His excellent rapport with them was obvious.

She saw him glance in her direction, but just as quickly he looked away again. She tried to concentrate on her task, but his presence was distracting. Twice she overfilled a bowl and had to apologize. From her station a little further along the serving counter, Sister Mary-Catherine threw her a quizzical look.

"Are you all right, Grace?"

Grace blushed at the concern in the nun's voice. "I-I'm fine," she said hurriedly, wiping up yet another spill.

The problem was, whenever Callum was around, her usual

calm and sensible demeanor took flight. He made her nervous, jittery, clumsy. He awakened feelings in her she thought long dead and herself undeserving of. She wanted to believe he was a guardian angel come to improve the lives of so many, but the jaded part of her, the part that had seen her wealthy in-laws steal her children away, saw him in a different light.

As he moved closer, she caught more snippets of his conversation. She heard him asking people about where they'd be spending the upcoming night and watched as he listened intently to their replies. He nodded his acceptance when they told him the shelters were often overflowing and how cheap accommodation was hard to find. Even if they found a bed in a shelter, it was only short term. A night or two, maybe three and they were expected to move on. There were too many needy people for anyone to be allowed to stay long.

She watched the compassion fill his face and caught the kindness in his eyes. He appeared to really care about these people and their plight. Either that, or he was an incredible actor.

Grace instinctively shook her head in denial. This wasn't the first time she'd seen Callum interacting with the people in the soup kitchen, talking to them, pulling out their stories. Yes. He was curious by nature, but he wasn't a fraud. Somewhere along the way, she'd accepted he was genuine in his willingness to help these people who were down on their luck. If only she could be just as reassured her position there as cook and caretaker was also safe.

"Smells good. Do you mind if I have some?"

Callum's deep voice rumbled over her like a caress. She blushed furiously and tried to keep her heart rate under control. Despite her best efforts, she sounded breathless when she spoke.

"Um, sure." She spooned a generous serving of chicken and pasta into his bowl.

He murmured his thanks and turned away. She warred with herself for a few seconds and then called out to him.

"Callum."

He turned back around to face her. "Yes?"

Once again, her cheeks heated under his steady regard. "I… I want to thank you…for the food. It was more than generous."

"You told me what you needed and I agreed to get it for you. I gave you my word."

She bit her lip and nodded, ashamed at how she'd ended their previous conversation. "I… I'm sorry for tossing you out. It was childish of me."

His gaze remained fixed on hers. "I'm sorry, too. You'd made it clear your private life was off limits and I should never have gone behind your back. Everyone's entitled to their privacy. You're right. It's none of my business."

She looked at him. His expression was so open and earnest, her shoulders slumped on a sigh. "You meant me no harm. I shouldn't have gotten so worked up about it."

He moved closer and frowned. "No. You had every right. I was out of line."

"Maybe next time you want to know something about me, you'll ask me. If I choose not to answer, that's up to me. No offense taken either way. Deal?"

He smiled and it lit up his face, making him look even more breathtakingly handsome. "Deal."

She looked away, flustered. "Um, I overheard you speaking with some of the patrons. About their limited choices for accommodation. Are you really going to do something about that?"

"Yes. Absolutely and I still think some upper floors of this place would be perfect. We could have the kitchen on ground level, just as it is, and offer accommodation on the floors above. There are still a lot of details to be worked out, and heaven forbid, I haven't even secured the property, but I've never been one to shy away from a challenge. I'm willing to pay double the market value just to get started. I doubt the owner's going to knock back that kind of offer. After that, it's a matter of securing planning permission and we'll be good to go."

"I'm surprised the people here were so willing to talk to you. They're usually reticent with strangers. It seems you've earned their trust."

He regarded her with a somber expression. "And what about you? Do you trust me?"

Her eyes widened in surprise. "I… I don't know. I want to," she answered honestly.

His lips compressed and disappointment clouded his eyes. "Fair enough."

She was immediately flooded with guilt. "I'm sorry. You seem…nice. And you've been so generous. With your time and with the food donations. And the people here seem to like you. I… I guess that's good enough for me."

His gaze became more searching. She wanted to look away. It was like he could see into her very soul.

"Who hurt you, Grace?"

His tone was so soft and gentle, tears pricked her eyes. Hastily, she turned away, and moved further back into the kitchen, swiping at her eyes with the back of her hand. He followed closely behind her, immediately contrite.

"I'm sorry, Grace. I didn't mean to upset you. It's none of my business. Darn, I'm a slow learner. You told me to keep out of your private life. I shouldn't ask such personal things."

She drew in a deep breath and let it out on a shudder. For three long years, she'd kept the hurt and pain buried deep inside. In all that time since her husband's death, no one, not a single person had asked about *her*. Until Callum.

She tried to stifle a sob, but it was hopeless. On a gasping breath, her shoulders shook and tears poured down her cheeks. Callum was beside her in an instant, looking stricken. He drew her against him. She was helpless against the kindness in his embrace.

The sobs continued to grip her, no matter how hard she tried to stop. She bit her lip, pushed her fist against her mouth, clenched her jaw as tight as she could, but still the tears fell.

Callum didn't speak, merely murmured sounds of comfort. Holding her against him, he gently stroked her shoulder. When she finally quieted, she was so filled with embarrassment, she could barely lift her head. Staring at his shirt, she realized it was soaked.

"Oh, my goodness! I'm so sorry! I ruined your shirt," she gasped, once again holding a hand to her mouth.

He merely brushed away her apology. "Don't worry about it. It's just a shirt." He paused and his expression turned tender. "Are you all right?"

She nodded. "I'm…fine. It's been a tough week, but nothing I can't handle. Thank you for asking."

"If you ever want to talk about it… I've been told I'm a good listener."

She felt an immediate frisson of alarm and began to shake her head. He held up a hand as if to stop her.

"It's okay, Grace. No pressure. Talk, or don't talk. Whatever you want. I just want you to know I'm here for you if you ever need a friend."

Before she could respond, he turned and left.

Callum left the soup kitchen and climbed into the BMW. He'd been upset to see Grace so distressed, but until she was ready to open up to him, there was nothing he could do. In the meantime, he intended furthering his plans to buy the building and for that he needed a lawyer. Lucky for him, his cousin was a junior partner in one of the city's most prestigious law offices.

With a careful look over his shoulder, he pulled cautiously out into the traffic. Flynn's office was in a swanky part of town not far from the Supreme Court. Though he hadn't yet earned a corner office with spectacular views of Sydney Harbour, Callum knew he had a pretty decent outlook over the botanical gardens.

As he pulled up at a set of lights, he called Flynn and confirmed their appointment.

"How far away are you?" Flynn asked.

"On my way there now. Give me ten minutes."

"Great. I'll meet you downstairs and give you my pass so you can park in the underground staff parking."

"Sounds good. See you soon."

Callum ended the call and in no time at all, he pulled alongside the curb outside the impressive glass and steel skyscraper that housed the offices of Sydney Legal. Spying Flynn, he reached over and opened the passenger side door.

Flynn whistled in appreciation at the sight of Callum's wheels. "I didn't know seminarians could afford to own vehicles like this."

Callum grinned as Flynn climbed in beside him. "They aren't. This belongs to Joel. He's loaned it to me while he's overseas."

"Nice."

"Yeah, he's a good brother. He's letting me stay in his apartment, too."

"Lucky bugger. That has to be better than the seminary."

Callum winked. "Absolutely."

Pulling away from the curb, he followed Flynn's direction to the parking station where the staff of Sydney Legal left their cars. Flynn handed him the magnetic pass and Callum lowered the window and held it so that it could be read by the electronic security system. The wooden arm of the boom gate slowly lifted and Callum drove on through.

"So does this mean you've given up on the idea of the priesthood?" Flynn asked as Callum slid the car into a parking space.

Callum shrugged. "I don't know. I haven't decided yet. My mentor at the seminary told me to take as much time as I need. I guess I'll have a lifetime to live with my decision. I don't want to make it in a rush."

"Fair enough."

They climbed out of the vehicle and Callum locked it with the remote. They took the elevator up to the tenth floor and Flynn led the way to his office. An attractive young blond sat behind a desk in a stylish waiting area. Flynn waved briefly in her direction.

"Hold my calls please, Emily."

"Of course, Flynn," the girl replied.

Callum followed his cousin into an expensively furnished office. The large cedar desk dominated the room. It was neatly stacked with files and papers. A computer screen sat in one corner and office supplies including pens and a stapler sat in a caddy in another. A dark-green leather blotter was centered in front of Flynn's large black ergonomically sound office chair.

"Take a seat," he offered, indicating one of the two plush chairs opposite.

Callum did as he was bid. Flynn took off his jacket and hung it up in a closet in the far corner of the room and then turned back to Callum.

"Would you like a drink? I could get Emily to order up some coffee."

"No, thanks. I'm fine."

Flynn took his place behind his desk and pulled his chair in close. Leaning his elbows on his desk, he looked at Callum.

"So, what can I do for you?"

"I need you to buy me a building."

Flynn laughed. "Excuse me?"

"I need you to buy me a building."

"I heard you the first time, idiot. I mean, why does a man who's training to be a priest need to buy himself a building?"

"I already told you the jury's still out on whether or not I'll return to the seminary. Anyway, that's not the point. The thing is, I want to put my inheritance to good use. I have no need for ten million dollars, but there are many people who do. I could help a lot of people with that kind of money."

Flynn regarded him with interest. "What's your plan?"

Callum filled him in on the details. When he'd finished, Flynn gazed at him in admiration. "That's very generous of you."

Callum shrugged off the praise. "It's not about me. There are so many people living rough in this city. For whatever reason, they no longer have homes to go to. The shelters are full and there's nowhere else to go. I want to try and change that, even in a small way."

"Do you have a place in mind?"

"Yes, as a matter of fact, I do." He gave Flynn the details of the building that housed Jennifer's Kitchen. Flynn pulled out a blank piece of paper and took notes.

"Do you know who owns it?"

From his pocket, Callum pulled out a copy of the lease and handed it to Flynn. "You should find all the information you need in here."

"How much is the building worth?" Flynn asked.

"I don't know. The ground floor is tenanted, but the rest of the building is empty and in disrepair."

"What do you want me to do?"

"I want you to contact the owner and make him an offer."

"Do you know if he wants to sell?"

"I don't have a clue."

Flynn smiled. "What's your budget?"

"I don't have one."

"You should get a market appraisal before you do anything."

"I guess. But it really doesn't matter. I'm prepared to pay whatever it takes."

Flynn looked at him dubiously. "A building that size and in that location could cost more than five million. Are you really prepared to spend that much?"

"Yes. That will leave me five million for the renovations."

Flynn's eyebrows rose in surprise and Callum could tell his cousin thought he was crazy, but Callum didn't care. He wanted to do this. For Grace and for the other patrons who relied on Jennifer's Kitchen. From the very start, this felt right.

"You know I specialize in family law," Flynn said with a chuckle.

"So? Don't you know how to negotiate a contract?"

"Of course. But most people don't use a family law lawyer for that kind of thing."

Callum's shoulders slumped. "So you can't do it?"

"I didn't say I couldn't do it," Flynn hastened to assure him. "It's just a little…unusual."

Callum sat back in his chair while Flynn flicked through the pages of the lease. "So the ground floor is tenanted to the Little Sisters of the Poor?"

"Yes. They run a soup kitchen there."

"Is there someone in charge?"

"Grace Gunning. There are also a number of volunteers and some nuns, of course."

Flynn frowned. "Grace Gunning?"

"Yes. Do you know her?"

"What does she look like?"

Callum hesitated, not wanting to make it too obvious how

closely he'd observed her. He offered a casual shrug. "Oh, you know. Average height, petite. Late twenties. Dark hair. Brown eyes."

"Attractive?"

"Yeah, I guess you'd call her attractive. Why?"

"It's not important. If it's the same woman, I gave her some legal advice a few years ago. No big deal."

Callum didn't question his cousin any further, knowing Flynn wouldn't breach a client's confidentiality. But in the normal course of events, Flynn was a family law lawyer. Callum couldn't help but wonder if Grace had sought advice over a divorce. After all, she had mentioned a son…

"Does this Grace know about your plans?" Flynn asked.

"Yes. She's…quietly enthusiastic."

Flynn grinned. "What does that mean?"

Callum offered him a wry smile. "She's a little distrustful of my motives and doesn't think I'm for real. I don't blame her; she barely knows me. I guess she's not used to someone like me coming along and offering to make lives better without wanting anything in return."

"Yeah, well I'm guessing she's long past the age when she believed in Santa Claus," Flynn replied dryly.

Callum merely winked. "I don't know about that. I've always looked good in red."

Flynn rolled his eyes. "Okay, cut the crap. Why don't you tell me the real reason you want to help this woman."

Callum blushed and silently cursed at the way Flynn had seen through him.

"Come on, Callum. Spill."

"There's nothing to tell," he protested.

Flynn merely lifted a single eyebrow and waited him out. Callum made a sound of irritation.

"Well, if you must know, I like this woman."

"Grace Gunning."

"Yes. Grace."

"And you think it might impress her if you buy her a building?"

"I'm not buying *her* a building. I'm buying the building to help people without the means and wherewithal to have places to stay or even provide food for themselves…and yes, also for Grace. So she can continue to work, has somewhere decent to live and doesn't have to pay rent."

"Where is she living now?"

"In a tiny apartment attached to the building."

"Sounds dismal. Can't she afford something better?"

"No." Callum gestured impatiently. "Look, she's been through some tough times. I don't know all the details, but her life's gone a little off track. I just want help the patrons of Jennifer's Kitchen and, in the process, cut her some slack."

Flynn nodded. "Fair enough. You've always been the most charitable among us." He grinned. "So, how is the family? Still reeling from the terms of your father's will, no doubt."

Callum nodded. "Yeah. There were a few…surprises."

"The gift to my brother, most of all."

Callum frowned. "I don't bear any ill will toward Logan. I'm sure he had nothing to do with Dad leaving the bulk of his estate to him. But I'm damned if I know why Dad did it."

"Yeah. Logan's just as bewildered as the rest of us. If you ask me, it's downright strange. Nicholas has given his life to Craigdon Enterprises. He's worked there since he left school, and even before. If anyone was the natural person to inherit, it's him. Instead he was left out in the cold."

"Yeah, what happened to Nick is rough. But I also feel sorry for Logan. It's not his fault. I hope he knows none of us blame him for what happened."

"Thanks, Callum. I'm sure he'll be glad to hear that. Did you know he's appointed Nicholas the managing director?"

Callum started in surprise. "No, I didn't. That was good of him."

"Yeah, well Logan has no interest in running Craigdon Enterprises. It makes sense to hand the reins over to Nick."

"That reminds me," Callum said. "Mom's planning a family dinner in a few days. It would be good if we could all get together and touch base. Make sure everyone's doing okay."

Flynn nodded. "Sounds good. Let me know the details and I'll try to make it."

Callum pushed away from his chair and stood. He held his hand out toward his cousin. "Thanks for everything, Flynn. I really appreciate your time."

Flynn shook his hand and smiled. "No problem, Padre. I'll let you know as soon as I have anything to tell you."

As Callum made his way out of Flynn's building and headed toward the parking station, he spied a familiar figure. His half-brother, Christopher Barrington stood on the other side of the street, waiting for the lights to change. Callum spent a few seconds debating whether he should draw Christopher's attention, but the decision was taken out of his hands when his half-brother looked up from his phone and saw him. A sardonic smile curled up Christopher's lips. Callum briefly lifted his hand in acknowledgement.

The lights changed and Christopher crossed with the wave of pedestrian traffic. He came to a halt beside Callum. "What a surprise," Christopher drawled, his gaze anything but friendly.

Callum tensed. Though his family had always treated his father's oldest child with courtesy and respect, Christopher had never felt that was enough. He had a chip on his shoulder the size of Ayers Rock and nothing the rest of the family said or did could budge it.

With a concerted effort, Callum greeted his half-brother calmly. "How are you, Christopher?"

"I'm pissed, Callum. Dad might be dead and buried, but his insults live on. He's worth at least a billion dollars and he leaves me nothing. *Nothing!* Not even an acknowledgement! I'm his son! I deserve my fair share."

Callum silently agreed. It was mean of his father to overlook Christopher. The man was, after all, his son. That had never been in dispute.

Steering clear of an argument he had no intention of exacerbating, Callum changed the subject. "What are you doing in this part of town?" he asked, feigning interest.

Christopher waved a sheaf of papers in his face. "I'm here for *this*. Have you forgotten? I've been to see my lawyer. I'm filing a claim against the estate."

Callum acknowledged Christopher's angry response with a brief nod. "I see. Well, you do what you have to do, Christopher, but are you sure it has to come to this? We're your family. Surely we can work something out?"

Christopher's eyes flashed. "I'm not interested in 'working something out,' Callum. I want my share. I'm not going to rest until a court awards me every dollar I'm entitled to. While he was alive, my father ignored me, dismissed me, scorned me, *pitied* me every day of my life. Now that he's dead, it's time for acknowledgement and revenge."

Callum stared at him, feeling sorry for him. Anger like that could eat a person up inside. It wasn't healthy. "So this is what your claim's all about? It's that petty?"

Christopher's lip curled up in disgust. "It's easy for you to say it's petty while you're counting your ten-million-dollar inheritance. How do you think *you'd* feel if every single one of your brothers and sisters inherited significant sums of money, in fact millions and millions of dollars, and you got *nothing?*" he spat out.

Callum remained calm, despite the fury that now emanated in waves off his half-brother.

"You're talking to the wrong Craigdon, Christopher. It's very probable I might become a priest. Money has little importance to me, even millions of dollars. Perhaps you'd be best to talk to Nicholas. Or even Sophia. They're the ones who got next to nothing. You'll probably find they're much more sympathetic to your cause."

Christopher's face turned puce. He opened his mouth to give Callum another angry spray, but Callum cut him off.

"You know, mate, I'm late for an appointment. It was good to see you. You take care." And with that, he turned on his heel and walked away.

Chapter Eleven

race took a vacant seat beside a man she didn't know and set her handbag on the floor near her feet. She looked around the old church hall. It had a familiar feeling of age and neglect and smelled faintly moldy. Like the building that housed the soup kitchen, this hall had seen better days, but it served its purpose and she was sure the rent was cheap and for the purpose of this group, that's all that mattered.

Matthew Reilly, her sponsor and the man who ran the meeting, called for them to be seated. The scattering of people who hovered around the tea and coffee stations at the back slowly joined the circle. Matthew looked around at each of them and smiled.

"Well, it's good to see you all again, and in particular, our newest member." He looked at the man seated beside her and nodded and smiled in greeting. The man shifted nervously and lifted his hand in a half-wave.

"So, who'd like to start us off this evening?"

There was a moment of nervous silence and then Grace slowly stood.

"Hello. My name is Grace and I'm an alcoholic."

There were murmured hellos among the group. Grace had been attending the AA meeting for more than twelve months and most of the people in the room were familiar, but more often than not she didn't speak during the meetings. It was enough that she got herself there, listened to the struggles, the hopes, the fears the others experienced and took on board the advice offered by Matthew.

But ever since Callum's unexpected arrival in her life, she'd been struggling. He'd turned her world upside down and it was difficult to remain strong and focused on her goal when her thoughts were consumed by him. Then there was dealing with the death of her brother. A brother she hadn't seen in years but who was integral to some fond memories of the happier times when they were children…

"When was your last drink, Grace?" Matthew asked kindly. His question startled her out of her reverie. "Three-hundred-and-eighty-nine days ago."

"That's great, Grace. You're doing so well. How has it been for you?"

She compressed her lips and stared at the floor. "Hard. Very hard."

"And how have you managed to stay away from the drink?"

"Through extreme willpower," she confessed. "Every day I yearn for the taste of it, the sweet oblivion. It never goes away, does it?"

"No," Matthew agreed, his voice gentle. "I think everyone here will tell you the same: It never goes away."

There was a murmur of assent among the group. Matthew turned back to Grace. "Has anything happened recently to make things harder than usual for you?"

She clenched her hands into fists. Drawing in a deep breath, she nodded.

"Would you like to tell us about it?"

Once again, she nodded. She *needed* to tell them about it. She needed their help, their advice. That was the reason she was there.

"When you're ready, Grace," Matthew encouraged.

"Two things. I lost a brother a month ago. He was killed in an accident…We hadn't connected for years and I'd lost track of him, and he too was an addict. Didn't turn himself around. He died at the scene. Thinking about him stirs up old memories of happier times and that makes me sad. Now I'll never reconnect with him."

There was a murmur of sympathy and shaking of heads. She took a deep breath and continued: "And something else is going on that scares me. You know how I'm trying to get my kids back…Well, about a month ago, someone came into my life. He's kind and funny and compassionate. Most people think he's a good guy. He's also talking about buying the building where I work. He has all these plans which sound great, but I don't know if he's all talk, whether I can trust him to do what he says he will. And I worry about if he does, how that will affect me. I need that job so badly and I don't know where I fit into his plans. He assures me I'll be fine but I don't know if I can trust him. I'm so worried and confused and scared and all the time I'm trying desperately to stay sober. Sometimes it's just so hard…"

Her voice drifted off and she wrapped her arms around herself and promptly sat back down. She was limp and exhausted from the effort of opening up to them. Tears burned behind her eyes.

"It sounds like you have a lot going on, Grace," Matthew said gently. "It would be enough for any of us to deal with. We're sorry to hear about the loss of your brother. That must be hard too. You've done remarkably well to stay strong. You ought to feel proud of yourself. I do. And I'm sure the rest of us are proud of you, too."

There was a murmur of agreement from the others. She took comfort from their support. This was why she came to these meetings so often. It helped her maintain her resolve.

She couldn't afford to fall off the wagon. That would certainly mean disaster for her after coming so far and being so close to her goal. Each day she felt stronger, more satisfied with herself as a person…

"It's at times like this our resolve is sorely tested," Matthew continued in the same quiet voice. "I'm so glad you came along tonight, Grace. Let us help you, guide you, encourage you, strengthen you. That's what we're here for."

She nodded. The tension inside her eased. She looked around the room and saw kindness, compassion and understanding on the faces of those seated in the circle. One of the women was in tears. These were her people. They came from different backgrounds, cultures, walks of life… But they all had one thing in common: They were recovering alcoholics who needed help to get through life…one hour, one day, one month, one step at a time.

It had been a couple of weeks since Callum met with Flynn and he still didn't know if the owner of Grace's building was willing to sell. He'd been volunteering at the soup kitchen every day and the more he got to know the patrons, Grace and the other staff, the more he wanted to help them.

The sun was setting on another day, casting red and orange hues dancing like diamonds across the water. The guilt and fatigue that had dogged him since the night of the accident eased. He leaned on the railing of Joel's balcony and cracked open a beer. He'd just taken his first mouthful when his phone buzzed. He pulled it out of his pocket and checked the screen. Recognizing the number, his heart leaped.

"Flynn! It's good to hear from you."

"Yeah, sorry it's taken me so long to get back to you. Our vendor has been overseas. He's only just arrived back in the country."

"I hope you have good news."

"Well, cuz. That depends."

Callum's stomach dropped. He was flooded with disappointment. *The owner wouldn't sell... All his plans would come to nothing... Grace... He'd promised her...*

He forced himself to speak. "Depends on what?"

"The owner's willing to sell, but he wants six million."

Callum gasped in shock. "Six million!"

Callum had already done up a rough budget and he was going to need every cent of the five million left over from the purchase if he wanted to see his plans for the redevelopment of the building come to fruition. His inheritance had seemed like a lot of money, but it appeared it wasn't going to be enough. He felt weighed down with disappointment.

"Yeah, that's what I thought," Flynn continued. "I got it appraised by an agent. He valued it at three-and-a-half. Six million's way out of line."

Callum blew out his breath on a heavy sigh. "I guess if that's what the owner wants, that's what I'm going to have to pay. I want that building. I'll just have to modify some of my plans, lower my expectations. I won't have the money to do everything."

"I think you're crazy paying that kind of money for the building," Flynn replied. "Offer him four. He's still getting more than it's worth."

"But what if he turns me down? I'd rather pay what he wants and know it's mine."

This time it was Flynn's turn to sigh. "Sometimes you can be a pain in the neck, Callum. Did anyone ever tell you that? Why this particular building? I'm sure I can find you something more affordable—with a more reasonable vendor."

Callum shook his head reflexively. "No. It has to be that building."

Once again, Flynn sighed. "Well, if you insist on spending six million on it, I'm going to donate my inheritance to the cause."

Callum blinked in surprise. "You're going to give me a million dollars?"

"Yep. That's what Uncle Henry left me. It was probably guilt money for the way my mom died. He never got over the fact he was driving when they had that accident."

"Maybe," Callum agreed. "I guess that makes sense."

"Yeah. Don't ask me to explain Logan's windfall though."

"I don't think any of us can explain that. Are you sure you want to give me your entire inheritance?"

"Yes. I don't need the money. You do. I'd like to contribute to your project. What you're doing is a good thing. There ought to be more redevelopments like that going on."

Callum was filled with warmth and relief. "Thanks, mate. I really appreciate it."

"It's cool. So, when do you want me to go back to this greedy asshole?"

"As soon as you can."

"Okay, but please, just let me present a counter offer. Let's say we go in with five. That's what you planned to spend. Besides, if you decide to leave the seminary, you're going to need something behind you to make a new start. Have you thought of that?"

Callum pursed his lips. "No. But you're right. All right, let's offer him five. But if he refuses it, just give him the six he's asking. I'll think about my future later. Right now I want to get started on the renovations."

"You'll need permission from Sydney City Council before you can do anything."

"Yes, but they'll agree. Why wouldn't they? I'm helping to solve one of their biggest problems and tidying up an eyesore along the way."

"Don't be too certain of finding friendly attitudes at the council. The people in the planning department seem to go out of their way to make life difficult."

"Ah, but I have God on my side, remember? He and I are tight."

Flynn chuckled. Callum reminded him of the upcoming family dinner and after thanking him once again for his help, brought the call to an end.

"Yes!" He punched the air with exuberance. He was one step closer to making his vision come true. He was sure any problems he met at city council would be overcome and soon the work could begin. Grace would get the soup kitchen of her dreams and so many less fortunate people in their city would have a roof over their heads. It was a win for everyone. He couldn't wait to tell her the news.

Grace finished peeling the potato and dropped it in the sink with the ones she'd already done. Picking up another, she began to remove the skin. She'd settled on shepherd's pie and pavlova for the lunch menu and was busy preparing the mash. The mince was already in five large pans on the industrial-sized stove, browning with onions and garlic. All she had to do was add diced tomatoes, a few additional herbs and spices, a dash of honey and a good dollop of tomato paste.

Sister Mary-Catherine had the heavy-duty electric mixer going, beating egg whites for the pavlova. Fresh strawberries, bananas and passion fruit had been delivered to the kitchen from a local green grocer. When the van pulled up and the man came in with the first carton of fruit, Grace had pulled him aside, certain there'd been a mistake.

"I'm sorry. We didn't order this. I think you have the wrong address."

"Is this Jennifer's Kitchen?" the man asked.

"Yes," Grace replied.

"Then this is the right place."

Grace frowned. "I don't understand. Who authorized this?"

The man consulted a clipboard. "It says the order was arranged and paid for in full by Callum Craigdon."

And then Grace understood. Once again, she was taken aback by Callum's generosity. First the food a couple of weeks ago and now a generous delivery of fruit. If the donation had come from someone else she'd be wondering what they expected in return. Even their corporate sponsors expected some form of recognition. But Callum, it seemed, wanted nothing. His motivation appeared to be a genuine desire to help the less fortunate and that knowledge warmed Grace through.

A knock on the door to the dining hall reached her above the din of the mixer. She washed and dried her hands, crossed the room and opened the door. Callum stood there on the bottom step, grinning. Despite circles under his eyes they twinkled with excitement and good humor. She couldn't help it. She smiled back.

"Hi! You're just the person I was looking for," he said.

Her smile widened. "I guess you found me. Everything okay, Callum?"

There was a slight hesitation. Only slight. "Sure. Things are fine. Can I come in?" he asked.

She stepped back and opened the door wider, allowing him to enter. She returned to the kitchen to finish peeling the potatoes. Sister Mary-Catherine greeted him with a pleasant smile.

"Callum! How wonderful to see you! Thank you for all the lovely fresh fruit! You've been way too generous."

Grace blushed. She should have thanked him already. She added her mumbled appreciation.

"My pleasure, ladies," Callum replied, encompassing both of them in his gaze. "I'm happy to help."

"Oh, it's been a big help," Sister Mary-Catherine effused. "We're using some of it to decorate pavlovas for dessert today. A real treat, to be sure."

"Sounds delicious." He turned to Grace who had a peeler in one hand and a potato in the other. "Do you need any help?"

She shrugged in a nonchalant manner, but opened the utensil drawer and handed him another peeler. He picked up a potato and in short order removed the skin.

"It looks like you actually know how to use that thing," she teased.

He grinned. "Have you forgotten the exceptional pot of custard I cooked last time? I told you I used to cook at the seminary. Didn't you believe me?"

She blushed. When he looked at her like that, she felt warm and tingly all over. Sexual awareness raised goosebumps on her arms. Even in the heady days of her courtship with Daniel, she couldn't remember feeling like that.

Sister Mary-Catherine shut off the mixer and the room was thrust into momentary silence. With the last potato peeled, Grace filled a huge boiler with water.

Callum noticed how hard she worked. "When we renovate in here I think pot fillers would be a good addition to the space. No more lugging water to the stove at least..."

Grace shook her head but looked pleased as she bent her head and went back to work.

"Do you want me to cut the potatoes into pieces?" Callum asked.

"Yes, thank you. In quarters, at least. They'll cook faster that way."

He began to do as she asked while she emptied several tins of tomatoes into each pan of minced beef, along with the remaining ingredients.

"If I had to guess, I'd say you're making shepherd's pie," Callum commented.

Grace nodded. "You guessed right. What gave me away?"

His expression was somber. "The potatoes, for sure."

He looked so serious, she burst into laughter. It felt strange, sharing that humorous moment with him, but it also felt good.

"What brings you by the kitchen today?" she asked, striving for casual.

"I heard back from my cousin about the purchase. The owner has agreed to sell."

He flashed her a smile so wide and sweet it snatched her breath away. His eyes gleamed with excitement.

"That's… That's wonderful, Callum."

His face lit up. "Isn't it? It's going to take at least six weeks to finalize the legalities, but after that, it's all systems go. I can't wait to go over the plans with you. You know this place better than anyone. I'd really value your input."

His excitement was contagious. She thought about her recent AA meeting and recalled her sponsor's advice. Matthew and the group agreed that if she felt she could trust Callum, it might be best to open up to him, and in particular, tell him about her daily struggle with the booze. It might help him to understand her fears concerning the changes he proposed and also reassure her that he was on her side.

As she saw him smiling at her, something inside her shifted. This was a good man. A man with a kind and compassionate heart. A man who wanted to do good in the world. A man who had earned her trust.

"Do you really want to hear my suggestions on the expansion of the kitchen?"

He shrugged. "Not just the kitchen. I want to hear your thoughts on the whole redevelopment of the building. All four floors above us too. I want to turn them all into self-contained rooms. Sort of like hotel rooms, only with a kitchenette.

And of course there would be a communal laundry room with washers and dryers. I want the people who live there to be self-sufficient as much as they can."

She stared at him, her eyes wide. "Wow, that sounds… amazing. I can't even imagine what it might be like. To be able to offer these people a little apartment all their own. It's…" To her embarrassment, she teared up. At the same time, she tried hard to swallow the lump that had lodged in her throat.

His expression softened. He moved closer and patted her on the shoulder, then gave her arm a squeeze.

"It's all right, Grace. I'm glad you feel the way I do. It means a lot." His gaze intensified. "In fact, it means everything."

She stared at him, mesmerized by the expression in his eyes. "But, you don't even know me," she protested weakly.

His gaze remained locked on hers. "I'm a good judge of character, Grace. Believe me, I know enough."

Chapter Twelve

Grace was both pleased and grateful when Callum offered to stay and help them with the serving. When the last meal had been eaten and all the dirty dishes stacked in the huge dishwashers and ones washed earlier, packed away, Grace thanked Alice and the nuns for their help and bid them farewell.

As she closed the door behind them, she sighed. It had been a long day and it was only mid-afternoon. Still, she wasn't as tired as she usually was after a full day of cooking and serving and cleaning up and she knew that was because of Callum.

Throughout the day, he'd chatted and laughed and teased staff and patrons alike. He'd stirred pots, served food, shared stories, listened, stacked the dishwashers and cleaned the vast number of pots and pans required to feed so many people. Wherever he was, laughter followed and the sound of it had lightened her heart. For the first time in a long time, she'd gotten through most of the day without thinking of the liquor store across the road.

Oblivious to her thoughts, Callum finished the last pan and tossed the dishtowel into the basket of dirty laundry. "Wow, I'm glad that's done."

She smiled. "Thanks for your help. We couldn't have done it without you."

He grinned. "That's a big fat lie, but I'll forgive you for it. By the way, the pavlova was a hit."

She smiled, filled with warmth at his praise. She'd learned to cook from her mother and she knew she was good at it, but it still felt special when someone recognized her talents. It was even more special coming from Callum.

"Would you like a coffee?" he asked.

"Coffee sounds great. White with one," she added.

"I remember," he said over his shoulder and followed the comment with another grin.

Her stomach somersaulted and nerves jangled in her belly. In an effort to distract herself from this infatuation with a man she hardly knew, she turned away and took a seat at the small table on the far side of the kitchen. Before her pulse had returned even halfway to normal, he set a steaming cup of coffee in front of her and slipped into the chair opposite.

"We made quite a team today," he said, sipping his coffee.

She nodded. "Yes." His gaze locked on hers and she couldn't look away.

"I really enjoy working with you, Grace."

The intensity of his gaze burned her like she'd been scalded. Her hands shook so badly, she spilled her coffee.

"Oh, damn it," she muttered.

He continued speaking as if he hadn't noticed. "To think this place will soon be mine... As luck will have it, my cousin Flynn is a lawyer. He doesn't usually do property conveyancing, but he agreed to help, as a favor. He's negotiating with the owner and hoping to close the deal soon. I still can't believe it."

She looked at him with admiration. "You really do keep your word," she mused.

He shot her a lazy smile that made her pulse skyrocket again. "I'm doing all I can. Do you still doubt me?"

She shrugged and looked away, uncertain how much she wanted to reveal to him. Then she remembered the urging of her sponsor. She drew in a deep breath.

"I haven't always had trustworthy people around me, or been strong and worthy of trust myself. Let's just say, there have been people in my past I should have been able to trust and yet they betrayed me. It takes awhile to recover from that."

His expression flooded with compassion. "Oh, Grace! I'm so sorry! That's terrible!"

She bit her lip against a surge of emotion, trying hard not to cry. "Yeah. Well, I guess I lucked in."

She heard the bitterness in her voice and wasn't surprised by it. She despised her in-laws for doing what they'd done. They'd accused her of murdering their son and then they'd stolen her children. And then her mind snagged on something he'd said and fear iced her veins. She shot him a glance and did her best to keep her tone casual.

"You said your cousin is a lawyer. Flynn, right?"

"Yeah. Flynn Craigdon. Our fathers were brothers."

Oh, God. His cousin is a lawyer. The same lawyer I engaged three years ago when I tried to keep my children… What if his cousin told him about her? About her past?

Panic nipped at her heels, increasing the turmoil of her thoughts. Then she got hold of herself. Her conversations with Flynn Craigdon were protected by legal professional privilege. He'd told her at their very first meeting that everything she said to him was confidential. That was the reason she'd been so frank with him. She'd told him everything…

In the end, he hadn't been able to help her with her children. Phillip and Nerida Gunning had been awarded full custody. The best Flynn had been able to manage was supervised access for a few hours one day a week. She'd been shocked speechless, stunned, devastated. Her babies had looked at her, scared and confused. They knew something bad had happened, but the full import of the judge's decision hadn't yet set in. Seth and Alyssa had clung to her, crying and begging her to take them home. They'd never been separated from their mother or their family pet, Bluey who'd been with them from the cradle. Their dog wasn't welcome at their grandparents' and her children were sad and confused. It took repeated requests from the judge for her to release them into the care of their grandparents, before the sheriff's officer eventually prised them from her arms.

The memory of that tragic day still haunted her. It was yet another reason she'd tried and failed over and over again to get herself clean. Through it all Bluey had been the only constant and she loved him dearly. But now she was more than twelve months sober and she'd turned her life around. Perhaps it was time to trust Callum with her secret. Lord knows, it would be a relief to share the burden of her pain.

"Grace? Are you all right?"

The caring and concern that filled his tone was reflected in the beautiful blue of his eyes. Her throat closed up. Tears threatened and then spilled over. She was helpless against the deluge. Once again, she found herself in his arms, taking refuge leaning against his broad chest. The warmth of his skin seeped into her, bringing her amazing comfort.

He let her cry without interruption. He just held her and pressed sweet, comforting kisses against her hair. She felt so good in his embrace, safe, secure and protected.

Finally, the tears subsided and she raised her face to his. Her eyes felt swollen and tears still dampened her cheeks, but he looked at her with such love and tenderness it stole her breath.

"Talk to me, Grace," he whispered.

And so she did.

"I met Daniel Gunning when I was at university. I was studying to be a nurse. He was halfway through a four-year urban and environmental planning degree. It was love at first sight. Though we didn't plan for it to happen, I fell pregnant. Seth was born right before my twentieth birthday. Alyssa was born two years after that."

"When did you marry?" Callum asked.

Grace nodded. "Right after Seth was born."

"How did Daniel's family feel about everything?"

Grace looked at him, silently marveling at his intuition. "Let's just say they didn't take kindly to me."

"What about Seth?"

"Oh, they doted on their grandson, of course. Their effusiveness where Seth was concerned was almost embarrassing. When Alyssa came along, she was treated like a princess. It was only to me they gave the cold shoulder."

"Where was Daniel in all this? Surely he supported you against his parents?"

Grace stared down at the table. "I wish I could say he did."

Callum frowned and anger glinted in his eyes. "You mean he sided with them?"

She nodded and he cursed. "The bastard."

"Oh, yeah. And you don't even know the half of it." With a sigh, she continued. "If I hadn't fallen pregnant, there's a good chance the love I had for Daniel would have died a natural death. We would have drifted apart, found other interests, busied ourselves with our studies and eventually our careers. As it was, a lot of that happened, only we were married with two little babies. We'd complicated things way past a simple breakup."

Memories assailed her. She cleared her throat. "And then of course on top of that were his parents. They were sure our marriage wouldn't last. I was determined to show them they were wrong. I tried so hard to be the kind of wife Daniel wanted and needed to support him in his career, but as the years went by, nothing I did seemed good enough.

"He graduated at the top of his class and was offered a job at the Sydney City Council as a junior urban planner. He was ambitious and worked long hours, even on weekends. It felt like we hardly saw each other. It didn't help that by then the love-struck teenager had matured and I looked at him through different eyes. I saw a man who cared far too much about what his parents thought and relied far too heavily on their approval. When he didn't get it, he'd spiral into a depression that would sometimes take weeks for him to come out of.

"In the meantime, I was trying to raise two children and manage the household. All without help from Daniel." She looked up. "It was tough."

"I can't even begin to imagine," Callum said softly. "I take it you never finished your degree?"

She laughed without humor. "No. There was no time for that. Daniel was busy with his career. Someone had to stay home with the kids."

She looked at him, her eyes wide. "Not that I ever regretted it. I love my kids with everything that I am. I'd never trade those years with them for anything."

"Where are they now?" Callum's voice was pitched low. It was like he'd already worked out where the story was going. He knew she lived in a small apartment off the kitchen and she lived there alone.

"Before we get to that," Grace continued, "you need to know what happened to Daniel."

Callum regarded her steadily. "Okay. Tell me what happened to Daniel."

Grace bit her lip and cast around for her courage. This was harder than she thought. She drew in a shaky breath.

"Daniel was a risk-taker. Fast cars, motorbikes, speed boats. He made okay money as a planner, but not enough to indulge his passion for speed. Fortunately for Daniel, his parents had showered him with expensive gifts prior to our marriage. Our garage was full of them. We used to go water-skiing on the rare weekends when he wasn't working."

She paused, remembering that fateful day. A coldness settled inside her, causing her to shiver.

Callum noticed her distress. He reached out and touched her arm. "I understand if you'd rather not talk about it, Grace."

"No, no," she reassured him. "I want you to know."

She drew in another breath and blew it out through loose lips. "That day was like any other, a warm summer day with a sky so clear and blue it was breathtaking. We were out on the boat on the Parramatta River with the children and my best friend. We'd packed a picnic and the kids were enjoying having all of us together. That didn't happen often.

"Daniel was skiing behind the boat. I was at the wheel. My best friend, Justine, had agreed to be the observer. Daniel was a show-off, and with good reason. He was an excellent skier. That day he'd been performing tricks on the skis for the kids. Leaping into the air, twisting and turning, spinning all the way round. To me, he seemed to be acting even more reckless than usual, but Seth and Alyssa loved every minute of it.

"My attention was mostly on the river in front of me. There were a lot of watercraft out that afternoon. I didn't want to hit anyone." She paused and gathered the strength she needed to continue.

"Somehow Daniel got caught up in the ski ropes. They twisted around him, dragging him under."

"He drowned?"

She shook her head. "No. He went under the propeller."

"Oh, Grace!"

She closed her eyes against the barrage of memories. *The shock, the horror, the screams…*

"I don't know how it happened," she continued quietly. "Justine was meant to be watching him, but she'd been distracted by the children. By the time we realized Daniel was no longer on the skis it was too late."

Callum's eyes were filled with compassion. "How utterly devastating. For all of you."

"Yes. I'm ashamed to say I blamed Justine for not paying proper attention. If she'd realized soon enough that Daniel was in trouble, I could have stopped the boat. Of course, I really only blamed her to alleviate my own guilt and I regret that now."

"It wasn't your fault, Grace. It was an accident."

She merely shrugged. Callum wasn't the first person to try and convince her of that.

"How long ago did this happen?"

"Three years. You can guess how his parents reacted."

"They blamed you."

"Of course they did. Daniel was their golden child. They wouldn't even consider the notion he'd contributed to his own death. The police report stated that if he hadn't been skylarking, he more than likely wouldn't have been caught up in the ropes. They ruled his death an accident. Phillip and Nerida didn't see it that way."

"What did you do?" Callum asked gently.

Grace squeezed her eyes shut tightly against a wave of pain. The next few minutes were going to be the hardest. But she'd come this far, she might as well finish it.

"I fell apart. I couldn't take it. Everywhere I turned, my in-laws blamed me for their son's death. They were angry, vicious, relentless. Doled out a barrage of guilt and abuse. My children were so sad and I felt so much guilt. My thinking wasn't rational all the time and I had no idea where to take my life. Everything was turned upside down. I'm ashamed to admit I found solace in alcohol. It was the only way I could escape the torment.

"Before I realized what was happening, I was drinking three or four bottles of wine a day. Then it increased to five, then six. I was drunk most of the time I was awake. Seth and Alyssa were frightened. They didn't know what to do. They did the only thing they could think of. They called grandma."

"Grandma to the rescue," Callum said dryly.

Grace smiled bitterly. "Oh, yes. She rode in on her white steed, eyes blazing. She took my babies home with her and I never got them back. Within weeks I was served with court papers informing me she and Phillip were seeking full custody. I went to Flynn and he was great, but my case was hopeless. I was an alcoholic without a job or even a home."

Callum frowned. "What about the place you lived in with Daniel?"

Once again, Grace laughed bitterly. "Oh, yes. My marital home. See, our home had been given to us by Daniel's parents. The only thing they failed to mention was it was only on loan. When Daniel died, they kicked me out, right after they took my kids. I was homeless, penniless and all my hope was gone."

"You said Daniel made okay money. Surely he had some savings?"

She shook her head. "No. When he died, he had less than a five thousand dollars in his bank account."

"What about life insurance?"

"Oh yes, he had insurance. Only the beneficiaries were Alyssa and Seth. The money is now held in trust until they come of age and is administered by their guardians."

Callum's expression was grim. "Let me guess. Your in-laws."

"Yep."

Callum slowly shook his head, his eyes filled with sadness. "Oh, Grace. No one should have to go through what you have. It's just not right. Sometimes I don't understand God at all. Why would He do this to you? Why would He expect you to carry such a burden of grief and pain?"

"I have no answers, Callum. I wish I did. For the next two years, my life spiraled out of control. I was a hopeless drunk. I was unemployed. I lived on the streets. And then one day I stumbled upon Jennifer's Kitchen and I was warmly welcomed inside. I was given a hot meal. I found kindness, compassion and understanding. Nobody asked difficult questions. Nobody looked at me with disapproval or judgment in their eyes. It was then I vowed to get my life back together. To get off the drink. To get myself clean and put the mess behind me. I had a powerful incentive. My kids."

Callum looked at her with tenderness and admiration. "You've done an amazing job of getting your life together. I see you as the most put-together woman I know. How could a judge not want you to have your kids now?"

She gave a small smile. "You're very kind. The thing is, I've been clean for twelve months. I regularly attend AA meetings and the support I receive there really helps. I have a stable job. My living situation isn't ideal, but I'm working on that. I've been saving every cent I can so I can move to a proper flat. Somewhere the judge will approve of. That's why the thought of you changing things upset me at first. I thought I'd lose the stability I'd worked so hard to create.

"The biggest hurdle I have is my in-laws. As you can imagine, they haven't warmed to me over the years. They still blame me for Daniel's death. They've already made it clear if I ever try and go for custody, they'll fight me every step. I see Seth and Alyssa a few hours once a week and I'm trying hard to rebuild our relationship, but it was difficult when I was still drinking and now they've spent so much time with their grandparents who've taken every opportunity to paint me as an unfit mother. And to be clear, until I got clean, I really didn't deserve to have them."

"There must be some way I can help you," Callum murmured.

Grace smiled softly. "You're a good man, Callum Craigdon. I love that you want to help me. The thing is, I don't see how you can."

Callum shook his head. "No. I refuse to believe that." He looked at her with eyes that were fierce with determination. "You should know this about me, Grace. I'm not someone who's daunted by a challenge and when I set my mind to something I never, ever give up."

She wanted so much to believe he could change things, appeal to her in-laws to end their bitter battle against her, convince a judge to give her back her children because she was better, so much better, and that reuniting her children with their mother was the best thing for all concerned...

But she knew that wasn't possible. Not even someone as good and kind and wonderful as Callum Craigdon was capable of all that. It would take a miracle and right now, she no longer believed in miracles.

As if following the train of her thoughts, Callum's expression turned fiercer. "Don't give up on yourself, Grace. We're going to get through this. I promise."

She tried to smile, loving how much he cared. It felt so good to have someone fighting in her corner for a change, referring to her as part of a "we." She thought of her brother and the senseless loss of his life. It filled her with so much sadness. She needed to make her life count. After all, none of them knew how much time they had left. Tears filled her eyes and slid down her cheeks.

"Please don't look so sad," Callum murmured. Gently, he reached out and touched a fingertip to her tears.

"It isn't just about losing my kids," she said quietly. "My brother, Ken Wheeler, was recently killed in an accident."

Callum's mouth gaped open in shock. "Oh, Grace! That's terrible!"

"Yes. The police told me he stepped off the curb and into the path of an oncoming car."

The color left Callum's face. He stared at Grace, his eyes wide with disbelief. "Wh-where did it happen?"

"I'm not sure exactly. The police did tell me. I just can't remember. Somewhere north-west of Sydney, in the Richmond area."

Callum merely shook his head, as if unable to find the words to offer her even a modicum of comfort. She let out a shaky breath, still upset at the tragedy of her brother's death. He'd had his fair share of troubles, but no one deserved to die like that.

"I'm… I'm so sorry, Grace," Callum finally responded. "I don't know what to say."

"It's all right," she reassured him. "It wasn't your fault."

He looked like he wanted to be sick. She frowned at him in concern.

"Are you okay, Callum?"

He swallowed and then pushed away from the table. "I'm sorry, Grace I have to go. Take care, okay? I'll speak to you soon." And with that, he turned and left.

Grace watched him leave. As the door closed behind him, she sighed and hugged herself. It had been so hard to open up to him, but she was glad she had. Now there were no secrets between them and she hoped he had a better understanding of her and how the events of her past had shaped her and continued to shape her.

She glanced around the empty room and spied Bluey waiting patiently just inside the back door.

"Come here, boy." She patted her thighs in encouragement.

The dog padded toward her, his tongue out, grinning in anticipation. When he reached her side, she leaned down and patted him.

"You're such a good boy, aren't you? My beautiful Bluey." She hugged him. He nuzzled her shoulder and licked her face. Just being with him reminded her of her children. Somehow he made her feel closer to them and after opening herself up to Callum, she felt off-balance and vulnerable. Bluey whined quietly and once again nuzzled her shoulder. Tears burned behind her eyes. She hugged him again.

"I know, boy. I miss them too. But we're going to get them back. I promise. We're going to be a family again."

Shakily, she got to her feet and went to lock the front door. She passed by the kitchen window that overlooked the street. Evening had fallen and the street lights were on, illuminating the cracked and broken pavement. The red neon sign above the liquor store stood out stark and bright in the darkness.

A strong yearning came upon her. It snatched her breath. She could almost taste the sweet liquid, the burning as it slid down her throat. The oblivion that came afterwards when all the darkness and pain disappeared. And she only had to cross the street and she could have it. It was right within her reach.

And then she thought of her babies, of the hard work and sacrifices she'd made to get clean. More than twelve months down the track and she was that much closer to getting them back. They needed their mother and she needed them. She wouldn't do anything to jeopardize her chances, no matter how strong the urge. She wasn't that same weak person any longer. She had learned she could change for the better. Feel pride in accomplishments, small and large. She believed in herself and she wouldn't allow any amount of haranguing by her in-laws to undermine what she was and wanted to be—for her children.

It continued to be a struggle every day to stay sober, but she owed it to herself and her kids to stick with it. She knew she could withstand the tide. And she owed it to Callum too. He'd listened to her story and hadn't judged her. Not once had she seen pity or condemnation in his eyes. Instead, he wanted to help her. He wanted to help her get her kids back. That's all that seemed to matter.

With a last long look at the neon sign, she gritted her teeth and with fierce determination, turned her back—and with Bluey beside her, she left the room.

Chapter Thirteen

Callum loved this time of year, when the sun set later and he got to enjoy more daytime hours than usual. He'd loved it even more during his time at the seminary, when much of his day had been spent indoors, learning lessons, saying prayers, and poring over library books.

Red and purple and orange hues painted the early evening sky as he drove the final few miles toward Craigdon Manor. The beauty of the end of day filled Callum with a sense of peace even as his mind spun around Grace's news about her brother's death....

His mother had pulled off a minor miracle by gathering all the members of her family together for dinner. All except Joel, who was partying his way through Europe, and Jett who'd called Callum to offer his apologies. He wasn't going to make it. Danielle and the kids had come down with a virus.

The last thing Callum felt like, though, was a family dinner. This kind of event usually extended over a few hours and considering the tension still simmering about the terms of his father's will, no doubt there would be plenty of drama. He didn't know how much more he could take right now.

He was tired and preoccupied and his brain kept running in circles. Sleepless nights had become his new normal after the accident. Now he'd discovered it was Grace's brother he'd killed. Ken Wheeler. Now he had a name, and a family who grieved for the poor man. Grace…

Dear, God! What am I going to do? I have to tell her… But…how?

What if she never forgave him?

His gut still churned with dread and uncertainty as he swung Joel's convertible into the wide paved driveway that led to his family home. He drew in a few calming breaths and forced himself to take a moment to appreciate the tall established trees, the acres of manicured lawns and the seasonal flowers that bloomed in profusion in neat garden beds around the estate. For many years, his mother had spent hours in the garden each day and though she was assisted by two able gardeners, the design of the outdoor spaces and placement of every tree, shrub and flowerbed had come from her.

He guessed her green thumb and ability to produce beautiful gardens stemmed from her innate creativity. In her youth, his mother had wanted to become a concert pianist, like her mother. Elizabeth had studied for a time at the Conservatorium of Music in Sydney and was well on the way to following in her mother's footsteps. Then she'd had a change of mind, had met Henry and fallen in love. The rest was history.

Except his mother had recently confessed the rock-solid marriage their children had always believed in wasn't as rock-solid as it had appeared. Callum wasn't naïve enough to think that marriage was always perfect. Though he'd never made that kind of commitment to anyone, he was sure marriage had its ups and downs. Two people joining their lives together, learning to adjust to one another, even years down the track, well that couldn't always be easy. And yet his parents had been married for more than thirty years. He'd assumed they'd worked out most of the rough patches by then, including his father's infidelities.

But now Callum's father was dead. He couldn't help but wonder if Henry had ever had any regrets. *Had he wished he'd spent less time at the office and more time with his family? Had he even once regretted putting so much effort into making money and far less effort into making friends?*

For all Henry's standing as a prominent businessman in Sydney, there had been a mere handful of friends at his funeral. The majority of the crowd had been made up of business acquaintances and those members of society who were there more for the photo opportunity and a chance to get a look at the Craigdon estate than they were to remember their personal connection to Henry. Callum wouldn't dwell on the lack of friends at his father's funeral, but it hadn't gone unnoticed.

As he swept around the final curve of the driveway, the three-story mansion stood tall and majestic before him. Lights blazed from every window, giving the house a warm and welcoming feel. Several cars, shiny in the lamplights that bordered the perimeter of the long driveway, were already in the parking bay. It seemed like most of his family had already arrived.

Climbing out of the sports car, he pushed the turmoil of his earlier thoughts to the back of his mind and headed up the wide stone steps to the front door. An elegant foyer inlaid with travertine tiles marked the entrance and led to the palatial formal dining room. Immediately to his left was his father's study, a room he hadn't been in since the reading of the will. Spying his mother, he headed toward her.

"Callum. It seems like an age since I saw you last."

He smiled and leaned forward and kissed her on the cheek. She was dressed in a tailored cream-colored suit with gold trim. "You're looking well, Mother. "How have you been?"

"I'm fine. It…takes some adjusting to, but at least I have Issy here to keep me company. I was upset for her when she broke things off with Luke and returned home, but right now, I'm glad to have her here. She's been good company."

Callum felt a twinge of guilt and gave her a brief hug. "I'm glad you managed to bring us all together tonight. We need to make more of an effort to do things like this. I think Dad's unexpected death has made us all realize how finite life really is."

"You're right. It's too bad Jett was unable to make it."

"Yes, although I guess we should be grateful he stayed home. None of us would have thanked him if we'd picked up a stomach bug."

"You're right. Have you heard from Joel?"

"Yes, he emailed me the day before last. He sent me some pictures. He's living it up on some Greek island. Had a cute girl on either arm." Callum grinned. "It looks like he's making the most of his inheritance."

His mother's expression softened. "I'm glad. Henry would hate it if everyone went around morose the whole time. He was never particularly sentimental. What he did enjoy was making money and he also enjoyed spending it. I'm sure he'd approve of Joel's shenanigans."

"You're right," Callum agreed.

His mother's housekeeper came up on silent rubber-soled feet and murmured in his mother's ear. She nodded. "Thank you, Greta."

The woman turned and disappeared as quietly as she'd arrived. Elizabeth clapped her hands together and called for attention. "If everyone would like to make their way to the dining room, I believe dinner is served."

With that, among murmured conversations and the occasional chuckle, Callum and his brother and sisters, cousins and Uncle Archie walked toward the formal dining room they used whenever the whole family dined together. Callum nodded a greeting in Flynn's direction and wondered how the purchase was going. Flynn had worked a miracle and had managed to secure the building for five million. With the addition of Flynn's million, Callum had a healthy budget for his renovations with a little in reserve, if needed. Callum couldn't wait to start.

The twenty-seat dining table was resplendent with a crisp white linen tablecloth and more than a dozen thick white candles in elaborate silver candelabras centered along the entire length of it. The candlelight reflected off the surface of the shiny silverware and even picked up the gold trim around the china plates. His mother had gone all out for this family dinner and Callum understood why. The memories of burying their husband, father, brother and uncle were in the minds of all present. It was nice to think about more pleasant things the first time they'd come together again in Henry's house.

The starter was served by his mother's kitchen staff in a flurry of heavenly smells and laughter. The seafood cocktail with his mother's special sauce was a family favorite and was quickly consumed. The main followed, a mouthwatering rack of lamb with green beans and baby roast potatoes, garnished with rosemary from her gardens. Once again, it was a meal they'd enjoyed on many family occasions. The fact Henry would never share a meal with them again crossed Callum's mind more than once, and from the occasional somber expression on the faces of some of his siblings, he guessed they also felt their father's absence. But by and large, the conversation flowed freely, interspersed with laughter along the way. Callum forced himself to join in.

When the last of the triple chocolate cheesecake and raspberry coulis had been consumed and coffee and port had been served, Callum's mother tapped her fork against her wine glass and asked for everyone's attention. The table fell silent and all eyes turned expectantly to Elizabeth, who was now the head of the Craigdon family.

"I'd like to thank everyone for coming tonight. The last time we were together was a very sad occasion and it's nice that we can be here now to enjoy each other's company." Her gaze encompassed everyone at the table—Callum's brother and sisters—Nicholas, Isabella, Sophia and his cousins, Flynn, Noah and Logan. Uncle Archie was also there, seated beside Callum's mother.

There was a murmur of agreement from those gathered around the table. Suddenly, Nicholas slammed his wineglass down on the table. Seated beside him, Isabella jumped. Callum, who was at the far end of the table, blinked in surprise.

Nick pushed back his seat and stood, an angry flush staining his cheeks. "Thanks for the feel-good words, Mom, but has everyone forgotten how mean Dad was in his will? He's worth millions and all he left you was this house! You should have gotten more! And what about Craigdon Enterprises?"

Callum shot a look toward Logan. His cousin's jaw tightened and he kept his gaze fixed on the table.

Nicholas' lip curled up in disgust. "I busted my gut working for that company. Fifteen, even twenty hours a day. It should have been mine. At the very least, it should have been given to all of us." He glanced half-apologetically toward Logan. "I'm sorry, mate. Don't take it personally. This has nothing to do with you." He laughed without humor. "No, my dearly departed father came up with this stunt all on his own."

"You're right, Nick," Logan said quietly. "I had absolutely no idea."

Nicholas shook his head in helpless anger and then his expression flooded with defeat. His shoulders slumped. When he spoke again, his voice was thick with pain. "I just don't understand why he did it. I gave my heart and soul to Craigdon Enterprises. I fully expected one day to be part of the senior management team. It should have been a natural progression for me to take over, if and when Dad retired. Instead, he leaves the entire company to one of his nephews, pulling the rug out from under me and leaving me flat on my ass, gasping for breath and wondering what the hell hit me. I mean, what kind of a father does that? A prick, that's who."

Elizabeth gasped and Callum frowned. He understood his brother's anger and disappointment, but the name calling was out of line. He said as much to Nicholas.

His brother's expression remained angry and unapologetic. Once again, he tossed a look in Logan's direction. "Look, Logan. I really appreciate you appointing me managing director of CE, but surely you understand where I'm coming from?"

Logan nodded. He eyed Nicholas with genuine sympathy. "Of course. I feel terrible about how Uncle Henry treated you. It's grossly unfair. I'm more than happy to appoint you managing director. To me, it's the only thing that makes sense. The company is more yours than it is mine, no matter what Uncle Henry's will said."

And just like that, Nicholas' anger dissipated. He gave Logan a grateful half-smile. "I'm deeply thankful for that, Logan. I promise I won't let you down."

"Of course you won't." Logan spoke with complete assurance. Callum eased out his breath.

Just when he thought the tension around the table had dissolved, Sophia spoke up. "I want to know about the fifteen million Daddy left to the Stella Taunton House for Widows and Orphans. I mean, who the hell is that? We all know Daddy was never philanthropic, except when it came to the Church. And Widows and Orphans? Really?" she sneered. "I don't mean to be insensitive, but since when did he care about people like that?"

Callum regarded his youngest sister with heartfelt

sympathy. She had every reason to be angry at their father. He'd treated her even more shabbily than Nicholas under the will. Callum was as much at a loss to explain Sophia's inheritance, or lack thereof, as he was with regard to the Logan versus Nicholas issue.

Anger continued to burn in Sophia's eyes. Her body was stiff with tension. As Callum looked closer, he saw the glimmer of tears on her cheeks. His heart clenched. His sister was angry and hurting. She was bewildered by their father's unexplainable, insensitive actions. The hardest thing was, the man responsible for so much grief was no longer around to provide answers.

Before Callum could offer any words of comfort, Sophia angrily dashed at the tears on her cheeks and spoke again.

"Of course, we all know he never liked me. Isabella was always his favorite." She turned an accusing gaze on her sister. Callum's heart dropped.

"How dare you!" Isabella cried, her eyes wide with shock.

"Sophia," Callum admonished. "That's grossly unfair. I understand your anger and disappointment, but it has nothing to do with Issy. She had as much input into Dad's will as Logan. We all know Dad did what Dad wanted. He never consulted anyone. I'd bet my inheritance that even Mom didn't have a clue about what Dad's will contained. Right, Mom?"

Callum turned to his mother. She'd fallen silent at the head of the table. Uncle Archie moved his hand to cover hers in an act of reassurance. Callum kept his gaze on his mother, his eyebrow raised in silent expectation, demanding she answer.

Elizabeth flushed under the combined regard of her family. She moved her hand out from under Uncle Archie's. Clearing her throat, she stared directly at Callum. "You're right, Callum. I had no idea." She turned and her gaze encompassed all of the people present. "I don't need to remind any of you about the kind of man your father was. For all his good qualities, he was far from perfect. Over thirty-three years of marriage, he never once consulted me on anything important, not even the purchase of this house. It's laughable to think he might have consulted me over the terms of his will."

"I'm sure he had his reasons for doing what he did, Mom." The quiet statement came from Isabella. Callum blinked in surprise. Sophia's lip curled up in disgust.

"Of course you'd say that. You just inherited twenty million dollars."

Isabella regarded her sister calmly. "I'm more than willing to share it with you, Soph. In fact, why don't you take half?"

There was an audible gasp at the table. Nicholas turned an angry gaze on his sister. "Why the hell should she get half when I only got a million dollars? That isn't fair."

Isabella rolled her eyes and sighed. "Oh, Nicholas, for heaven's sake! Grow up!"

"Guys! Please!"

Callum implored. "Don't let this tear us apart. We're a family. We love each other. We all know what Dad could be like. Sometimes he wasn't a nice person. That's just the way he was. Like Mom said, none of us are perfect. Some of us might not like the choices Dad made when he divided up his estate, but what's done is done. We have to learn to live with it and come to terms with the fact we might never know why he did what he did. As much as we might want answers, there's no disputing Dad's never coming back. We need to accept what happened and move on. What we don't need is for this to drive a wedge between us that might never be healed. That would be the real tragedy."

"What Callum says is right," Elizabeth said. "I don't know why your father did what he did, but let's not let his meanness divide us. We're all in this together. We need to remember that."

Everyone fell silent. Callum looked around the table. He sought to change the subject. "If anyone would like to hear some good news, I have something to share."

Several pairs of eyes lifted to his. He smiled and continued. "I've been encouraged to take some time off and work out what I want to do. So, I've taken a leave of absence from the seminary. I've come to the conclusion Dad's gift to me was his way of urging me to rethink my future and make a decision based on what *I* want."

"Okay, so what's the good news?" Sophia asked, still a little surly.

Callum rolled his eyes at her response, but smiled. "I've been volunteering at a soup kitchen in the city. It's called Jennifer's Kitchen. It's run by the Little Sisters of the Poor and a handful of volunteers. Over the past couple of weeks, I've come to know some of the people who work there and others who use the place and I want to help them."

"How?" Isabella asked, her gaze wide with curiosity.

Warming to his subject, Callum's smile widened. He filled his family in on his plans for the kitchen and for the empty floors above it.

"You're going to spend all of your inheritance to create accommodation for the homeless?" Nicholas asked, incredulous.

"Yes, Nicholas. As difficult as that might seem to you, it's what I want to do. It's the *right* thing to do. And in the process we'll try to work out a self-sustainable plan to deal with the running expenses."

Elizabeth smiled at him from the far end of the table. "I think it's a wonderful idea, Callum. I'm so proud of you."

Warmth flowed through him. "Thanks, Mom."

"I think you're throwing away good money," Nicholas

muttered, lifting his half-full wine glass to his lips and drinking until it was empty.

"Everyone's entitled to their opinion," Elizabeth soothed.

Before Callum could reply, the door to the dining room burst open. Everyone at the table looked up in surprise. Christopher Barrington stood in the doorway. His eyes were glazed. He swayed dangerously on his feet before taking hold of the doorknob and steadying himself.

"Well, well, well! What do we have here? A cozy little gathering! The Craigdon family sharing fine food, fine wine and good conversation. My invitation must be lost in the mail."

Almost simultaneously, the Craigdon men pushed away from the table and stood shoulder to shoulder, forming a protective barrier between Christopher and the women.

Christopher sneered. "Look at you all! Sitting around, counting your millions while I'm left out in the cold. "It's not fair!" he slurred. "I'm the first born child! I should be the head of Craigdon Enterprises!"

Callum moved forward and reached out toward Christopher. Taking hold of his arm, he did his best to calm the man down. At the same time, he inched Christopher toward the door.

"Let go of me, Callum!" Christopher shouted, tearing away from Callum's hold. The movement threw Christopher off-balance and it took him a moment to steady himself.

Sophia's lip curled up in disgust. "Get your sorry drunk ass out of here, Christopher. You're not the only one who missed out. I was given enough money to clear my student loans. A mere one hundred thousand dollars. Big deal. It's a pittance. And what about Mom? Wife of thirty-three years, mother to six children. All she got was this house. Don't come here whining about how hard done by you are. We're of no mind to listen."

Callum glanced toward his mother, waiting for her

response. *Will she explain why Henry treated her so shabbily? Will she tell everyone the truth about her affair?*

And then his mother looked at him and he saw the resignation in her eyes. He closed his eyes briefly, knowing she was going to speak.

"I might not know why your father did some of the things he did, but I know exactly why he left me nothing but our home."

Her statement was met with looks of confusion and surprise. Even Christopher stilled.

"What are you talking about, Mom?" Sophia asked.

Elizabeth was silent for a moment, then quietly she spoke. "Many years ago, I had an affair. Your father never forgave me."

Shocked silence followed. Isabella was the first to find her voice. "Who with?"

Elizabeth shook her head, her closed expression rebuffed all further discussion. "It doesn't matter. I just wanted to explain why your father did what he did, at least to me. I wish I could offer some further explanation to help those of you who are struggling with his other decisions. Unfortunately, I can't. All I ask is that we stick together. It would break my heart for something like this to tear us apart."

Sophia's tone turned conciliatory. "Of course this isn't going to tear us apart. We're family. We love each other. This doesn't change that. Besides, we all know Daddy wasn't an angel." She sighed. "I just wish he'd treated us fairly." She looked around the room at her siblings and cousins. "That doesn't mean I blame any of you for what happened. We all knew what Daddy was like. He was a man who kept his own counsel and made his own decisions. It just hurts to know he didn't love us equally."

"Oh, Soph! I don't think that's what Daddy meant by all this," Isabella protested.

Sophia merely offered her sister a sad smile. "That's easy for you to say."

"He loved you, Soph! Of course he did! He loved all of us," Isabella insisted.

Fresh tears glinted in Sophia's eyes. Callum's protective instincts rose to the surface. "I think we should call it a night," he said. He'd dealt with enough drama for one day.

Their mother nodded, her face flooding with relief. "You're right, Callum. It's getting late. This isn't going to be resolved in one night." She paused and let her gaze rest on each of them, including Christopher. "I just want you to know, you're all very important to me. I love you like you could never know. It upsets me to see some of you hurting, especially when there isn't anything I can do about it. But know that our love for each other is stronger than any hurdle we come up against. Together we can overcome anything. Your father's will doesn't change that. Provided we stay strong and remain kind and loving toward each other and put our trust in God, things will work out. I truly believe that."

There were general murmurs of agreement as chairs scraped backwards and farewells were made. Gradually, the room emptied until only Elizabeth and Archie remained.

"That was more difficult than I imagined," Elizabeth said, her voice pained.

Archie pulled her into his arms and held her close. "I'm so proud of you," he whispered and kissed her gently, lingeringly on the mouth.

When at last they pulled apart, Elizabeth looked up at him with a small smile. "What have I done to make you proud of me?"

"You told them about our affair. All these years I've had to hide in the shadows, waiting until the time was right and now you've taken that first step."

A frisson of alarm swept through Elizabeth. She stepped

out of Archie's embrace. "What... What are you talking about?"

"Us. I'm talking about us. Finally we can stop hiding our love."

Elizabeth turned away, wringing her hands together. "Archie. I... I think you've misunderstood me."

His tone became wary. "How do you mean?"

"I mean, I didn't tell our children about my affair in order to ease them into accepting us. As far as they know, my indiscretion was a thing of the past and they have no idea who it was with." She turned back to face him, eyeing him steadily. "And that's how it's going to stay."

Hurt and disappointment clouded his features. "But... I don't understand. We're both now free. It's been ten years since Janelle died and now Henry's gone, too. What's stopping us from telling the kids we're in love? They might take awhile to get used to the idea, but they'll eventually come round."

Elizabeth was filled with unease. She couldn't quite say why she didn't want her family to know about her and Archie, but that was the truth. Still, it pained her to see him hurting. She loved him more than she'd ever loved anyone.

"It's too soon," she said instead, hoping to mollify him. "Henry's only been dead a little over a month. Give them time to come to terms with his passing and the terms of the will before we shock them with any other news."

Archie looked unconvinced, but he didn't argue further. As the door shut behind him, Elizabeth suppressed a sigh of relief and headed up the stairs to bed.

Chapter Fourteen

It was late. Well past midnight. After Grace's revelations and the night of drama at his mother's house, and questions raised by his own conscience, it was no wonder Callum couldn't sleep. He'd tried, of course, like he had every night since the accident, but he tossed and turned for so long, in the end he climbed out of bed and made himself a hot chocolate. He took it out to the balcony and leaned over the railing, staring into the darkness below.

The late summer breeze was balmy and a sprinkling of stars littered the sky. A lot of the time, the stars weren't visible in the city, but on this night they were as bright as diamonds.

It had been an eventful day…an eventful evening. He was surprised his mother had found the courage to tell everyone about her affair. He'd had time to get used to the idea, but he understood the shock that had been painted across everyone else's faces. And then there was Nicholas and Sophia, and of course, Christopher.

It pained Callum to know how much his brother and sister, and even Christopher, were hurting. There was anger for sure, and that was real, but it was the hurt that would stay with them for a long time, maybe forever.

How did one explain why a father left one child twenty million dollars and another barely enough to pay off her student loans?

It was mean and nasty and spiteful. It made not a lick of sense. All it did was cause trouble and spark jealousy among them.

Why would his father do such a thing?

It wasn't the first time Callum had asked the question and he still didn't have any answers. His mother was right. All they could do was put their faith in God and pray that everything turned out all right.

Then there was Grace. Her revelations had both shocked and saddened him. How would she take it when she discovered Callum was the driver who killed her brother…? And then there was the rest. He couldn't believe she'd trusted him with the secrets of her past. They'd only met a month ago and yet he felt like they'd known each other forever. Perhaps she felt the same? Maybe that's why she was able to share stories so personal they brought tears to his eyes. And, worse than that, she didn't even know the half of it.

The battles she'd fought in such a short time! First with her in-laws refusing to accept her marriage and then the shocking death of her husband that catapulted into the worst scenario possible—losing custody of her children. The grief and pain she'd experienced seemed too much for one person to bear. It was little wonder she'd turned to alcohol.

He didn't blame her in the least. If anything, it made him care for her even more deeply and his admiration for her as a recovering alcoholic continued to grow. She'd had every excuse to wallow in the gutter, consumed by her grief and guilt, and yet she'd pulled herself up and straightened herself out, all for the love of her children. It must have been hell, and yet she'd done it. If there was anyone who deserved to get her babies back, it was Grace.

Oh, God, I want to help her. I want to give her a reason to smile again… But what about when I tell her about her brother? What will she think of me? How can I ever make up for his life gone? What will happen then?

If he were truthful, the main reason he wanted to put his money into the soup kitchen and the accommodation project was Grace. And that had been obvious to Flynn.

From the first moment Callum had seen her, she'd touched something way down deep inside him. He couldn't remember ever feeling like that before, not even when he was deep in prayer, feeling utterly connected to God.

That was another reason he couldn't sleep. He couldn't stop thinking about Grace and how much she'd come to mean to him and how recent events might affect his future going forward: his terrible accident involving her brother, and Callum's future as a priest. And then there was this burning need to help her get her children back.

Seth and Alyssa.

Did they have their mother's beautiful brown eyes and dark hair? When they smiled, did they light up the world around them? Did they look at those less fortunate with kindness and compassion in their eyes?

Or had they been so hurt by the painful events three years earlier and the estrangement from their mother that they could never feel happy about anything again? It wasn't right that two children were being raised by their grandparents instead of their mother who loved them with every fiber of her being, wanted to raise them and was more than capable of doing that.

Okay, so there had been a time when Grace wasn't up to looking after her children. Callum accepted this and understood why the court made its decision to grant sole custody to the grandparents. But that was all in the past and something needed to be done to change it. Grace had done the hard part—getting her life together and returning to sobriety. It was time he helped her down the final straight. But first, he needed to tell her about the awful part he'd played in her brother's death and pray to God she'd forgive him.

He knew from experience she didn't hold back when she was hurt or angry, and she'd likely hate him for what he'd done. But he also knew that she'd think on things and perhaps would come around to seeing him not so much as the killer of her brother, but more of someone who'd made a mistake, distracted by events surrounding his father's death. A fatal mistake, yet someone still worth having in her life. That was his hope.

Grace stood at the sink peeling carrots for the next meal. She looked up and saw Callum's car pull in at the curb across the street. Her heart leaped involuntarily, like it did every time she saw him. He parked right outside the liquor store that constantly beckoned to Grace, but he didn't even give it a glance. Instead, his attention was focused on the soup kitchen. Then he pulled out his phone and began taking photos from several angles. At last, he put the phone back in his pocket and headed for the door.

Wiping her hands on a tea towel, she made a deliberate effort to tamp down her nerves and went to let him in. A moment later, his knock sounded on the wooden panel. Though she was excited to see him, another part of her dreaded it. Yesterday she'd spilled her innermost secrets to him. Just thinking about all she'd shared with him made her flush with embarrassment to see him this first time since.

What must he think of me?

There had been no judgement in his eyes after she'd finished telling him, but maybe he was better at hiding it than most. After all, he'd spent years training to be a priest. He must have picked up some skills of that nature along the way. Or maybe he was as good and kind and compassionate as he seemed and she was worrying needlessly? With a sigh, she opened the door.

"Hi," she greeted him uncertainly, her face warming.

"Hi," he said.

She stood there a moment, holding the door. Eventually she found the courage to raise her gaze to his.

"Are you going to let me in?"

Her embarrassment deepened. "Oh, sure. Sorry." Awkwardly, she stepped back, leaving him room to enter. Turning away, she headed back to the kitchen and busied herself peeling the rest of the carrots she planned to use for lunch. The potatoes were boiling on the stove and she'd already made the rissoles.

"*Mmm*, something smells good. Then again, this place always smells good."

She turned in time to catch Callum's smile. The beauty of it caught in her throat. Her heart told her this man was everything he appeared to be. Surely she couldn't be wrong this time.

Callum didn't give her any further time to contemplate her sad past. He moved toward the oven and opened it, finding the trays of cooked rissoles she'd prepared earlier.

"Ah, so this is what smells so good. Where's the gravy? You can't have rissoles without gravy."

She laughed. "You're right. I haven't had time to make it yet. Feel free to get a start on it."

With that, he rolled up his shirtsleeves—this time a tailored business shirt in a blue that matched his eyes.

"Flour?"

"In the pantry."

"Frypan?"

"In the cupboard over there," she said, pointing right.

"What about broth? Do you have any juices left over from the meat?"

She smiled and slowly shook her head. "You really are a cook! I expected you to ask me where the gravy mix was.

Instead you're going to make it from scratch. You've earned some serious credits, Callum Craigdon."

He shot her an adorable grin and it was all she could do not to move closer and press her lips against his. The notion startled her. Of course she'd noticed how attractive he was and had been more than aware of how her body responded to him, but she hadn't given serious thought to anything more than a friendship developing between them. It was possible he might still return to the seminary. Just her luck that the first man to stir such feelings since Daniel was also in training to be a priest.

Oblivious to her thoughts, he gave her a searching look. His expression was so serious, she felt a jolt of alarm.

"Callum? What is it?"

He stared at her a moment longer before dropping his gaze. He shook his head. "Nothing. I… Don't worry about it."

She frowned. "Are you all right?"

His smile looked forced. "Yes, of course. Actually, I'm going to be even further into your good books when you hear my news." He winked at her.

She grinned. "What news?"

"I have the final plans for the redevelopment. They're with the city council right now. Provided they approve them, as soon as the sale goes through, we can make a start. Isn't that great?"

Grace nodded, but inside, her excitement dimmed. As if sensing her mood, Callum put down the utensil he held and moved closer. "Grace? What's wrong? I thought you'd be thrilled?"

She shrugged and tried to smile. What he was doing with the place was a good thing and would benefit so many people. It was just…

"Talk to me, Grace."

His quiet plea, accompanied by the sincerity in his eyes,

did her in. She bit her lip against a rush of tears. Immediately, he looked stricken.

"Grace! Oh, honey, please don't cry. What's the matter? What have I said?"

"N-nothing," she stammered, swiping at her eyes.

"Don't tell me it's nothing. My Grace doesn't cry for no reason."

My Grace. She tried to ignore the rush of warmth that filled her with his words. He was so good and kind and caring. He deserved an explanation.

"It's just that, I'm not sure what will happen to me. I know you've assured me my job here is safe, but I just can't see how that's going to work. From what you've told me, the renovations will take months. I know what a building site is like. There are rules and regulations, safety concerns. There's no way the kitchen's going to be able to continue to operate the way it does. I... I'll have to move out, find another job. That's if I can find one. With the economy in the state it is, it's not as easy as it once was. And I don't have any real skills. I didn't finish my degree. I don't have any formal qualifications. My high school certificate is it. I'm unlikely to find a job outside Jennifer's Kitchen. That's really the first and only job I've had since high school."

Her chest rose and fell with her increasing agitation. Another tear escaped and rolled down her face. Callum's eyes filled with tenderness. He reached out and cupped her cheek. His hand was warm and comforting against her skin. She wished it didn't feel so good.

"Oh, you're such a worrywart," he murmured, taking the sting out of his words by accompanying them with a gentle smile. "I've got everything worked out," he continued. "Trust me. You don't have to worry about a thing."

She blinked in surprise. "You do?"

"Yes. You see, you say you don't have any skills, but I've

already noticed how well you run a kitchen. You're organized, calm and efficient. You deal firmly but kindly with the staff. You know how to prepare a budget and stick to it and believe me, that's a skill all in itself and one very few people have! You know how to deal with the general public and you have excellent communication skills. All the things I'm looking for in my project manager."

Her eyes widened in shock. "Your what?"

Callum merely smiled. "My project manager."

"But… No! I… I could never do something like that!"

"Of course you can!"

"But I don't know the first thing about project management."

He grinned. "Neither do I. We'll learn together. What do you say?"

Grace shook her head, confused. "But, why? You barely know me. Why would you do this for me?"

Callum took his time before replying. When he did, his voice was thick with emotion. "You're the most amazing woman I've ever met. You're smart, funny and beautiful, inside and out. You're determined, courageous and resilient. Most people faced with the challenges you've had would have given up."

She dropped her head and stared at the floor. "I did give up."

"Maybe. But not for long. You found the strength and courage to pick yourself up and keep going. I admire you, Grace. I don't know anyone with that kind of courage." He paused and then added quietly, "I also like you. I like you a lot. I think about you all the time. I don't know what it means. I've never been in love. Heck, a month ago, I thought I was going to be a priest. It's what I expected. It's what I'd been trained for."

He sighed and ran a hand through his thick hair, sending it all askew. He looked even more adorable than usual. It was all she could do not to smile, but the intensity of his gaze stopped her.

"Then you came into my life and turned it upside down. Now I don't know which way is up. I still haven't figured everything out yet and I'm probably scaring the hell out of you, but this feels right, Grace. You, me, the soup kitchen. Helping out the less fortunate in whatever way we can. It makes me feel good. It feels like this is my calling, what I'm meant to do."

She stared at him in wonder. "Wow." Hesitantly, she reached out her hand and touched his lips. They were full and soft and sensuous beneath her fingers. His nostrils flared and she felt him suck in his breath.

"Grace..."

And then his arms were around her, pulling her close. Their lips touched, tentative at first and as the heat enveloped them, so did their rush of need. His lips were full and firm and soft. He tasted faintly of coffee. His tongue pressed shyly against her lips, seeking permission. She opened her mouth and his tongue slipped inside. Both of them sighed.

The kiss built in intensity, each one caught up in the magic of discovery. Then Callum pulled her full against him and she felt the force of his erection.

Things were moving too fast...

The thought had barely formed in her mind when Callum ended the kiss and lowered his arms. They were both breathing hard. Embarrassment heated Grace's cheeks.

Oh, Lord. What have I done? What will he think of me? He's almost a priest!

"Whatever you're thinking, you're wrong," he said quietly.

Her embarrassment deepened. "I'm sorry, Callum. That shouldn't have happened. I shouldn't have—"

"You didn't do anything wrong, Grace. I was a willing participant." He shot her a grin that was tinged with disbelief.

"I'm not sure you realize it, but you're the first woman I've kissed."

She laughed in surprise. "You mean you usually kiss boys?"

Now it was his time to blush. His cheeks turned an unbecoming crimson. "No! Of course not! I meant—"

"I know what you meant," she smiled, taking pity on him. She touched his arm gently. "I guess I'm surprised and flattered that I'm your first." Then she shook her head as the full import of what he'd said hit home to her. "You mean you never kissed a girl, even at university?"

"Nope."

"Not even once? You didn't get drunk at a party and hook up with whoever happened to be handy?"

"Nope." He grinned. "Does that kind of thing really happen?"

"Yes. Not to me, of course."

"Of course."

"I got together with Daniel almost immediately after my arrival on campus." She winked. "I didn't have the chance to engage in casual hook-ups. But plenty of people did."

He grinned. "I thought that kind of amoral behaviour only happened in the movies."

She grinned back at him. "Oh, Callum Craigdon. You've lived a sheltered life."

He pulled her into a hug. "Yes. I have. Lucky for me I've met the perfect person to expand my education."

Before he could kiss her again, she ducked out of his embrace and returned to the sink.

"As much as I'd like to continue our conversation, I have lunch to prepare. If we don't hurry, it won't be ready on time."

"Yes, ma'am. You're the boss." Callum saluted her and returned to the gravy preparations. In short order, he had the flour browned and had used the stock left over from the pan she'd cooked the rissoles in to add liquid to the mixture. Salt and pepper and a few other seasonings followed and soon the gravy was bubbling merrily and giving off a delicious smell.

Grace tossed the carrots into several pots of boiling water and put them on the stove. She then pulled out more than a dozen large bags of frozen beans. They were quickly added to more pots boiling on the second stove. When the preparations were finished at last, she leaned against the kitchen counter, pushed back her hairnet and sighed.

"Wow. We did it."

Callum grinned and gave her a high five. "We make a good team."

Her heart jumped at the expression in his eyes. "Just because I can run a kitchen doesn't mean I can run a building site."

"You won't have to do it on your own. I'll be there every step of the way."

"What if I make a mistake?"

"Then we'll sort it out together and learn from it."

"What about my room out back? Where am I going to live?"

"I've thought about that, too. The initial construction period won't affect your apartment. We'll leave that till last. That way you can live there for as long as possible. The construction noise will only be happening during the daylight hours, so it shouldn't bother you."

Grace nodded. The tiniest seam of excitement crept through her veins. Being able to tell the court she was the project manager of a multi-million dollar development was so much more impressive than being cook at a soup kitchen. It might just be enough to sway the judge to her side.

She smiled shyly at Callum. "It seems like you've thought of everything."

"Not quite. I'm still working on how I can help you with your custody petition."

Though he'd said something to that effect the day before, she was surprised he'd given it another thought.

"Are you serious?"

He nodded. "Of course I'm serious. I'm a firm believer that children are better off with their biological parents. In this case, their mom. Particularly if there's no good reason they shouldn't be."

A kernel of hope blossomed inside her. She stared at him, wondering where he'd come from and how she'd gotten so lucky to have him come into her life. It felt so good to have somebody on her side.

"Do you have any ideas how I can get my children back?" she asked.

"Not exactly, but remember my cousin, Flynn?"

"The lawyer?"

"Right. He helped me with the negotiations to secure this building, but he actually specializes in family law."

Grace held his gaze for a moment and then lowered it. Callum didn't know about her connection to his cousin. It was time to come clean.

"Yes. I've met Flynn already."

Callum looked vaguely surprised. "You have?"

"Yes. I… I went to him for advice when the Gunnings first took my children. He was very blunt. He told me that unless I cleaned up my act, found a job and a safe, stable place to live, I didn't have a hope of regaining custody. He was right."

"I see. Well, my idea was to get Flynn on board and see what he can do about bringing the matter back before the court. He's very good at his job. One of the best. I'm sorry he wasn't able to help you before, but maybe now things will be different. That is, if you're willing to give him another try…?"

Grace blew out her breath on a sigh. "I have no ill will toward your cousin. He was right. I had no hope of getting my children back while I was in that state. Though it was difficult for me to hear, he merely told the truth and I admired him for that. He didn't pretend he could help me and he didn't just try to waste my money. He told me straight up."

Callum smiled. "Flynn would never gouge a client. He's a good guy." He clapped his hands together. "Good. It's settled then. We'll go and see him."

Grace frowned. "It's not that easy."

Callum looked at her in confusion. "What do you mean?"

Grace lowered her gaze, suddenly uncomfortable. Callum lifted her chin with his finger until she had to look him in the face.

"What's the matter, honey?"

She bit her lip as embarrassment flamed across her cheeks. Callum's gaze became more insistent.

"Grace? What aren't you telling me?"

"N-nothing. I'm not keeping anything from you, It's just that…" Once again she stumbled. Callum looked concerned.

"Grace?"

"I don't have the money to pay for a lawyer," she blurted.

Callum smiled in relief. "Oh, is that all."

"Is that all? It's everything. Without a lawyer on my side, I'm going to lose before I get anywhere near the courtroom."

He looked at her sternly. "Grace Gunning, listen to me. I'm in this with you and we are *not* going to lose this case. Better still, we *are* going to have a lawyer. And a damn good one. Like I said, Flynn is excellent at his job."

She blew out her breath in exasperation. "Callum! You're not listening to me! I can't afford a lawyer like Flynn. I can't afford *any* lawyer! The only reason I could pay his bill the first time was because of the money left in Daniel's account."

She tensed as Callum folded her into his arms. "*Shushhh…*" he said against her hair and gradually her resistance eased.

"You don't need to worry about Flynn's fees. I'm more than happy to cover them."

She stiffened. "No. I won't take your money."

He set her away from him. Irritation clouded his face. "Grace, don't be silly. I want to help you in every way I can. That includes financial support."

"I'm sorry, Callum. I might not have much, but I have my pride. I'm not a charity case. While I appreciate everything people have done for me here at the kitchen, I work hard for my keep. I've come a long way since I had no choice but to accept a helping hand."

Callum cursed under his breath. "Grace. You're being unreasonable! You're jeopardizing your chances of getting your children back, all for the sake of your pride!"

Anger coursed through her. "That might be so, but pride is all I have left!"

Callum's shoulders slumped on a sigh. "I'm sorry. I shouldn't have lost my temper. I want to help you, Grace. Please, let me help you."

He fell silent. A few moments later, his expression changed to one of excitement. "I've got it! What if I give you a loan?"

"A loan? How am I going to pay it back?"

"Okay, not a loan. What about an advance on your wages? You're going to be my project manager. I'll put you on the payroll from today. You can consult with me over the redevelopment plans, issues that might arise with the council and any number of other things. What do you say?"

His enthusiasm was contagious. Reluctantly, she smiled.

He grinned back at her. "Yes?"

She nodded and then laughed. "Yes."

He winked. "See? Problem solved."

Chapter Fifteen

They were a little late leaving. Grace had a goodbye ritual with her dog that couldn't be shortened. She insisted Callum wait in the car instead of chancing another allergic reaction, and with a few words and a pat on the head, she left an accepting dog at the door.

Once on the road, they made good time. Now Callum tapped the steering wheel impatiently as he waited for the lights to change. Grace sat beside him, wringing her hands in her lap. He'd called ahead to set up an appointment with Flynn and now they were on their way to meet with him.

At the back of Callum's mind hung the spectre of Grace's brother's death. He should already have told her what happened that night. It should have been the first thing out of his mouth when he'd seen her that morning. But every time he thought about bringing it up, something held him back. She'd been through so much already. Their relationship was still so new, so fragile. The feelings he had for her were growing stronger every day and they scared him half to death, but he didn't want to jeopardize where this might lead by ruining things. Besides, how was he supposed to tell her?

Oh, Grace. You know when you told me about your brother being killed in an accident? Yeah, well, that was me. I'm the guy. I'm the asshole who ran over your brother…

He decided that once they'd met with Flynn, he had to devise a way to tell Grace everything about that night. And before he did he'd let her know that no matter what happened between them, he was there to see her through this tough time while she worked to regain custody of her kids.

Even if he were able to come up with a plan, the thought of confessing his part in her brother's death filled him with dread. Still he would have to do it sooner or later. He glanced in her direction. Her expression was tense and nervous. Though she'd agreed to let him help her, he could tell she was having second thoughts. No, his decision to hold off his confession was the right thing to do. She had enough on her plate.

Coward…

The word mocked him. Forcing his dark thoughts aside, he plastered a smile on his face and offered her a few words of encouragement.

"There's no need to look so worried, Grace. It's going to be fine."

She continued to look grim. "How can you be so sure? The last time I met with your cousin he dismissed my chances in no uncertain terms and though he represented me in court, we lost…as he'd predicted."

"Hey, that was before you turned your life around. Flynn will be impressed with your courage and how far you've come. And so will the judge."

She looked at him, her eyes wide with uncertainty and the faintest glimmer of hope. "Do you really think so?"

"Yes," he said firmly.

She offered him a wobbly smile and his heart turned over. He couldn't believe how quickly he'd come to care for her. In such a short time, she'd invaded his head…and his heart. He couldn't stop thinking about her and how he might help her solve her problems. He wanted to cosset her, protect her, keep her safe from all of the evils of the world. Not be thought of as evil…to be accused. He wanted to be the man she turned to for advice, for comfort, for love.

Love? Is that what this is? Have I fallen in love with her?

The thought didn't terrify him like he thought it would. Nor did it feel strange. But it made telling her the truth about her brother's death even more imperative. There could be no future between them until he'd come clean.

Before he had time to contemplate it further, he was lucky enough to find a parking spot not far from Flynn's building and switched off the engine. He gave Grace another encouraging smile.

"You ready?"

She drew in a deep breath and let it out on a heavy sigh, looking as enthusiastic as someone on their way to the execution chamber. "I guess so."

They climbed out of their vehicle and headed toward Sydney Legal. The law firm was one of the oldest in Sydney. In an effort to distract Grace, he regaled her with the firm's history.

"Did you know I actually have a family connection to Sydney Legal?"

"Yes, you told me. Flynn Craigdon is your cousin."

"No, I mean an even older connection. Before it was Sydney Legal, it was known as Harton and Wentworth. Even earlier than that, my mother's father, who was a lawyer, sold his firm to Harton and Wentworth."

He could see Grace thinking about what he'd said. "So your grandfather was a lawyer?"

"Yes. Back in the 1950s, my grandfather, John Doherty and his brother, Peter, set up a small but reputable firm in the city. They called it Doherty and Associates. They had a decent share of the market. My grandfather had a reputation for being a man who went above and beyond for his clients. He did what had to be done to win."

"He sounds like a formidable man."

"Yes, I guess he was. But he was always fair. Anyway, after a number of years of incredible success, he was approached by the partners of Harton and Wentworth. They were a larger firm and also had an enviable reputation. The story goes like this: The partners and my grandfather and his brother got together and struck a deal. Instead of competing against each other for the most illustrious clients, they joined forces. My grandfather and his brother joined Harton and Wentworth as senior partners and worked there until their deaths. The amalgamation of two exceptional law firms turned out to be an outstanding success."

Grace looked at him. Her expression was full of admiration. "What a fantastic story! And I love how you still have a family member working there, walking the same corridors once traversed by your grandfather and his brother."

"Actually, it isn't the same building they worked in. This impressive glass-and-steel structure was only erected five or six years ago. The firm outgrew its previous, much more modest space."

As they approached the automatic double glass doors, Grace's expression once again dimmed. Callum reached for her hand and squeezed it reassuringly.

"It's going to be fine. Trust me."

She managed a small smile that didn't hide her nerves and they walked directly across the wide polished marble foyer to the bank of elevators.

Flynn's secretary buzzed to let him know they'd arrived for their appointment. In no time at all, they were ensconced in Flynn's comfortable office. Flynn greeted Callum with a friendly handshake before turning to Grace. He couldn't hide his surprise.

Instead of the dirty T-shirt and torn skirt she'd turned up in the last time he'd seen her, she wore a nice charcoal-gray suit that molded to her slim figure. A white ruffled blouse peeked out between the lapels. But the biggest changes were in her demeanor. Her brown eyes were clear, her hair clean and neatly coiffed into a bun at the base of her neck. Eyeliner and mascara emphasized the almond shape of her eyes. Red lipstick drew attention to her mouth. She looked good. She looked healthy. She looked like a different person.

"Grace. It's nice to see you again. You're looking well."

She gave him a tight smile. "You're too kind. What you mean to say is, I look a heck of a lot better than I did the last time you saw me."

Flynn glanced at Callum. His cousin's expression held no surprise. *So he knows about her past… Interesting.*

Flynn turned his attention back to Grace. "You're right." He indicated the two chairs that sat opposite his desk. "Please, take a seat. Can I get coffee for either of you?"

They shook their heads and sat down. Grace folded her hands neatly on her lap, but she fidgeted with the strap of her handbag. Flynn took his place behind his desk and tried to put her at ease.

"Callum tells me you'd like to petition the court for the return of your children."

She glanced at his cousin who gave her a reassuring look. Flynn observed their body language. They sat close together, almost shoulder to shoulder. Whoever this woman was to his cousin, it was obvious they trusted one another.

"Yes," Grace replied. "I'm not sure if you remember, but my children have been living with their paternal grandparents. They've been with them for nearly three years."

Flynn nodded and opened her file. "I took the liberty of retrieving your file from our records department. When you came to me back then, I'm afraid I wasn't of much use to you."

She shook her head, her expression resolute. "No, you did your job as well as you could. It wasn't your fault you had a client who was so messed up she had no right to ask the court to consider her fit to raise her children, no matter how much she loved them."

Grace's voice broke with emotion. This time, Callum reached for her hand and gave her a look filled with concern and tenderness. Flynn watched the exchange with interest. It didn't seem that long ago that Callum was in the seminary, destined to become a priest. Now he held hands with a woman he seemed to care a great deal for.

Interesting…

"The thing is," Callum said. "Grace has come a long way since the last time you represented her. You can see for yourself."

Flynn nodded in agreement. Callum continued. "For the past twelve months, Grace has been clean. She has a job, a place to live and she regularly attends AA meetings to help her stay on track. One thing that hasn't changed in all of this is the deep love she has for her children. Seth is now ten. Alyssa is eight. They are being raised by people who are in their sixties. No one is denying the Gunnings have done a good job, but the fact is, these children need to be with their mother."

Flynn flicked a glance in Grace's direction. "What kind of access do you have right now?"

"I see them for three hours, one day a week."

"And are those visits still supervised?"

"Yes.

"Well, that's the first thing we need to change. From what I can tell, there's no reason you shouldn't be able to spend time on your own with your kids now."

Hope flourished on her face. "That would be…wonderful."

Callum frowned at Flynn. "We want more than just access. We want full custody."

Flynn held up his hand in an effort to ward off any more objections. "I understand that, but we need to take small steps. Unless the children are in danger, the court won't just remove them from the only home they've known for the past three years. We need to show the judge that firstly, you can be trusted to be alone with Seth and Alyssa and then, if that goes well, we'll petition the court to change their living arrangements so that they can come and stay with you."

Callum's expression darkened. He sat forward in his seat. "But—"

"Callum," Flynn interrupted. "Hear me out. This is my area of expertise. I know how it goes. No court is going to make drastic changes overnight to the present custody arrangements. It's a step-by-step process. First we get Grace unsupervised visits. Then we push for overnight stays—maybe a couple of nights every week. If we show the court that has gone well, we'll go for full custody." He paused and then added. "It will also depend on the attitude of the children. They're old enough for the court to put some weight on where they want to live."

Flynn turned his attention to Grace. "Do you know how they feel about living with their grandparents? Are they happy there?"

She bit her lip. "They're not *unhappy*. But every time I see them, they ask me when they're going to be able to move back in with me and Bluey. Our family pet," Grace explained.

Flynn acknowledged her response with a nod. "That's good. We're going to need your children on board if your petition's going to have any chance of success. They're still relatively young. Most judges are loathe to disrupt the status quo unless there's a good reason."

"But I'm their mother! They're my babies!" Grace cried.

"I understand that," Flynn replied in his calm, lawyerly voice. "Unfortunately, that's not always enough. As you already found out."

"She's not that person anymore!" Callum protested.

"You're right. She's not. And that's definitely going to work in her favor. The courts do prefer that children live with a biological parent, if at all possible, but the interests of the children always come first. When it comes down to it, the court will base its decision on whatever is best for your kids."

"Of course," Grace murmured. "And they were right to let my in-laws take care of them in the beginning. After Daniel's death, I was in no state to look after them properly." She eyed Flynn steadily, a gleam of determination in her eyes. "But I'm in a better place now. I've worked so hard to get here. I want my children back. I *need* them. And they need their mother."

Once again, Flynn acknowledged her comment with a nod. "I understand. I really do. But it isn't going to be easy. And like I said, it's a slow, gradual process."

"Is there anything we can do to strengthen Grace's case?" Callum asked.

Flynn nodded. "Sure. The more stable and secure you are, the better." He looked at Grace. "Where are you working?"

She glanced at Callum. "At Jennifer's Kitchen."

"The soup kitchen?"

"Yes."

"What do you do there?"

"I do most of the cooking. I order supplies. I…manage the kitchen."

Flynn looked unimpressed. "How much do you get paid?"

Grace flushed. "I… I take home a little over two hundred dollars a week."

Flynn shot her an incredulous look. "Two hundred dollars a week? Are you kidding? Is there any way you can supplement your income with an additional job?"

"Yes," Callum replied before Grace could speak. "I've already offered Grace the role of project manager for my redevelopment. It comes with a generous remuneration package." Once again Flynn hid his surprise. "Good. That will help." He turned back to Grace. "What about your current living arrangements?"

"I-I have a small apartment attached to the soup kitchen for my use. I pay only a nominal rent."

"How many bedrooms?" Flynn asked.

Grace's embarrassment deepened. "One."

He tried to keep the negativity out of his voice. "I see."

"I know it's not ideal…" Grace's voice faded off.

"You're right. It's not ideal," Flynn replied dryly. "Where are the children supposed to sleep?"

Grace looked at him helplessly. Flynn swallowed a sigh. *Great. Just great.*

Callum sat up in his chair. "Maybe we can come up with an alternative? There must be somewhere else you and the kids can live."

Grace looked at Callum blankly.

Flynn's earlier optimism faded. "Let's not worry about that for now. The first thing we need to do is get you unsupervised access visits." He cleared his throat. "Do you have any idea how your in-laws are going to react to your desire to have your children returned to your care?"

Grace stared down at her hands where they still rested in her lap. "I'm pretty sure they won't be happy about it. You might remember how they were the last time we were in court."

"Yes. They were vicious," Flynn agreed. "I also seem to recall they had a very prominent barrister. Money's no object for them, right?"

Grace nodded. "Right. And it gets worse. From snippets I've heard from my children, my in-laws are doing their best to turn Seth and Alyssa against me."

"Okay. So it's going to be a tough fight," Flynn said and then smiled. "Lucky for you I like a challenge. Now, I have to warn you, once they're made aware of your intention to seek full custody of your kids, this is likely to get nasty."

Grace looked at him. "What do you mean?"

"I mean, your in-laws. They're going to tear you apart. They'll have a private investigator follow you. Go through your garbage looking for evidence. You'll need to be on your best behavior. You have a tough battle ahead."

She looked at Callum, panic flooding her gaze. He regarded her solemnly, but once again reached for her hand and squeezed it.

"We've got this, Grace."

Some of the fear in her eyes receded, but her posture remained tense. Flynn sighed inwardly. He'd never been the type to go softly or tiptoe around the truth. She needed to realize that taking on her in-laws over this was going to result in one god-awful fight. He hoped she was up to the task.

"I'll start drafting the application with regard to the request for unsupervised access. I'll need to request a report from the social worker who's been supervising your visits. Hopefully the report will be supportive. If it is, there's a good chance you won't be required to give evidence at this initial hearing." He looked at Grace and grimaced. "The petition for overnight visitation will be a different matter."

"You mean, I'll have to give evidence then?" Grace asked.

Flynn compressed his lips and nodded. "Yes."

She looked distressed. Flynn did his best to reassure her. "Look, don't worry about it right now. We'll have plenty of time to prepare. It will take a month or two to get a hearing date for that. Maybe longer. After all, unless we can prove the children are in imminent danger...?" He left the question hanging.

Grace bit her lip, her eyes downcast. Slowly, she shook her head.

"In that case, we'll file for unsupervised visits as soon as we can and hope for the best." He glanced at Callum and then returned his attention to Grace. "In the meantime, I suggest you give serious thought to finding more suitable accommodation."

Callum looked resolute. "Leave it with me. I'm sure we can think of something."

Grace opened her mouth as if to protest, but then closed it without speaking. Flynn hid his surprise and merely nodded in Callum's direction. "Good. That's what we need. Secure, stable employment with a salary high enough to convince a judge she's capable of supporting her children in an acceptable manner."

He pushed away from his desk and extended his hand to Grace then his cousin. "I'll send over the draft paperwork when it's ready."

"Thanks for seeing us, Flynn," Callum replied. "We really appreciate it. And please, send your invoice to me."

Once again, Flynn concealed his surprise. This woman meant more to Callum than Flynn had realized. He wondered if Callum had any clue.

"Don't worry about the bill, Padre. I'm more than happy to help out. A friend of yours is a friend of mine. That's what family's all about, right?"

Callum grinned. "That's mighty generous of you, Flynn, but I'm quite prepared to pay for your services. After all, I just came into a sizable inheritance."

Flynn laughed. "Yeah, and I also know how much of it you've already spent." He slapped Callum on the back. "It's all good, mate. The firm prides itself on the number of cases it does *pro bono*. I'll add this one to the list."

Chapter Sixteen

From his position across the street, Christopher Barrington watched with interest as Callum and an attractive, dark-haired woman exited the Sydney Legal building and disappeared into the crowd of pedestrians waiting for the light to change. Every time he saw a Craigdon, he seethed with anger. They were so smug! The whole Craigdon clan! Sitting sweet with their millions, while he got nothing. He wasn't going to take that lying down!

He'd met with his lawyer again only that morning and had instructed him to get the matter rolling. He intended to sue Henry Craigdon's estate for as much as he could get. Callum might be Mr Nice Guy, but he'd inherited a tidy sum along with his siblings and cousins. As far as Christopher was concerned, Callum was as bad as the rest of them.

What's he doing at Sydney Legal, anyway? And who's the brunette with him? What if he's obtaining legal advice about the will? Is he already trying to get the jump on me? After all, Christopher had already warned the family of his intention to sue the estate.

Flynn worked at Sydney Legal. Perhaps the two cousins had been merely comparing stories about how they were going to spend their millions…

Christopher felt a fresh wave of fury, so hot he could barely think straight. He pulled out his phone and made a call.

Flynn's young secretary had helped him out on a number of occasions. There was every chance she might do so again.

"Emily," he said by way of greeting. "It's Christopher Barrington. I need some information."

He waited for what seemed a lifetime, but eventually she came back with what he wanted. He couldn't help but smile.

So, little brother Callum was besotted with some wastrel from a soup kitchen. *Grace Gunning.* Callum was trying to win her favor by purchasing the building that housed the soup kitchen and there was also talk he could help her win back her children. *How interesting.*

It just happened Christopher was known to the Gunnings. Though Christopher had had more than a decade on Daniel, they'd played in the same football team together. They'd never been close but they'd known each other well enough. Christopher had attended the funeral.

Maybe I should do his parents a favor and let them know what their wayward daughter-in-law has in mind? Give them a heads-up so they can be better prepared?

His nasty chuckle drew stares from onlookers, but he didn't give a damn. He was happiest when he was making other lives miserable. After all, he shouldn't be miserable on his own.

As he and Grace made their way back to the soup kitchen, Callum's mind raced. He'd solved her job problem, but her living arrangements still needed work. He'd designed the renovation timeline to allow her to live uninterrupted in her small apartment for as long as possible, but there would come a time when living there wouldn't be practical or safe. She'd need to find somewhere else to live if her children were to live with her. It made sense to make the move sooner than later. If she could find a solution more pleasing to the court, her chance of getting her kids back was even better.

A germ of an idea began to form, but he remained silent. It would be best not to say anything to Grace until he'd spoken to his mother. After all, her consent was instrumental if his plan was to work and he didn't want to get Grace's hopes up if it didn't pan out.

Swinging into the narrow inner city street that housed Jennifer's Kitchen, he cautiously swerved to avoid Bluey. Grace sighed in relief when the dog made it safely to the other side of the road. Finding a parking spot across from her building, he pulled into the curb and switched off the engine. For a moment, they sat there in silence. Grace was the first one to speak.

"I don't know how to thank you, Callum. You barely know me and yet you've done so much for me. More than anyone. Even more than the people who are meant to love me."

He guessed she referred to her in-laws. Apart from her brother, she'd never spoken of her family. He turned in his seat to face her.

"Where is the rest of your family? Your parents?"

"My father died of a heart attack when I was young. He was thirty-six. A heavy drinker and a smoker and there was a history of heart problems on his side of the family. My mother struggled to raise my brother and me on her own. She worked hard, but there were plenty of times we went to bed hungry. She died of liver cancer right before my husband was killed."

His mouth dropped open, aghast. *How was one person supposed to carry on in the face of so much grief?* Sometimes he didn't understand God at all. And he had to admit, he'd played a part in her brother's death… He almost choked on the guilt.

"Any other brothers and sisters?" he asked in a strangled voice.

She shook her head. "No. Just Ken. And now he's gone too." She paused and then added, "Tell me about your family."

Resolutely pushing thoughts of Ken to the back of his mind, Callum forced a grin. "What do you want to know?"

"Whatever you'd like to share."

He laughed. "You're going to be shocked."

She smiled. "I don't think so."

"Well, I have two sisters and three brothers."

"Wow."

"I told you I was going to shock you."

This time she laughed. "I'm not shocked. In fact, I have a confession to make. I did an Internet search on your family. I already knew there were quite a few of you."

He stared at her in surprise. "You Googled me?"

She shrugged. "Yes. Do you mind?"

"No. I guess not."

"I probably shouldn't have, given how sensitive I was about you checking into my past," she added, a faint blush staining her cheeks.

He softened. "Grace, I understand why you didn't want anyone poking their nose into your business. I have no problem with you wanting to know more about mine. In fact, I'm flattered." He smiled and was relieved when she smiled back.

"Six kids. That's a rather large family for these times."

"Yes. Let's just say my parents were good Catholics."

"Where do you fit in?"

"I'm the second oldest. My brother, Jett, is thirty-one. He's a year older than me."

"Are you close?" she asked.

"Yes. There are only ten years between the six of us. We all grew up together."

Grace smiled. "Tell me about them."

"Well, like I said, Jett's the oldest. He's a detective."

"Is he married?"

"Yes. To Danielle. They have two kids. Then there's Joel.

He's twenty-eight. Dad wanted him to be a lawyer, but after only a year at law school he defied Dad and followed Jett into policing."

Grace's eyebrows rose in surprise. "How did that go down with your father?"

Callum grimaced, remembering the ugly arguments that ensued at the time between his brother and his father over Joel's career choice. "Let's just say, Dad was forced to get used to the idea."

Grace nodded, understanding glimmering in her eyes. "Who's next?"

"Out of the boys, that would be Nicholas. He's twenty-five."

"Let me guess, he went into law."

Callum shook his head. "No. All Nicholas wanted to do was help Dad run Craigdon Enterprises. He spent all of his school holidays working there and after he left school, he was always employed by the company in some form or another."

"So now that your father's dead, he's stepped up as CEO?"

Once again, Callum shook his head. "No. Unfortunately, for some reason Dad didn't see Nick as management material. He gave the company to one of our cousins."

The shock on Grace's face was gratifying. At least it wasn't just him who thought Nick had been treated shabbily.

"Why would he do something like that?" Grace asked, her voice lined with confusion.

Callum shrugged. "Who knows? I wish he'd left some kind of explanation along with the terms of his will."

"Who's the lucky cousin?"

"Logan. He's Flynn's youngest brother."

"How old is he?"

"Twenty-five."

"The same age as Nick?"

"Yes."

"Was he already working in your father's company?"

"No. That's the strange thing. Logan's never shown any interest in Craigdon Enterprises. He's barely interested in his father's business."

Grace looked at him expectantly. Callum continued. "Uncle Archie designs and builds super yachts. Logan used to be a competitive sailor. He could have gone professional. Then he had a bad accident. Broke a lot of bones. They healed pretty well, but he was never the same. Still, he seemed content designing yachts for his father, even if he wasn't interested in the business side of things."

"I don't know the background, but it seems totally weird that your father left him your family company. Especially with your brother ready and waiting in the wings."

Callum compressed his lips, feeling grim. "Yeah. And I'm afraid Nick hasn't taken it well."

Grace's dark eyes filled with sympathy. "I feel for him."

Callum blew out his breath on a sigh. "So do I."

"So," Grace said in a lighter tone, "that's your brothers. What about your sisters?"

Callum acknowledged her effort to change the subject with a grateful smile. "Isabella and Sophia."

"Who's older?"

"Isabella. She's twenty-six. She's a doctor at the Sydney Harbour Hospital."

Grace's eyes widened. "Wow."

"Yes. She worked hard at high school and even harder at university. She's recently broken up with her boyfriend and has moved back home. It's worked out well, especially now. She's good company for Mom."

"And what about Sophia? Tell me about her."

This time Callum grinned. "Sophia's the baby. She's twenty-one. You might suppose she'd be spoiled, given she's the youngest, but surprisingly, she's not. She's sweet and kind and compassionate. At least, most of the time. She wasn't treated so well by Dad in his will, either. Let's just say, right at the moment she's a little…upset."

"What does she do?"

"She recently graduated from university with a teaching degree. She's in the process of finding a job."

He shrugged and sent her a wry grin. "So that's my family. Flynn has another brother, Noah. He's also a detective."

Grace smiled softly. "Wow, you're so lucky. Your family sounds pretty wonderful."

Callum nodded, feeling a rush of warmth toward his family. "Yeah, they are. Of course, we have our disagreements from time to time, but I wouldn't give up any of them for the world. I feel truly blessed."

She stared at him, her beautiful brown eyes filling with emotion. "Whenever I look at you, I feel exactly the same way."

Chapter Seventeen

Callum's heart thumped. He couldn't drag his gaze away from Grace. *Oh, God. I need to tell her about Ken. It isn't fair to keep something so important from her.*

He opened his mouth to tell her and then seeing her smile at him, lost his courage. It took all his effort to keep his voice even. "That's a nice thing to say, but I'm not sure it's justified."

"How can you say that? From the very first moment you walked into my life you've been looking out for me, trying to do what you can to help me." She shook her head helplessly, as if searching for the right words. "Nobody has ever done that for me. And you… You hardly know me. That just makes it all the more special. I don't think I'll ever be able to thank you."

Callum was filled with guilt. He couldn't look her in the eye. "I don't need your thanks."

Grace nodded. "It's just that I'd never seen you before and yet you were so kind to me. And I was so suspicious of your motives."

He put his hand on his heart and sent up a silent prayer for forgiveness. "I just want to help you, Grace. You've had a tougher time than most."

She stared at him and once again her gaze increased in intensity. Her eyes lowered to his mouth and he could almost taste her on his lips. Then her tongue stole out and she traced the line of her lips and it was all he could do not to reach for her.

A turmoil of need and desire erupted inside him. The feelings were so foreign and unfamiliar, they took him off guard. As a teenager, he'd been attracted to girls, but in the back of his mind, he'd always known that kind of life was forbidden to him. His father had chosen another path for him.

During his time at university, it was easy to remain apart from the party scene and the abundant temptations university life offered. He'd remained firmly focused on his theology studies and his goal to become a priest. He'd also not wanted to raise hopes or expectations he couldn't fulfil.

But now he'd been set free from those restrictions and a completely different future was a real possibility. It appeared his body was in full agreement with the changes.

His chest was tight, his cock was hard, his head was filled with her image. What would she look like naked? What would she feel like? Would she be sweet and sensual, or fiery and passionate, burning with desire?

As if sensing the chaos inside him and feeling an answering need, she leaned closer, until their lips were inches apart. Her soft breath whispered across his lips.

Kiss her!

The words echoed in his head and he was powerless to resist. He closed the short distance between them and pressed his lips to hers.

Oh, God. She tasted just as sweet as she had the first time. He was totally enthralled. The softness of her lips beneath his was indescribable. And then her warm tongue shyly coaxed him to open his mouth. When he did so, her tongue slipped inside and gently stroked his.

Over and over again, their tongues tangled in molten heat. Her spicy scent of vanilla and honeysuckle surrounded him, filling his pores. He drew her closer, as close as he could, and silently cursed the gearstick. And then she yelped when it dug into her and he was forced to release his hold.

They were both breathing hard. Grace's neat bun had come loose and tendrils of her hair curled beguilingly around her face. Her lips were swollen and there was a dazed expression on her face. She'd never looked more beautiful.

"I-I…" she started.

He put a finger against her lips. "*Shh*. It's okay. I'm as blown away by that kiss as you are. I probably should apologize, but I can't find it in me to feel sorry. In fact, I'd like to do it again."

She blushed and lowered her gaze and he loved her all the more. Grace was far from an untried virgin, but she felt like one all the same. He was sure the nature of their kiss had been outside her experience.

"I… I should be going," she said and he was immediately flooded with disappointment, even though it was for the best.

"Of course. I'll call you later."

She smiled. "How do you intend to do that?"

He frowned. "What"

"Call me. You don't have my number."

His frown deepened. "I don't?"

"No."

And then he looked away, embarrassed. Of course he didn't have her number.

"Would you like it?" she asked.

He looked back at her and saw the shyness and uncertainty in her face. He hurried to assure her. "Of course I would."

She rattled off her number and he put it directly into his phone. She smiled. "*Now* you can call me."

He smiled back and tamped down another wave of guilt over not disclosing all. "You bet."

Grace watched the BMW disappear into the thickening traffic and hugged herself. She couldn't believe the kiss they'd just shared. It had blown her off her feet.

What is it about this man that rocks my world? Is it his kindness? His goodness? The fact I'd trust him with my life? Perhaps it's the fact he appears completely unaware of his appeal? She guessed that had something to do with the fact that before they'd met he'd been headed for the priesthood.

The reminder was a little sobering, but not enough to remove the grin from her face. She couldn't remember the last time she'd felt so filled with hope and happiness. Yes, happiness. The feeling was so rare, she almost didn't recognize it. She didn't want to consider the possibility he might become a priest…

With Callum in her corner, anything was possible. She now believed that. Maybe even the return of her kids. Seth and Alyssa. How she missed them! The very thought of them filled her with yearning. Her next visit was scheduled for the day after tomorrow. She couldn't wait to see them.

With any luck she was now well on the way to getting them back for good.

On his way home, Callum's head was filled with Grace. Her scent, her softness, the sweet warmth of her lips. She'd driven him wild with her kisses. It had been more than half an hour since he'd left her, yet his body was still hard with need. He wondered how it would feel to lie with her naked on a wide bed with nothing between them. To touch her, to kiss her, to make love to her…

With a curse, he forced his thoughts away from such temptation. Until he'd told her about his involvement in Ken's death, and she had forgiven him—if she did—he had no right to think such thoughts. The longer he delayed his confession, the worse it would be. She'd be shocked, angry, upset… wondering why he hadn't said something sooner… And she'd be justified in her reaction. It was cowardly of him to remain silent. He needed to tell her before things went any further between them. Or before she found out some other way…

And then there was the other battle ahead of them. He was under no illusions: The quest to see Grace's children returned to her wouldn't be easy. Flynn had made it clear the courts were loathe to disrupt the status quo without a good reason and Grace's children had now been living with their grandparents for three years. It was a long time in the life of a child. Callum could only hope and pray the judge would look kindly on a child's need to live with their mother and a mother's need to have them with her.

Speaking of mothers…

"Siri, call Mom," he said and then listened as the phone rang out. His mother answered on the third ring.

"Callum! How are you?"

"I'm fine, Mom. I'm on my way out to see you. There's something I want to talk to you about."

He told his mom about Grace, leaving out the part about her struggle with alcohol, but talking about the custody battle and impressing on his mom the need for Grace to have her children back living with her. He told his mom about how he wanted to help her out and the job he'd offered Grace on his new project.

"We've already met with Flynn. He's going to file the necessary paperwork, but he made it clear the courts will look more favorably on her petition if she has a safe and secure, stable home environment," he added.

"You've always had a big heart, Callum. Your desire to help this woman doesn't surprise me in the least. But are you moving in with her, or asking me to plan a wedding? I'm a little confused about why you're telling me all this."

"No, no! Nothing like that." Callum drew in a breath and gathered his courage. He wasn't quite sure how his mother would react to his suggestion, but at least he had to ask.

"The thing is, I was wondering if I could bring Grace over to meet you with the possibility of having her move into one of the empty wings?"

"At Craigdon Manor?" his mother replied, sounding surprised.

"Yes."

"How long did you say you've known this woman?"

"A bit over a month. What does it matter?" he asked, trying to stem his impatience.

"It doesn't matter, but you're going way over above and beyond for her. Is there something you're not telling me?"

Callum's face heated as he remembered the kisses he'd shared with Grace. "I... I'm not sure of anything at the moment, but... Grace is important to me, Mom. For now, that should be enough."

"Of course, Callum. And you're right, the house is plenty big enough, with only Issy and myself here. But before I make a decision, I'd like to meet her, spend some time with her. Alone."

Relief coursed through him. At least his mother hadn't brought an immediate halt to the plan. "Of course, Mom. How about next Sunday?"

"That sounds fine. Invite her over for brunch."

Callum ended the call and relaxed back against the seat. The tension eased out of him. He wasn't sure what kind of reception his plan would receive from his mother, but she seemed at least open to considering the idea. She certainly hadn't dismissed it out of hand and that was a good sign.

He understood his mother's surprise over his request. Callum had never even had a girlfriend, let alone brought a woman home. His mother was no doubt worried he might be on the rebound through his liberty from the church and could be making ill-advised and ill-thought-through decisions. He couldn't blame her for her concern.

The last month since meeting Grace had been a rollercoaster ride. Not that long ago, he'd been sure his destiny lay in the priesthood. Now that was furthest from his mind. Maybe he needed to slow things down a bit, recalibrate, reconnect with his mentor and get some solid advice? After all, he'd been honest with Father Danny about everything. The old priest was in the best position to offer advice. Yes, he owed it to himself and to Grace to touch base with Father Danny and try and put things in perspective and see if any of this made sense.

With that thought in mind, he called his mentor and arranged to meet with him the very next day. When he ended the call, Callum was filled with relief. It had been the right decision. Things had been moving so fast. He needed to get some clarity and advice from an objective observer whose opinion he valued the most.

The leaves on the huge maple tree outside the seminary had begun to turn red. It was a bit disconcerting for Callum to discover this was the only change to the seminary he could discern in the month since his departure. It felt like his life had turned upside down and yet the rest of the world seemed not to have changed at all. He would have felt more at ease if he'd noticed differences, especially in the place where he'd spent the past four years. But apart from the autumn color and all was the usual calm and quiet in the cool, dim corridors.

He felt subdued as he took a seat across from Father Danny in the old priest's office.

"So, Callum. How have you been? You're looking well, but tired."

Callum nodded. Now he was there, he wasn't sure where to start. Father Danny gave him an encouraging smile. Callum drew in a deep breath.

"So much has happened since I left here."

"You've been enjoying yourself back out in society?"

"Yes, Father. I must confess, I have."

The old priest nodded, his eyes caring and kind. "Good, good. I'm glad."

Callum looked at him in surprise. "You are?"

"Yes, my son. Tell me, what have you been doing? Did you go to Jennifer's Kitchen?"

Callum started out hesitantly, but it wasn't long before he'd told Father Danny all about his volunteer work and meeting Grace. He spoke about buying the building and the plans he had to renovate it and open it up for affordable, possibly even free, short-term accommodation for those less fortunate. Father Danny nodded approvingly.

"It sounds like you've been busy, Callum."

"Yes, Father. I have."

"And you've been enjoying your time at the kitchen?"

"Yes. It's a wonderful service they provide and the staff are just amazing. They truly care for the people who eat there. They go above and beyond."

"Tell me more about this Grace."

And there it was. The reason he'd come there. Father Danny watched him carefully, waiting for him to speak. Unable to hold back any longer, Callum blurted out everything. Well, not *everything*. He'd kept back the part about their shared kisses. But enough for Father Danny to nod wisely when he was finished.

"This Grace, does she know about your connection to her brother's death?"

Callum bowed his head. "No."

"Why not?"

Shame burned across Callum's cheeks. "I want to tell her. I've tried to. I… I'm afraid she'll hate me."

"Does she care for you?"

Callum compressed his lips and shrugged. "I think so, but I'm not sure."

"I see."

"The thing is, Father, I think I've fallen in love with her and now I have this awful secret. I don't know what to do!"

"Yes, you do."

Callum sighed wearily. "You're right. I know what to do. But I'm so scared, Father."

"Fear isn't a sin, Callum. Being afraid only makes you human."

Callum's lips thinned as he acknowledged the priest's words with a nod. He closed his eyes briefly and then gazed at his mentor.

"I find myself yearning for something I've never yearned for before: love, a relationship, maybe even a family of my own. I want everything between me and Grace to be perfect. I don't want secrets between us. She's so important to me, Father. I look around me, at you and the seminary, and though it looks the same, it doesn't *feel* the same. It doesn't feel like home. I… I don't believe I'm cut out for the priesthood after all."

Father Danny nodded sagely. "There are times when we all feel like that, my son. What you need to do is pray about it. God will show you what you're meant to be. If your heart and soul is not with the Lord, then He will show you the way out. Being a good husband and father is a vocation, too, you know."

Callum was filled with relief and a renewed sense of purpose. He would do as Father Danny suggested and disclose all to Grace and pray hard that he make the right decision about the direction his life would take.

"Take your time, Callum. There's no rush. The Lord will always be here and I'm guessing if your Grace is the woman you say she is, she'll also be willing to wait. But you must tell her the truth about her brother. What she does with that truth is up to her, but she has a right to know. There's more to lose the longer you wait. You can't base your developing relationship on lies."

"I haven't lied to her about it!" Callum protested.

"Lies of omission are still lies, Callum. And they're just as destructive."

Callum absorbed Father Danny's words of wisdom. Slowly, he got to his feet. The old priest also stood and came around the side of his desk. The two men embraced.

"Thank you, Father."

"My door is always open, Callum. Feel free to reach out. Anytime."

With another murmur of thanks and a heart filled with gratitude, Callum left.

"Mommy! Mommy! Mommy!"

Grace's heart leaped for joy at the sight of her children running toward her. Blinking away tears, she smiled and opened her arms wide and was almost barreled over by the combined force of her babies as they threw themselves against her. She kissed their cheeks, their hair and anything else she could reach. With the initial excitement of seeing their mother over, both children wriggled to get free.

Grace released her hold on them, even though it was difficult. She wanted to hold them forever. She glanced over to where the court-approved supervisor was seated on a park bench about twenty yards from where Grace stood, watching and listening to everything that was said. The woman lifted her hand in greeting and Grace acknowledged her presence with a brief nod. It wasn't the supervisor's fault she'd been appointed to watch Grace with her children and ensure they remained safe. No, she had her in-laws to thank for that. They were the ones who'd painted a picture to the court that was so harsh, it was no wonder the judge had found it necessary to have her visits with her children supervised.

Okay, so her life had been a mess back then. She'd just lost her husband, had been unjustly accused of causing his death, had fought a custody battle with her in-laws…and lost. It was no wonder she'd been driven to the depths of despair.

But that was then and this was now. She'd come a long way since those dark days. She'd gotten her life together and she was determined to get her kids back and be the best mother she could be. God willing, with Callum and Flynn's support that would become a reality. But for now, she'd just enjoy the time with her babies and cherish every minute she had.

She ruffled her son's dark hair. "How's school, Seth? Are you still struggling with your maths?"

Seth looked away and shrugged. "Sometimes. It's just so *hard*."

"Did you put your hand up and ask the teacher for help, like I suggested?"

Seth's gaze remained downcast. "Grandpa told me I was stupid, just like you. He said I needed to work it out on my own. He said it's the only way to learn."

Grace bit her tongue against the protest that automatically formed in her head. She also held on to her anger. She'd made it a practice not to criticize their grandparents in front of them, but it wasn't easy. Especially when she heard things like that.

Instead, she patted Seth's hand. "Grandpa's right when he says you often learn the best when you work things out on your own, but it's not the *only* way to learn. Sometimes asking the teacher to show you another way can be just as effective. We all learn in different ways. Not everyone learns the same way. What works for Grandpa might not work for you. The thing is, you need to work out for yourself what works for you. Do you understand?"

"Yes, Mom. I think… I think next time I'm gonna ask the teacher."

Grace hugged him close. "I love you, Seth. I love you so much."

"What about me?" Alyssa piped up, brushing the hair out of her eyes.

Grace opened her free arm and drew her daughter in close. "Of *course* I love you too, my sweet munchkin." She kissed and tickled the two of them until they were writhing in giggles.

Slowly, the laughter subsided. "How's Bluey?" Seth asked. "Too bad you couldn't bring him with you. I miss him."

"Me, too!" Alyssa piped up.

Grace sighed. "I know you do. But I couldn't bring him on the bus and I don't have a car at the moment." She forced a smile. "But Bluey is fine. He misses you too!"

Seth frowned. "How can you tell?"

Grace kissed him hard on the forehead, "*I* can tell."

Alyssa regarded her solemnly through her big dark eyes. "When are we going to come and live with you, Mommy?"

"Yeah, Mom," Seth added. "It's okay living with Grandpa and Grandma, but we want to live with *you*."

"They don't tuck me in at night, or say my prayers," Alyssa said, her little face downcast.

"And they don't read to me like you used to," Seth said. "We want to come home, Mom. Please, can we come home?"

Grace's heart clenched with an agony of pain and overwhelming love. Gathering her babies close again, she hugged them hard. All the while, she did her best to hold back her tears.

"I want you to come and live with me, too." She choked on emotion and swallowed hard.

Seth pulled back and looked at her. "Then why can't we? You're all better now, aren't you?"

"Yay!" Alyssa cheered. "Take us home with you now, Mommy!"

Once again, Grace fought back tears. "Yes, honey. I'm all better, but it isn't as easy as that. I wish it was."

Alyssa frowned. "Why isn't it easy?"

Grace drew in a steadying breath and did her best to explain in as simple terms as possible, without blaming their grandparents.

"What does the judge still have to do with it? Why does he still get to say where we can live? We've lived with Grandpa and Grandma *forever*. We want to live with *you*." Seth's jaw was set at a stubborn angle.

Grace cupped his cheek. "Remember when Mommy wasn't well?"

Seth nodded. "Yes. That's when we went to live with Grandpa and Grandma."

"That's right. Well, it was a judge who made that decision. So if we want to change where you live, we need to go back to the judge."

"How long will that take?" Alyssa demanded, her forehead creasing into a frown.

"A little while. There's a lot to do. Papers to file. Arguments to make."

"Why do you need to argue?" Seth asked. "Surely Grandpa and Grandma will agree?"

Grace shrugged. "I hope so. But they've gotten used to you

living with them. And they love you too. They might not want you to leave."

"But you're our *mommy!*" Alyssa said, with an earnest expression on her face. "They can't keep us forever."

"And we miss Bluey!" Seth cried. "We want to live with him too!"

Despite her best efforts, tears welled up in Grace's eyes. She couldn't help it. Any minute and she'd turn into a blubbering mess. She could see the supervisor gazing intermittently in their direction and did her best to get herself back under control.

"It's going to be all right, baby," she whispered against Alyssa's sweet-smelling hair. "I promise."

Much too soon, their visit was over. Amidst tears and hugs and kisses, Grace farewelled her children and watched as they climbed into the private car sent by their grandparents to collect them. With her hands fisted by her side, she watched until the car disappeared from sight. The supervisor waved goodbye, but Grace ignored her. Even the slightest of courtesies was beyond her at that moment. It was all she could do not to shatter into a thousand pieces.

A fierce determination surged through her, straightening her spine. She swiped at the tears that silently ran down her cheeks. She couldn't keep doing this for much longer— spending time with her children and then watching them leave. It broke her heart.

I'm going to get them back. I don't care what it takes…

She thought of the daily battle she raged against the need for a drink and her desire to have custody of her children filled her with a steely resolve. Nothing was more important than her children. Each and every time she craved the sweet oblivion of alcohol, she would remember that.

Chapter Eighteen

race put the last of the clean dishes away in the cupboard. She'd already taken inventory in the pantry and had planned out the next day's meal. As she was preparing to lock up and return to her apartment a knock on the door to the soup kitchen caught her attention.

Crossing through the dining hall, she opened the door. Callum stood on the other side. Her heart skipped a beat. He looked so sweet and sexy in his rumpled T-shirt and jeans. Immediately memories of their kiss flooded her mind. She blushed. Almost simultaneously, a crimson stain spread across Callum's face. Somehow she knew he was also remembering what passed between them the last time they'd met.

"H-hi," she stammered.

"Hi," he said shyly.

She stood there staring at him as a tumult of emotions ran through her.

"May I come in?"

Her blush deepened. "O-of course. I'm sorry. I…" She stood back and let him enter. Feeling nervous and awkward, she headed to her place of refuge and took a seat at the kitchen counter.

"It's good to see you," he said.

She smiled and looked away. "It's good to see you, too."

And then his expression sobered. "Grace, there's something I have to tell you."

A frisson of fear swept through her at the gravity in his voice. "Oh?"

"Yes. This is really hard for me, but there's something I need to tell you."

She clenched her hands into fists. Tension gripped her insides. "What is it?" Her voice was barely above a whisper.

Once again, his expression revealed how difficult it was for him. Grace's delight at seeing him only moments earlier died inside her. She forced herself to ask the question again: "What is it, Callum?"

"Remember when you told me about your brother? How he was hit by a motorist and killed?"

She frowned, confused about the change in subject. "Yes, but what does Ken have to do with us?"

She saw him take another deep breath. The pain on his face was now stark. A coldness descended upon her.

"The thing is, I was the one in the car. I was the one who hit him."

Shock ricocheted through her like a bullet. She gaped at him, her mouth opening and closing without sound as she struggled to process what he'd just said.

"Y-you? It was *you*?"

He hung his head, as if he couldn't bring himself to look at her. "Yes."

She shook her head in increasing confusion. "But… I don't understand."

He lifted his head and the agony and guilt in his gaze almost overwhelmed her.

"I'm sorry, Grace. It was dark. He came out of nowhere. I didn't even see him until it was too late."

"You killed my brother?" she cried, incredulous.

"I'm so sorry, Grace. I stopped right away and called an

ambulance. I tried to render assistance, but he was hurt really bad. There was nothing I could do…And until you told me, I had no idea he was your brother."

Disbelief and a growing sense of anger unfurled in her stomach. She stared at him, her eyes narrowed.

"Why didn't you tell me earlier? When I told you about Ken, you said nothing about your involvement. Why?"

Callum stared at the ground. "I should have. You don't know how many times I've wished I did. As it was, I was having a hard time dealing with my part in a man's death… But I was so shocked when I realized the man I'd hit was your brother. Our relationship was so new, so fragile. I didn't want to jeopardize that. And you had so much going on with your kids…"

Anger ignited inside her. "So you decided not to tell me because you didn't think I'd cope, right?"

"No, Grace!" he protested.

She glared at him. "You have no right to decide what I can and cannot cope with! I've been fighting battles all my life! I've been dealt some harsh blows over my thirty years and I'm still here, still fighting!"

Callum stood. He held his hands out toward her, beseeching her. "Everything you say is true, Grace. You're the most incredible, the most amazing, the strongest woman I know. It's not that I didn't think you could cope with any more bad news, it's just that… I was scared, Grace. I… I've fallen in love with you. I was scared if I told you the truth about that night… I'd lose you."

His voice cracked with the force of his emotion, but Grace steeled herself against his pain. She took a few steps back and held on to her anger.

"You should have told me! How can I ever trust you again? What do you expect me to do? Forgive you? You're responsible for my brother's death!"

Callum looked stricken. Bluey came and stood at her side in a silent show of support. He nudged her thigh with his head. She glanced down at him. The dog's eyes were so sad and weary. Instinctively, she patted him on the shoulder.

"I think you should leave," she said in a calmer tone.

Callum opened his mouth as if to protest, but slowly closed it again. "Grace—"

Before Callum could say another word there was a pounding on the door. He and Grace looked at each other.

"Are you expecting someone?" he asked.

Wearily, Grace shook her head. "No."

Callum frowned. He'd finally told Grace the truth and now they were being interrupted before they could properly talk things through. The pounding came again. Then someone shouted, their tone filled with urgency. All of a sudden, the shouting became clearer.

"Fire!"

Adrenaline surged through him. Grabbing Grace by the hand, he dragged her across the dining hall and wrenched open the door that led outside. A man stood there with his fist raised as if he were about to pound on the door again.

"Fire!" he shouted and pointed up at the roof.

Both he and Grace looked in that direction. Grace gasped. Callum bit back a curse. Smoke billowed from one of the upper stories of the building.

"Quick! Get back!" he shouted, pulling her behind him. At the same time he took out his phone and dialed the emergency number.

"There's a fire. We need help." He gave the operator the address and then ended the call.

"Is there anyone else inside?" the man who'd alerted them asked.

"No," Callum replied. "Just us, unless there's someone up there that we don't know about."

The man nodded. All three of them moved further away. Callum took a moment to introduce himself and Grace and thank the man for warning them.

"No problem. I was at the liquor store across the street and when I saw the smoke."

"Well, Grace and I are extremely grateful."

The sound of sirens could be heard in the distance. All of a sudden, Grace looked stricken. "What about Bluey?"

Callum tensed. "Where is he?"

"He was just with us, but he didn't make it outside. I don't see him."

"I'll go and look for him," Callum replied and ran back toward the building.

"Be careful!" he heard Grace yell.

The smoke had thickened. It stung his eyes and burned the back of his throat. Shards of debris drifted down from above, filling the air. Through the smoke he spied the old dog cowering against the wall beside the door. The poor thing looked terrified.

"Bluey! Come here, mate. It's all right."

The dog continued to cower. His head was down and his tail was buried between his legs. Callum reached out to him, patting him gently on the shoulder.

"It's okay, Bluey. I've got you. It's going to be okay."

The dog was shaking so hard it was impossible to tell if he was even aware of Callum's presence. Realizing the quickest way to get the animal out of there was to carry him, Callum bent low and gathered the dog in his arms. Bluey whimpered.

"It's all right, Bluey. I've got you."

He started for the door that led back toward the street. As Grace caught sight of the two of them, her face lit up with relief and gratitude. He gently set the old dog down on the ground next to her. Grace fell to her knees and embraced the blue heeler, burying her face against his neck. Callum moved slightly away, his nose and eyes itching. A sneeze exploded out of him. He fumbled in his pocket for the packet of antihistamines he'd taken to carrying since he met Grace.

She looked up at him, her eyes filled with emotion. "You saved him!" she whispered.

Callum looked away, embarrassed. "It was nothing."

"Your eyes are red and your nose is running," she murmured.

"It's the smoke," he muttered.

Grace got slowly to her feet. The anger that had flooded her face during their argument had been replaced by something else. It wasn't forgiveness, or even acceptance, but neither was it the fury that consumed her only moments before.

Then the wail of the sirens became deafening, preventing further conversation. Bluey pressed himself against Grace's side. Several fire trucks pulled up to the curb, one after the other.

They stood in silence and watched in amazement as the firemen did their stuff. In short order, ladders and cherry pickers were put in place and men in protective gear and wielding hoses spraying gallons of water, worked hard to bring the fire under control. When the last flame was extinguished, Callum breathed a sigh of relief.

Grace turned to him. "Oh, Callum! Your building! It's ruined!"

Grimly, he regarded the charred and blackened ruins above them. "It doesn't matter. It's just a building. As long as you and Bluey are safe. That's all that matters."

The fire chief came up to them then and introduced himself. "Are you the owner of the building?" he asked Callum.

"Yes. At least, almost. It's under contract."

"Well, I guess you'll have to speak with your lawyer about who's responsible for the damage. It looks like it was started by some faulty electrical wiring."

Callum nodded grimly. "How bad is it?"

"Surprisingly, it's not as bad as it looks. We got here fast and contained it to just one floor."

Some of Callum's tension eased. "That's good news. Are we able to continue to use the soup kitchen?"

"Yes," the fire chief replied. "That part of the building didn't sustain any damage, but it's probably a good idea to stay out of there for the rest of today. The smoke's penetrated to the ground floor. You'll need to open up the doors and windows to air it out."

Callum acknowledged the suggestion with a nod. "Yes, of course."

"If I were you, I'd have someone look over the rest of the wiring in the building," the fire chief continued. "You don't want another fire to start."

"That's for sure," Callum agreed. "I'll have an electrician come over and take a look as soon as it's safe to do so."

The fire chief nodded and took his leave. Callum turned to Grace. "Well, that was lucky."

She didn't look convinced. "Lucky? I don't call having your building almost destroyed, lucky."

Without thinking, he squeezed her shoulder in an act of reassurance.

She immediately tensed. He dropped his hand and looked away. "I was going to gut the inside of it, anyway. The fire's just hastened my progress." He offered her a weak smile.

She regarded him solemnly. His smile faded. Glancing around him, he drew her away from the crowd of curious onlookers who still watched the firemen who tended to the last of the dying fire.

"Grace, I… I'm so sorry about what happened to your brother. I swear it was an accident. I wish to God it hadn't happened, but there was nothing I could do. Please, please believe me."

"I believe you, Callum. I do. Of course I'm sad about his death, but that isn't why I'm so upset." He caught the flash of pain in her eyes as she lowered her gaze. "You should have told me. As soon as I mentioned Ken and the way he'd died, you must have known we were talking about the same person. You should have told me then. Keeping it from me was wrong."

Callum agreed. "You're right. If I could rewind that conversation, I'd respond very differently. But in my defense, when I first made the connection, I was shocked. I could scarcely believe it. I mean, what were the odds? But as the shock wore off, I knew I had to tell you…and I didn't. And for that, I am truly, deeply sorry."

Chapter Nineteen

Grace stared at Callum. She believed in his sincerity, but that wasn't the point. He'd had ample opportunity to tell her about his involvement in Ken's death. And he hadn't. Still, she couldn't deny the shock of his news had started to wear off.

The police had already provided her with the details of what had happened the night of her brother's death. Ken had been high on drugs and had stepped off the footpath without warning and into the path of an oncoming vehicle. It had been dark. Of course, the driver had been taken to the station for mandatory drug and alcohol testing and those results had been negative. From all accounts it looked like a tragic accident.

Just the day before, she'd received a call from the detective in charge of the case. He'd told her they'd wound up their investigation. Her brother's death would be ruled an accident. The case was now closed. They hadn't given her the name of the driver, and at the time she didn't think that mattered. She'd resigned herself to accept it hadn't been the driver's fault.

Had anything really changed for her now that she knew that driver had been Callum?

Probably not.

It was just the shock of finding out it was him. It was different when the driver had been a nameless, faceless stranger. She couldn't quite put her finger on why, it just was… And then when she realized Callum had kept it from her, the hurt and anger had set in. Except he'd kept it from her because he loved her and he didn't want to lose her…

That pulled her up short. "Earlier, you said you were in love with me. Did you mean it?"

"Of course I did."

"Is that the reason you decided to come clean? To tell me the truth about Ken?"

He stared at her solemnly. "Yes."

"Why? Why did you bother telling me at all? You could have just as easily have kept it a secret from me forever. Unless you were charged and the case went to court, there was very little chance I'd find out."

He nodded slowly. "That's true."

She continued to regard him steadily. "And yet, you told me. You told me, knowing full well how I'd react. You said you were scared you'd lose me. You must have had some inkling I might not forgive you and that would have been the end of us once you knew."

He stared at her unflinchingly. "Yes to all of that. I had to tell you, Grace. No matter if there wasn't a chance in this lifetime that you'd have found out, I had to tell you. I'm responsible for your brother's death. You had a right to know. I would never have been able to live with myself with that secret between us. It would have eaten away at me, destroyed me, destroyed our love… I couldn't live with that…"

She groaned and cradled her head in her hands.

"Oh, Callum! I'm so sorry! I'm sorry you believed I might never forgive you! Who am I to judge? I've been there myself. I've been accused of causing someone's death when it was simply a tragic accident. Even when, just like you, the police ruled it as such. I know how it feels to be unjustly accused and yet, I did the same thing to you… A man so good and kind and compassionate. A man I love with all my heart and soul…"

His expression filled with wonder. "You… You *love* me?"

"Yes!" Tears overflowed and ran down her cheeks. She smiled and laughed and swiped at them with the back of her hand. "Yes! I love you, Callum Craigdon!"

He pulled her in close against him and hugged her. After a long moment, he gently eased back. "Does this mean you forgive me?"

She nodded. "Yes, I forgive you. You've been my rock almost from the time I met you, helping me, supporting me in so many ways. The least I can do is return the favor."

She moved back into the circle of his arms. He tightened his hold on her. She raised her arms and looped them around his neck and pulled his head down to hers. And then she kissed him.

The world stopped. The sound of the firemen still packing up around them disappeared. There was nothing and no one but Callum and the wonderful feel of his warmth and strength surrounding her, protecting her, keeping her safe.

And then she slowly pulled back. "What about the seminary?"

Callum sighed. "I went to see my mentor yesterday. A priest at the seminary. I told him all about you and how confused I felt about my future."

Grace's blinked in surprise. "You did? What did he say?"

"He was very supportive. He told me to pray about it and to give myself time to make a decision. He assured me there's no rush."

She took a step back, to give him space. "And have you?" she asked.

"Made a decision?"

"Yes."

Her heart thumped. She looked up at him, anxious yet filled with anticipation.

Callum's expression filled with tenderness. "I think I have. Yes."

Her breath caught. "And?"

He framed her face with his hands and stared down at her. "And I've decided to leave the seminary."

Her breath rushed out in a *whoosh*. She stared at him in disbelief and gulped to get air back in her lungs.

"You're… You're leaving the seminary?"

"Yes. I've decided God has other plans for me. I can do plenty of good without being a priest."

Grace's laughter was filled with joy. "Of course you can."

This time, it was Callum who initiated the kiss. Soft and pliant, he molded her lips to his. His masculinity surrounded her. The firm muscles that bunched beneath her fingers, the impressive width of his shoulders and chest. He pulled her even closer until her breasts were crushed against him. Her nipples puckered at the contact. She wanted the moment to go on forever, but it wasn't possible. They were as good as on a public street. There were people everywhere, including a number of firemen—several of whom were watching them.

And then he lifted his head and smiled down at her. He looked as dazed as she felt. "Well, that's one way to take my mind off the fire," he teased.

She smiled. Her heart felt lighter than it had for years. Her future had never looked brighter—all because of the man beside her.

"I can't believe you love me," she whispered.

He pressed a soft kiss against her mouth. "Today, tomorrow and forever." He kissed her again briefly and then set her away from him. "We'd better head back inside and get those windows open."

Hand in hand, they coaxed Bluey to follow them back to the kitchen. Grace laughed when the old dog made it to the back steps but would go no further.

"It's all right, Bluey. You can stay there." She went inside and fetched him a fresh bowl of water. He lapped at it greedily.

Despite the fact Callum had swallowed a couple of antihistamines without water, his nose tingled. He pulled out his handkerchief and prepared to catch the sneeze. Grace laughed again and shook her head.

"You weren't lying when you told me you were allergic."

He grinned and bent down to give Bluey a pat. "Yeah, I'm allergic, but it's no biggie. I can take medication that gets me over the worst of it. Besides, Bluey's a valued member of your family. He belongs with you."

Her heart melted with love. She stepped into his arms and kissed him with all the love in her heart. The kitchen smelled smoky and water leaked from a hole in the ceiling, but as far as Grace was concerned, she'd never been happier.

Grace was floating on air. She couldn't believe that less than an hour after her precious soup kitchen had been threatened by fire she felt so wonderful, but it was true and she owed Callum for that. She couldn't believe how he'd popped into her life and was now like her guardian angel. He wanted, truly wanted, to help her and he wanted nothing in return. He was good and kind and honorable and most wondrous of all, he loved her.

Even with all the windows wide open, the kitchen smelled of smoke, but thankfully, as the fire chief had told them, it had been spared serious damage. She glanced over to where Callum stood on a ladder, inspecting a leak in the ceiling.

"Thankfully none of our patrons were here when the fire started," she said.

"Absolutely. Getting that many people out in an orderly manner would have been a challenge."

She walked over to the stove and filled the kettle. "Would you like a coffee? I could sure use one to steady my nerves." She shuddered again. "I know we escaped relatively unscathed, but I can't help envisioning what might have happened if that man hadn't noticed the smoke."

Callum frowned. "That reminds me. How come we didn't hear any smoke alarms?"

"There are none. This is an old building. It hasn't been updated to comply with the current building codes."

Callum compressed his lips into a grim line. "That has to change immediately. A proper fire warning system, even a temporary one, will be the first thing on my list. When we do the renovations it will be include sprinklers."

She winked at him. "Right after you repair the ceiling."

He chuckled and climbed back down the ladder. She met him halfway and stepped straight into his embrace. They kissed softly, lingeringly, savoring the newness, the wonder of it.

When at last the kiss ended, Grace reached up and cupped his cheek, her heart overflowing with love. "I know I've told you this already, but you're a good man, Callum Craigdon and I love you with all my heart."

Over coffee, Callum told her the reason behind his visit. "I've come up with a plan," he said.

She smiled. "What kind of plan?"

"Well, we both know the court won't look favorably on your current living conditions, even without the recent fire."

"Right. And I'm trying to rectify that. I've managed to save almost enough to pay the bond on a small apartment. And now with your generous job offer and increase in salary… It won't be anything extravagant, but at least my children will have their own bedroom."

"The fact you've managed to save money on your miniscule wage is amazing," Callum replied. "But I have something else in mind."

Grace instinctively tensed, but she felt a tingle of curiosity. "Oh?"

He gave her a nervous smile that did nothing to allay her fears. "Yes. I've been speaking to my mother. She lives in a big old house with no one but my sister living with her. And the staff, of course, but they're in a building separate from the main house."

Grace continued to regard him steadily while her mind went into overdrive. "What does any of this have to do with me?"

Callum squirmed and looked away. "The thing is, I think you might be able to move in with my mom. At least, temporarily. It's a perfect solution. For you and Bluey now, and your children when you regain custody. We'll adjust the plan if and when there's a need."

Grace gave him a wry smile. "I didn't realize your mother required additional company."

Callum blushed. "Well, she doesn't. That is, she's perfectly capable of taking care of herself and she has my sister Issy for company, but… Anyway, I've raised the possibility with her and she'd… She'd like to meet you."

Grace felt a frisson of fear arc through her. Callum must have noticed something in her expression, because he frowned and his eyes filled with concern.

"What is it, Grace? What did I say?"

As memories of her marriage to Daniel bombarded her, Grace clenched her fists. She wouldn't meet his gaze.

"Grace?"

She sighed. "The thing is, my experience with wealthy mothers hasn't been a positive one. You know how my in-laws feel about me. Even when Daniel was alive, I was never able to meet their expectations. The constant disapproval from my mother-in-law was worst of all."

Callum's eyes filled with understanding. He reached out for her hands. "You'll be fine. I promise. My mother's not like that. She's smart and funny and opinionated, but she's also good and kind and caring. He gave her a disarming smile. "Where do you think I get it from?"

Grace melted. She had no resistance to his charm. "All right, I'd like to meet her at least," she agreed with reluctance.

Callum beamed. "Great. She's invited you over to brunch on Sunday so you can get to know each other. Her name's Elizabeth, by the way." He finished his coffee and leaned over and kissed her hard on the mouth. "I wish I could stay, but I have a meeting in the city with the architects in half an hour. I have to rush. They're going to be thrilled when I tell them about the fire. We're going to have to redesign substantial parts of the proposed renovations."

She nodded. "I understand. I'll talk to you later."

After Callum left, Grace paced restlessly around the kitchen. She kept thinking about the upcoming meeting and whether she'd receive Callum's mother's approval. Her mind kept returning to Nerida Gunning and how unworthy she made Grace feel.

The meeting with Callum's mother was even more important. If things went well, their meeting might be a giant step toward getting her children back. It would definitely speed things up. It would also help her blossoming relationship with Callum. She could tell how much his mother meant to him. It would be best for both of them if Elizabeth approved.

Grace stopped before the window that looked out on the street. The neon sign above the liquor store, already visible in the late afternoon light, still beckoned to her. Despite all the good things happening, and the hope she felt for her future, a yearning so strong she could almost taste it rocked her. She gripped the sides of the sink with both hands and fought it off. With her eyes squeezed shut, she blocked out the sight of temptation and prayed for the strength to get through another day of sobriety.

Sunday morning proved bright and sunny, another glorious late-summer day. Grace checked herself in the cracked bathroom mirror for the hundredth time. At least, that's what it felt like. The plain, charcoal-gray suit and white blouse was her best outfit. She only wore it on special occasions. Her very first thought after she'd woken that morning was that in a few hours she'd meet Callum's mother. Nerves had immediately gathered in her stomach and had been a constant presence ever since. She hadn't even been able to bring herself to eat breakfast and now it was too late.

A knock on her door signaled Callum's arrival and her heart jumped into her throat. It was all she could do not to turn and make a run for it.

Don't be silly, Grace. It's only his mother you'll be meeting. You're not expected to slay a two-headed dragon with a butter knife, no matter how nasty she might or might not be.

The knock came again.

Forcing a calming breath through suddenly dry lips, she resolutely turned away from the mirror and made her way to the front door. Callum stood on the other side, looking gorgeous in a polo shirt, jeans and a sports jacket.

"Hi, there." He leaned down and kissed her softly on the mouth.

She reveled in the feel of his lips and wished they could linger there forever. Maybe she could claim a headache and they could spend the time in her apartment instead. As if sensing her panic, Callum took her hand and squeezed it.

"Don't look so terrified. You're going to be fine. She's going to love you."

"You don't know that."

Callum kissed her again. "Yes, I do."

After her gestures to put Bluey at ease, to reassure him she'd return, he led her toward his car. He opened the passenger side door and closed it after she climbed in. Sliding behind the wheel, he gave her an encouraging grin.

She picked at a piece of imaginary lint on her skirt. "Do I look okay?"

"You look beautiful."

"I'm overdressed," she worried.

"No. You look just fine."

"Callum—"

This time, he reached over and cupped her cheek. The gesture was so intimate, so tender it brought tears to her eyes.

"My mother's a remarkable woman, Grace. In a lot of ways, you remind me of her. She's completely non-judgmental. She won't care about what you're wearing, where you work, what you've done with your life. All she cares about is the kind of person you are and we both know, when it comes to that you'll pass with flying colors."

Feeling slightly less terrified, she offered him a wobbly grin.

Callum beamed. "There you go. I knew I could get you to smile."

Grace relinquished Callum's hand so he could shift gears as they drove from the city. She tried to take confidence from his description of Elizabeth, but all Grace could think of was that this woman was a mother of six, wife to a high-flying billionaire and no doubt accomplished more things than

Grace could imagine. Still, she prayed Callum's mother was as nice as he said she'd be.

Callum swung the car through a set of enormous wrought iron gates and drove slowly along a paved driveway that seemed to go on forever. The nerves in Grace's stomach intensified. Through the car window, she spied acres of lush green lawn and colorful displays of perfectly manicured garden beds. And then the house came into sight.

To call it a house was an understatement. Even the mansion the Gunnings lived in didn't come close to this. She turned to Callum, her eyes wide with shock.

"This is where you live?"

"Not at the moment. I'm taking care of my brother's apartment while he's overseas. But otherwise, since I left the seminary, this is my family home. We moved here from Maroubra when I was twelve. It didn't always look like this. Mom's a magician in the garden."

Grace took in the magnificent grounds and shook her head. "She did all this by herself?"

"Not exactly. She had a bit of help. They've always employed a couple of gardeners, but Mom's hands-on a lot of the time. She's usually the one who comes up with the designs and plant choices."

"She's done a wonderful job. The grounds are beautiful."

Callum pulled up in front of a set of wide stone steps that led to the front door of the mansion he called home. The place was even more majestic close up and another rush of nerves hit her. The moment she'd dreaded was here.

Callum shot her a look of reassurance. And then he winked. He was so damned gorgeous. He stole her breath.

Climbing out of the car, he came around to her side and opened the door. He offered his hand and she took it, clinging to him gratefully. As they headed up the steps, hand in hand, she drew in a breath and forced herself to ease it out.

Callum squeezed her hand, but remained silent. He gave a perfunctory knock on the wide front door before turning the brass handle and letting them in.

"Mom? We're here."

The clacking of high heels across the travertine tiles was heard from a distance and gradually came closer. A tall, slim woman with a thick head of snow-white, perfectly coiffed hair and an elegant bearing—the woman from the online photo she'd found—came into sight. As she moved closer, Grace took note of the pale pink linen dress and matching jacket that fit Callum's mother like a glove. The outfit would have cost more than most people made in a month.

She greeted Callum with a smile that reached her eyes. Callum kissed her cheek.

"Mom. You're looking well." He stepped back and took Grace's hand, bringing her up against his side. "I'd like you to meet Grace Gunning."

Chapter Twenty

As Callum made the introductions, Elizabeth carefully concealed her surprise. The way her son looked at this woman, the way he held her hand, spoke volumes. It was strange seeing him with a woman in this sense, given that it had been understood from the day he was born he'd enter the priesthood. He'd never been one to bring women home. He'd never even had a girlfriend. That he cared for this woman was obvious. Elizabeth couldn't help but wonder what Henry would have made of it.

"It's lovely to meet you, Grace," Elizabeth murmured.

The woman on Callum's arm murmured a quick greeting. Her gaze darted around the room. It was obvious she was nervous. Elizabeth tried to put her at ease.

"Do come into the music room. It's much nicer in there."

Leading the way, Elizabeth went into a smaller, yet equally grand room off the main foyer. It was a room she chose to spend much of her leisure time, though between her garden and her charitable commitments, there was precious little down time.

The soft furnishings were pale silver and contrasted nicely with the light-gray couch. Elizabeth had chosen it herself. A shiny black, baby grand piano sat in one corner beneath the window, where there was an abundance of natural light.

Though her dreams of becoming a concert pianist were well behind her, whenever she felt the need to relax and forget her worries, she came there to play. It was far enough away from the rest of the house that she didn't bother anyone. Most of the time it was only her there, anyway. Even when Henry had been alive.

She showed her visitors to a seating area and called for some tea. Instead of taking a seat beside Grace, Callum remained standing. Grace looked at him expectantly.

"I'm sorry, Grace. I can't stay," he told her. "I'm afraid I have another meeting in the city."

A look of sheer panic crossed the woman's face. Elizabeth felt a moment of guilt. After all, meeting with the woman one on one had been her idea. She'd wanted time to assess the girl's character, without Callum running interference. Elizabeth wanted the chance to get to know the woman who might have captured her son's heart—or at the very least, had given him cause to reconsider entering the priesthood. It was important they have this time alone.

She forced a look of surprise. "Oh, darling! Are you sure you can't stay for a little while? I've just called for tea."

Callum gave her a look she blithely ignored. Instead, she hugged him briefly in a sign of farewell. "Well, have a good meeting. Drive safely. I'm sure Grace and I will be fine." She turned to the other woman and smiled. "Won't we, Grace?"

To her credit, Grace managed to smile back at her and reassure Callum. Most of the panic Elizabeth had witnessed a few moments earlier had receded. It appeared the woman had resigned herself to being left there alone with Callum's mother and was determined to see it through.

Good girl…

Elizabeth watched with interest as Callum kissed Grace gently on the cheek and spoke some quiet words of reassurance to her then took his leave.

Yes, he's definitely interested in this woman…

Like any mother would, Elizabeth needed to make sure Grace was worthy of her son's love. And what better way to ascertain that than to spend some time alone together?

The tea things arrived, along with a tray laden with fresh pastries. Elizabeth poured. Grace confirmed she took milk and sugar. Elizabeth handed the woman a cup.

"Thank you, Mrs Craigdon."

"Oh, please. Call me Elizabeth." As Elizabeth fixed her own cup and settled back against the couch, in a deceptively casual tone she posed her first question.

"So, Grace. Callum tells me you work in a soup kitchen?"

"Yes. Jennifer's Kitchen. It was set up many years ago by a woman by the name of Jennifer Rawlings. It's run under the auspices of the Little Sisters of the Poor."

"How long have you been working there?"

"A little over a year. I started there as a volunteer. The sisters needed someone to be around on a regular basis—shop for essentials, plan menus, co-ordinate the lunches. Someone they could rely on. I was volunteering there when their cook had to leave. They approached me about the job and I was happy to take it on."

Grace smiled and continued: "I love working there. I love being able to help so many people. It might only be a hot meal and some conversation, but it means so much to them. It makes me feel good, too. They've helped me in ways they don't even know."

"Callum tells me you lost your husband. That must have been difficult. I recently lost my husband, too."

Grace nodded. "Yes, Callum told me. Please accept my condolences."

Elizabeth waved away Grace's sympathies. "Tell me about your husband."

Grace sighed quietly. Elizabeth wondered what was behind the sad resignation she saw on the other woman's face.

"Daniel and I were married nearly eight years," Grace began in a soft voice. "We met at university and fell in love. We have two children, Seth and Alyssa."

"They live with you?"

"No. They live…with their grandparents."

Of course Callum had already filled her in on Grace's situation, but she wanted to hear the story from the girl herself. She feigned confusion. "Oh? Why is that?"

She watched as Grace carefully set aside her teacup and then drew in a deep breath, as if gathering her courage.

"I'm not sure how much Callum told you, but my husband died in a tragic accident. The children and I were there when it happened. His parents blamed me." She shook her head, as if to ward off the memories.

"Did the police charge you?"

"No, of course not. It was an accident. The coroner ruled it as such. Still, my in-laws never got over their son's death. Relations between us had never been great. They only deteriorated after Daniel's death."

Elizabeth sat forward, incredulous. "So they petitioned the court for custody of your children out of *spite*?"

"Yes. No…" Grace sighed wearily. "There was more to it than that."

Elizabeth nodded. "There usually is." She took a sip from her cup and nibbled on a pastry, waiting for Grace to continue. The color had leached out of the young woman's cheeks. It was obvious dredging up old memories was difficult for her. Elizabeth felt a wave of sympathy, but she forced herself to remain distant. It was important she know the full story. She needed to know everything there was about the woman who might not only share her home but who seemed to have engaged Callum's heart.

"When Daniel died, I fell apart. I was under constant pressure from his parents to take responsibility for his death. They hounded me about everything. He should never have married me. It had been a mistake, they said. The only good to come of the union was Seth and Alyssa and they were determined to take them from me."

Elizabeth frowned. "But a court doesn't just hand over someone's children to a relative when their mother is alive and well. They must have had good reason."

Grace's lips compressed into a thin line. The sadness and resignation in her gaze intensified. Tears shimmered in her eyes.

"You're right. They had good reason."

Grace's voice was little more than a whisper. Elizabeth leaned forward so she could hear. And at that point she felt like she was intruding. It was obvious from Grace's demeanour this was painful. Was it really necessary for her to relate what happened?

Yes, Elizabeth decided. Elizabeth's personal safety and her son's happiness were at stake. She and Henry had raised six children. Only one of them was married. She was determined to see each and every one of them happy, married or not. She knew firsthand how unhappy one could be in the wrong marriage.

She'd spent thirty-three years making the best of it, but she didn't wish that kind of unhappiness on anyone, especially on her children. She loved them too much to let that happen. She made no apologies for the fact she'd do everything in her power to ensure the person each of her children chose to marry was their perfect match. Right now, it appeared it was Callum's turn.

"This might be none of my business," she said, "but Callum is my son. I'm not sure how much he's told you about his past, but you're the first woman he's brought home.

He asked me to help you get your children back by giving you a place to stay, something more suitable than your current arrangements."

She spread her arms wide. "As you can see, this house is large enough to accommodate several families. It's not a question of whether I have enough room. But the thing is, I can tell you're important to Callum. His request goes beyond his kind and caring heart and his desire to help someone less fortunate. I think he might really care for you and I need to know you're not going to break his heart."

She spoke calmly and without inflection, but steely determination straightened her spine. Her gaze remained locked on the young woman before her. To her credit, Grace gazed steadily back at her without flinching.

"What do you want to know?"

"Tell me why the court decided to remove your children."

Elizabeth watched as Grace swallowed. Even more color fled her cheeks. But at last she looked Elizabeth in the eye and quietly said, "I lost my children because I couldn't take care of them. I was an alcoholic. My children were scared. They didn't know what to do. At the request of Daniel's parents, the courts stepped in and made the decision to put them in their care. They were given sole custody. That was three years ago. I've been straightening out my life, having supervised visits with my children and planning how to get them back ever since."

Elizabeth stared at Grace in shock. While Callum had told her about the custody battle, he'd said nothing of Grace's struggle with alcohol.

"Does my son know you're an alcoholic?" she asked.

Grace nodded. "Yes."

Once again, Elizabeth was taken by surprise. She felt a grudging admiration for the woman who sat across from her. It couldn't have been easy for her to admit such a thing to

Callum. Elizabeth was sure it had been just as difficult for Grace to admit it to his mother.

"How do you feel about my son?" she asked softly. Once again, the question was probably out of line, but where the happiness of her children was concerned, Elizabeth didn't give a toss.

The smile that eased itself across Grace's face took Elizabeth's breath away. It spread slowly, lighting up the young woman's eyes, bringing color back to her cheeks.

She's in love with him… It was as clear as the nose on her face.

"It's hard to find words that adequately convey how I feel about Callum," Grace began in a quiet, but firm voice. She glanced at Elizabeth. "You're his mother. You know better than anyone how special he is. I've never met anyone like him. He's so good and kind and compassionate. He really cares. And there doesn't seem to be any limit. It doesn't matter who it is, he treats everyone the same."

"I take it you know that not long ago he was in the seminary?"

Grace nodded. "Yes."

So it seems Callum has kept no secrets from her… Another sign he was serious about this woman.

Elizabeth regarded Grace with interest. "How do you feel about that?"

Grace shrugged. "He would have made a wonderful priest."

Elizabeth frowned. "What do you mean, 'would have'?"

At Elizabeth's question, surprise and a flash of dread colored Grace's features. Elizabeth regarded her closely.

"Um, I… I'm sorry. I shouldn't have said anything."

Elizabeth's gaze narrowed. "Has he said something to you?"

"Please, Mrs Craig—Elizabeth. It's not my place to say."

Elizabeth frowned in consternation. It was clear things

were moving faster than she'd imagined. She leveled Grace with a look. "Are you in love with my son?"

Grace squirmed at Elizabeth's bluntness. Elizabeth smiled inwardly. One of the advantages of being older and being Callum's mother was her right to ask questions that others might not dare to ask. To her credit, Grace squared her shoulders and then returned Elizabeth's steady stare.

"Yes. I'm in love with your son. I can't imagine my life without him."

Elizabeth nodded. Her respect for this woman continued to grow. "Have you told him yet?"

"Yes."

Once again, Elizabeth was filled with surprise. "I see. And how does Callum feel?"

Grace's gaze remained on hers. "He feels the same way."

Elizabeth blinked. "Really? That's so…interesting."

Grace shrugged. "I know what you're thinking. We haven't known each other very long. It all seems so fast. But you can't help who you fall in love with and that's what we are…in love."

"What about your children?"

Grace nodded. "Of course. My children. Any decision I make about my future must include them. No matter what I feel for Callum, Seth and Alyssa are my priority. I won't do anything that might jeopardize getting them back."

"Fair enough," Elizabeth replied, admiring the girl's honesty. She finished the pastry, dusted her fingertips with a napkin, took another sip from her cup and then set it aside. "So, tell me about your family. What do your parents do?"

"My parents are both dead. Dad died when I was young. Mom died of cancer right before Daniel's accident."

Elizabeth was filled with sympathy. "You've had your fair share of grief."

"Yes."

"What about brothers and sisters?"

Grace shook her head. "My only brother was killed in an accident a little over a month ago." She glanced at Elizabeth and then continued in a quiet tone. "In fact, Callum was the driver of the vehicle."

Elizabeth reared back in shock. "You don't mean… Oh, my goodness! He told me about the accident of course, but… Does he know the victim was your brother?"

Grace nodded. "Yes. We talked about it. I've had time to come to terms with it."

"Aren't you angry? Don't you blame him? He ended your brother's life."

"You're right, and I was angry. We had a big row. But I've forgiven Callum for the part he played in my brother's death. The police told me my brother was high on methamphetamine and cocaine when he was struck." She cut a glance toward Elizabeth and just as quickly lowered her gaze again. "Ken had…problems. He struggled with…a lot of things."

Elizabeth nodded in understanding. "I see. Well, good for you. Not everyone would feel so kindly toward the man responsible for a loved one's death."

Elizabeth took another sip of her tea before setting the cup carefully back on the saucer. "So, do you have any other family? Any cousins?"

Grace shook her head. "If there are any cousins, I don't know of them."

Elizabeth shot her a look of sympathy. "So you're on your own."

"Yes. In some ways it feels like I've always been on my own."

Elizabeth frowned. "But what about your husband?"

Grace's eyes filled with resignation. "I'm afraid he wasn't as supportive as I'd hoped. We were very young when we married. Having to cope with his parents' disapproval was difficult for both of us. It took its toll. Toward the end, Daniel began to resent me for the rift I'd caused in his family. More often than not, he took their side against me. It was…a difficult time."

Elizabeth stared at the woman across from her who had endured so much and yet still remained open to love. Any doubts she'd harbored about Grace's suitability as Callum's wife or the strength of her feelings for her son had dissipated.

"When does your custody hearing come before the court?"

"I'm not sure. Your nephew Flynn, is taking care of the paperwork. He said it might take a month or two before to get a date."

Elizabeth nodded, her mind made up. "Callum said it would help your case if you were living in more suitable accommodations."

"Yes," Grace replied, her voice hardly above a whisper.

Elizabeth spread her arms wide. "Do you think this would do?"

Grace stared at her in shock. "W-what are you saying?"

"I'd like to invite you to move in here. At least until after you've been given back your children. And even afterwards, if it suits. You can take the eastern wing. There's plenty of room. Four bedrooms, each with their own bathroom. It's been empty since Callum moved out."

Grace continued to stare at her, as if struggling to process the information. "But… I don't even know you! Why would you be so kind?"

Elizabeth shrugged. When Callum had first approached her for help, she'd been inclined to agree at the outset. She believed in helping others, if she could. Callum's friend was no exception. But after speaking with Callum, it had become clear this woman wasn't just a friend in need. Elizabeth decided she wanted to know more about this Grace Gunning and her sad plight.

And now she had and she was impressed with what she'd discovered. Grace was every bit as compassionate and caring as her son. She'd overcome much adversity and those challenges appeared to have made her stronger. She also loved her children and in Elizabeth's mind that was incredibly important. She told Grace as much.

"I don't know how to thank you, Elizabeth."

"There's no need for thanks. Like I said, there's plenty of room and it makes me feel good to be able to help others out. Do you know what I mean?"

Grace's smile lit up her face. Her eyes sparkled with unshed tears. "Oh, yes!"

She's beautiful… Along with her sweet nature, there was no guessing about what had attracted her son.

And then the tears spilled over and ran down Grace's cheeks. Elizabeth shifted in her seat.

"There, there, Grace. There's no need to cry. I'm more than happy to help out."

"I-I'm sorry," Grace hiccupped on a sob. "I-I don't know what to say. "Nobody's ever shown me such kindness…apart from Callum."

Elizabeth stood and looked around for some tissues. Finding none, she excused herself from the room and went to look for some.

Grace wiped her eyes on the back of her sleeve and tried to come to terms with all that had happened. She felt drained, exposed…and oh so elated. She hadn't expected to be asked to spill all of her secrets, but now she was glad she had. Elizabeth had agreed to take her in, knowing the worst and for that level of approval and understanding, Grace couldn't thank her enough.

As she looked properly around the room for the first time

since arriving there, she noticed the expensive furniture, the matching draperies. The room was luxuriously furnished and as elegant as its owner. Priceless artworks lined the walls, but they were also interspersed with family portraits. Formal and informal poses displayed in extravagant gold frames, but also in much more modest ones. The contrasts gave the room a homey feel she hadn't expected.

The feeling summed up Elizabeth Craigdon perfectly. On the outside, she was an impeccably groomed, wealthy, elegant lady, but on the inside, she was just as kind and compassionate as her son. Callum had been right. That's where he'd gotten it from.

Her gaze went to the piano and she wondered how many of them played. And then she looked past the piano to a bar that was built against one wall. Feeling like a puppet on a string, she was pulled in that direction.

The bar was well stocked with numerous colorful bottles of spirits lining the glass shelves behind it. More shelves held glassware that sparkled in the light. There was a sink, a counter and a fridge. Another section held hundreds of bottles of wine, no doubt quite a few of them, vintage.

The urge to taste their sweetness was like a physical ache. She could almost feel the oblivion such sweetness would bring. Exposing old wounds had left her numb, but there were also flashbacks of pain. It was the kind of pain she'd once been able to obliterate with alcohol.

With a shaking hand, she leaned against the bar. Dragging her gaze away from the temptation of bottles, she willed herself to turn from it. She thought of her children. They were the reason she'd already gone through so much pain. She wouldn't throw it all away now. And today, filled with hope for a different future than she'd imagined, she preferred sober reality to oblivion.

With a sheer act of will, she forced one foot in front of the other until she was once again on the far side of the room, seated on the couch. She heard Elizabeth's high heels on the tiles outside and sighed quietly in relief.

One more day sober. One more day and counting…

Chapter Twenty One

Grace crossed the street with Callum and once again walked toward Flynn's office. Nerves and anticipation warred in her stomach. She was grateful when Callum reached for her hand. With their fingers twined together, they strode through the automatic sliding doors, across the marble foyer and halted near the elevators.

Flynn had called Grace earlier to tell her he wanted her to come in and go over the affidavit he'd prepared. Callum had been so busy dealing with the aftermath of the fire and meeting with engineers and other professionals, adjusting his plans, that she'd barely seen him. But when she called and asked him to come with her to Flynn's office, he'd immediately agreed. She was so glad he had.

The days dragged on when he wasn't with her. She missed him desperately, all of the time. It was madness, like she'd been taken over by some spirit that controlled her thoughts and movements and everything led to Callum. She looked across at him and her heart swelled with love. It has been two weeks since her meeting with Elizabeth. Even if she'd lied when Callum's mom had asked her the question, she was sure the woman would have sensed the truth.

I'm in love with Callum Craigdon! I'm shocked; I'm delighted; I'm scared to death...

Callum had helped her move her meagre possessions to his mother's house and that night he'd stayed for dinner. By now Grace had shared with him the details of her conversation with his mother, including their declarations of love. Callum had been surprised, but pleased that things were out in the open, but Grace urged him to take things slowly.

He'd only recently made the decision to completely change the direction of his life… And she had her children to consider. Until their future was secured and they were back living with her where they belonged, she couldn't move forward in a committed relationship. It wouldn't be fair. Callum deserved her utmost attention and right now with the custody hearing looming, she just couldn't give it. He'd assured her he understood and was there to love and support her in any way he could.

Ding! The opening of the elevator doors interrupted her tortuous thoughts. Callum waited for her to step in ahead of him. He pressed the button for Flynn's floor. They completed the trip in silence. Nerves escalated in Grace's stomach. Once the affidavit was finalized and filed, the hearing would become a reality, along with the confrontation and guaranteed fallout from Daniel's parents.

As if sensing her turmoil, Callum squeezed her hand. "Don't look so worried, Grace. You're only here to read over your affidavit."

She swallowed a sigh and managed a nod. "You're right."

Flynn greeted them in the waiting area and took them straight to his office. After offering them coffee, which they declined, they took their seats and he returned to his desk.

"So," Flynn said, leaning his elbows on his desk. "I've drafted the affidavit in accordance with your instructions. I want you to take a look at it and make sure everything's in order. The application and your accompanying affidavit will form part of the evidence in support of your case."

She looked up at him in surprise. "I won't have to take the stand?"

"I didn't say that."

Nerves increased tenfold in Grace's stomach.

"It depends on the judge," Flynn explained. "Some of them are satisfied with written evidence, others want to hear from the parties themselves." He paused and then added, "It's my guess, given the history of this matter and the fact your in-laws are going to vigorously defend their right to keep your children, I'd hazard to say you're going to have to testify."

She blew out her breath on a heavy sigh. Once again, Callum reached for her hand.

"It's all right, Grace. You can do this. All you have to do is answer the questions and tell the truth. You've got this."

"Callum's right," Flynn added. "If you're called to the stand, I'll take you through your evidence—basically everything contained in your affidavit. That's it."

"Then *their* lawyer gets to cross-examine me, right? That's what happened before."

"That's right," Flynn replied. "But I'll be there to make sure things don't get out of hand. You're not on your own."

"She's moved into Mom's house out at Richmond," Callum offered. "She's staying there for as long as she needs. Make sure her affidavit reflects her new address."

Flynn's eyebrows rose in surprise. "When I suggested she find more suitable accommodation, I didn't mean—"

"I know," Callum cut him off. "But the idea came to me and Mom was more than happy to go support it. After all, she has plenty of room."

Flynn made a notation on the legal pad in front of him. "Very well. I must admit, that's going to look good on the application. Not only the fact the children are living in comfortable surroundings, but that Grace has people around her willing and able to support her."

He looked at Callum, who nodded in tacit acknowledge-ment. Once again, surprise showed in Flynn's eyes but this time all he did was nod and murmur, "I see." He shuffled some papers and withdrew some from the stack. He handed them to Grace.

"I've received the report from your social worker. She's the same one who's been supervising your visits for the past three years. She speaks in positive terms when referencing you and is supportive of your petition for unsupervised visits. This will go a long way with the judge. The social workers are seen as objective witnesses. It's good news for us."

Grace flicked through the pages. Her gaze caught on phrases such as "positive relationship" and "good rapport" and "presents no danger." She swallowed a sigh. This is what her life had been reduced to. An assessment by a stranger whose evidence would be given significant weight by the judge. The same judge who'd decide if she was well enough to be around her children without a social worker looking on. It was sad and degrading, but she only had herself to blame. The court's only objective was to keep her children safe. She had to accept that and hope they found her worthy.

"I've noticed a man with a camera lurking around the soup kitchen," she said.

Flynn nodded. "It's probably an investigator your husband's parents have hired, looking for dirt. We talked about this, remember? Have you told anyone about your plan to seek custody?"

"Only Callum and Elizabeth."

Flynn's lips compressed. "Well, I'm sure they haven't told anyone. Still, you need to be on your guard."

Grace felt a flash of anger. "I have nothing to hide!"

Flynn continued to regard her steadily. "Good. Then you have nothing to worry about. The investigators can't come onto private property without your permission.

Just ignore them and go about your business."

Callum turned to her, his face reflecting surprise and a little hurt. "You didn't tell me about this."

She bit her lip. "I didn't want to worry you."

He shook his head and then reached out and brushed away a piece of hair that had fallen across her eyes. The tenderness in his gaze snatched her breath away.

"Grace, I can't take care of you if I don't know about these things."

She was prevented from replying when Flynn once again took control of the conversation and pushed some papers toward her, urging her to read them and make any necessary changes.

"I'll update your address details, so you don't need to worry about that."

Grace merely nodded, her head still full of Callum and what he'd said. With difficulty, she concentrated on the papers in her hands. Once she'd read through them and made the changes she wanted, she gave them back to Flynn.

"It all seems in order. There are only a few minor changes."

Flynn took the affidavit and nodded. "Great. Well, I'll get on this right away and email you the final draft. We should be able to file them in the court before the week is out. Then we wait for a hearing date."

"Great. Thanks. I… I know how hard you've worked on this and I really appreciate it," Grace said.

Flynn merely shrugged and smiled. "It's no biggie. This is what I do."

"Still," she persisted.

Flynn held up his hand. "Grace, it's fine. I'm more than happy to do it."

The two men shook hands and Flynn saw them out. On the way down in the elevator, Grace's shoulders slumped on a weary sigh.

Callum looked at her in concern. "What is it?"

"Nothing. I'm just relieved I'm finally dealing with this."

Callum kissed her softly on the mouth. "Me, too. In a month or two, this all should be over. You'll have your children back."

Grace stared into his beautiful blue eyes and wished she had his confidence. She was so grateful for his support.

"Thank you," she whispered.

"For what?"

"For being you. For being so wonderful. I love you, Callum Craigdon."

His tender kiss stole her breath. "I love you too, Grace Gunning. Don't you forget it."

Grace wanted to check on supplies for the lunch she had planned the following day, so they made the drive back to Jennifer's Kitchen in silence, each lost in their thoughts. Reliving the history of the breakdown of her relationship with her children in Flynn's office had been difficult. Dredging up those sad memories, even on paper, had left her feeling down. As Callum pulled up outside her building, she glanced across at him.

"Maybe you could come in for a few moments? Have a coffee."

He grimaced and shook his head. "I wish I could, but I have another meeting in the city. It might run late. Are you okay about catching the train home to Richmond?"

She tamped down her disappointment. "Yes, of course. It won't be the first time."

"Good. I'll see if there's anyone at Mom's who can collect you from the station."

She smiled at his protectiveness. "I have cab fare, Callum. I'll be fine."

He acknowledged her comment with a wry grin. "Sure. Okay, well I guess I'll see you later." He leaned over and kissed her goodbye.

She climbed out of the car and lifted her hand in a brief wave of farewell as he pulled away from the curb. Grace watched his vehicle disappear into the traffic and turned away with a little sigh. The day always seemed brighter with Callum around. And then she gave herself a mental shake and headed toward the soup kitchen.

Although she'd moved into the east wing of Craigdon Manor, she still had a key to her small apartment. Right now, she was grateful for that. Letting herself in, she threw herself down on the tattered couch. Tears burned behind her eyes.

A good cry might help. But where would that get her? She was on the brink of getting another chance to get her kids back. She had to pull herself together. She needed to stay strong. She had to prepare herself for the time when she'd once again come face to face with her in-laws in a courtroom.

The last time, she'd been barely sober, stumbling over her words and forgetting the question. Her behavior had only aided her in-laws' cause. She was determined to never let that happen again, but she didn't kid herself, it wouldn't be easy. Her daily battle with sobriety was real, but so was her dogged desire to get her children back.

A knock at her door interrupted her thoughts. She immediately thought of Callum. Her heart leaped with joy.

He's come back...

She ran to the door. In her excitement, she didn't pause to check who it was. Phillip and Nerida Gunning stood on the front step. It had been three years since she'd seen them. Phillip's hair was now completely gray and the lines around Nerida's downturned mouth were more pronounced, but otherwise little about the couple had changed.

"W-what are you doing here?" Grace stammered, trying to control her shock.

"We heard you're trying to get custody of Seth and Alyssa," Phillip growled, an angry flush on his face.

Grace gasped. The papers hadn't even been filed.

How can they know? Surely none of the Craigdons had told them? Her mind immediately rebelled against the idea, but they were the only three people who knew. *Oh, God. Which one of them betrayed me?*

As if she could read Grace's mind, Nerida sneered. "Don't worry about how we know, the point is, we do. And we're here to tell you to forget about it."

"Those children belong with *us*," Phillip said, his voice deadly.

"Who do you think you are?" Nerida spat. "You're a *nobody* from *nowhere*! You work in a soup kitchen! You might as well live on the street! Go back to whatever hovel you came from and leave us all alone!"

"Don't you remember how your children were terrified of you? They called us in the middle of the night! They were out of their minds with fear. They didn't know what to do," Phillip shouted.

"*You* did that to them!" Nerida cried. "You were so drunk you passed out, right before you vomited all over the place! You're disgusting!"

Phillip hacked up a large globule of phlegm and spat it at her feet. Grace jumped back in shock, humiliation heating her cheeks.

"You're just a no-good drunk and alcoholic!" Nerida screamed, spittle flying from her lips. "You're not fit to be their mother! There's no way you're getting them back!"

"If you were any kind of mother, you'd think of your kids and all that we can provide for them," Phillip shouted, his expression harsh. "Don't be so god-damned selfish!"

He looked around him, at the filth and decay. "This is no fit place to raise children! It just goes to show you've lost your mind." He raised a clenched fist toward her, fury emanating from every pore. She flinched and stepped back.

Bluey appeared from nowhere. He ran toward the Gunnings, barking furiously and baring his teeth.

"Get away from me, you flea-ridden, filthy animal!" Phillip shouted.

Bluey kept coming at him, barking all the while. Phillip struck out with his foot and connected hard with Bluey's side. The old dog yelped in pain then limped away.

Grace screamed. "Bluey! You've hurt him! You've hurt Bluey!" She ran over to where the dog lay on the ground, whining softly. She kneeled beside him.

"Look at her, all upset over a dog," Nerida crowed to her husband. Then she fixed her malicious gaze on Grace. "Seth and Alyssa want nothing to do with you. They told me they never want to see you again. They're sick of you telling them you love them. It's obvious you don't give a damn! You have no real job, you live with dirty derelicts in a shabby part of town." Her eyes narrowed as she glared at Grace. "Your kids are ashamed of you. Did you know that?"

"No! No! You're wrong!" Anger and pain, held in check for so long, suddenly found its head. She came to her feet and rounded on them.

"You call yourself their grandparents, and yet you happily smear their mother's name. You know how much I love them and they love me the same." She narrowed her eyes in sudden comprehension. "That's the problem, isn't it? You're jealous! You're jealous of the love they have for me, a no-good piece of white trash you wish would disappear.

She strode closer, moving in on their space. Both of them held their ground. Grace ignored their sneers.

When she spoke again, her voice was low and guttural with

the force of her anger. "Let's get one thing straight. Seth and Alyssa are *my* children. They'll always be my children, no matter what you say. Make no mistake, I'm going to do everything in my power to get them back. I'm no longer that scared and weak and grieving woman who allowed herself to be bullied into losing her dignity and her children. I've worked hard to get my life back on track and this time, I *will* succeed."

Phillip shot her a deadly look. "I guess we'll see you in court." With that, Daniel's parents turned and left her standing there, still seething. As their shiny black town car turned the corner, Grace cradled Bluey in her arms.

"It's all right, boy. It's all right."

He buried his nose in the crook of her arm and whimpered. She bent low and collected him off the ground and stumbled blindly back inside her apartment. Trembling with anger, she lowered him to the couch and collapsed beside him. After a gentle examination, she decided there was nothing broken and circled her shoulders in relief. Then, as delayed shock set in, she buried her face in her hands.

"Well, well, well. What do we have here?"

At the sound of the unfamiliar voice, her head came up. She stared at the tall stranger who filled the open doorway of her apartment. In her anguish over Bluey, she'd forgotten to close the door. The man's dark hair was flecked with gray at the temples and was a bit too long to be fashionable. Still, his clothes were of the latest cut and looked like they'd come off a designer rack. A smirk spoiled his otherwise handsome features. She wondered who he was.

Gathering her scattered thoughts, she eased away from Bluey and stood. "I'm sorry, do I know you?"

He came further into the room and held out his right hand. "Christopher Barrington," he offered in a lazy tone.

She frowned and shook his hand. "Grace Gunning. I'm sorry, but have we met before?"

"No. I'm Callum Craigdon's half-brother. We share the same father. That is, until dear old Henry decided to kick the bucket."

Graced wracked her memory but couldn't recall Callum ever talking about a half-brother.

"What are you doing here?" she asked.

He chuckled, but the humor didn't reach his eyes. She shivered at the coldness she found there.

"I thought I'd call in and introduce myself. Seeing as you're almost family. I understand my dear half-brother has a soft spot for you. Given that until recently he was headed for the priesthood, you can understand my surprise when I discovered he was seeing someone. And not just anyone. You were Daniel's wife, weren't you?"

Grace gasped. "How do you know Daniel?"

Christopher gave her a sly smile. The sight of it raised goosebumps along Grace's skin. "Let's just say we bonded on the football field."

Dread formed a hard ball in the pit of Grace's stomach. She watched as Christopher casually picked at an imaginary piece of lint on the lapel of his jacket. She grew impatient and was becoming increasingly scared to have this stranger follow her into her home. In a burst of courage she headed for the door.

"Look, Mr Barrington. I don't know what you want or why you're here, but it's time you left. My husband never mentioned you. He's been dead three years. Whatever you had to say, you've left it way too late."

He merely chuckled. "Oh, you misunderstand me. "I'm not here for Daniel, or even to talk about him. It's you I came here to see."

Once again, she struggled to contain her surprise. "Me? Why would you want to see me? You don't even know me."

Another slimy smile. "Oh, but that's where you're wrong.

I know plenty about you. For instance, I know you lost custody of your children when you became a hopeless drunk. I know you've been trying to put your life back together. I know you're planning to petition the court for a reversal of their earlier decision. You plan to steal your children from their grandparents. Yes, dear old Phillip and Nerida, who've done everything they can for your kids. Isn't that correct?"

Grace stared at him, aghast. "Who are you? How do you know this stuff?"

He chuckled. "Oh, Grace. You're such an innocent. It really isn't that difficult to obtain information in this town. All you have to do is know the right people. And of course, offering generous compensation for their trouble always helps. It never ceases to amaze me what people will do for money."

As the pieces fell into place, she was filled with anger. Somehow he'd bribed someone in Flynn's office to tell him all he knew. It was the only explanation that made sense. And then, armed with that information, he'd told the Gunnings.

Fury ignited her nerve endings, setting her on fire. Her chest rose and fell in time with the rapid beat of her heart. She glared at him. "Get out."

As if completely unaffected by her anger, he merely lifted a single dark eyebrow. "Really, Grace? You want me to leave. We're only just getting started. And I haven't even been given the chance to give you this."

From behind his back, he produced a bottle of Jack Daniels. The sight of the whisky made her freeze. Laughing softly, he set the bottle on the kitchen counter and then casually strode toward the door where she stood.

He was halfway out the door when he turned back to face her. "It was nice meeting you, Grace. We must do this again sometime. Enjoy the drink."

He closed the door quietly behind him. Bluey whimpered from the couch. She stared at the bottle of Jack Daniels.

The alcohol looked like liquid gold as it caught shards of late afternoon sunlight. It had been more than a year since she'd been this close to temptation other than when she'd noticed the bar at Craigdon Manor.

Affirmations she'd learned at AA meetings ran together in her head, mingled with desperate prayers. She'd put her heart and soul into getting to where she was. There was no way she'd let someone put all of that in jeopardy.

With grim determination, she picked up the bottle and took it over to the sink. She unscrewed the lid and was immediately met by the familiar and unmistakable smell of whiskey.

Oh, Lord, please help me. Please help me to stay strong. I need to be strong. For my babies, for Callum…for me…

Squeezing her eyes tightly shut, she poured the contents of the bottle down the sink. She didn't dare open her eyes until every last drop was gone. With a shaking hand, she set the empty bottle back on the counter. By then she was trembling all over and collapsed upon the couch.

Suddenly, the traumatic events of the past hour overwhelmed her. Burying her face in her hands, she sobbed her heart out. Though Bluey was there, whining softly beside her, the Gunnings' malicious words replayed themselves over and over in her head.

What they'd said wasn't true! She knew her babies loved her! They wanted to come and live with her! The last time they'd been together, they'd begged her to be allowed back home. The Gunnings were lying. They'd stoop to anything to keep her kids. Well, it wasn't going to work. Not this time. They could call her names, do whatever they wanted, she wouldn't be bullied again. And she sure as hell wouldn't let a twisted stranger and a bottle of whiskey destroy everything she'd worked for.

Chapter Twenty Two

Callum packed up the architect's plans and smiled with satisfaction. The amended design for the expanded soup kitchen and new accommodation units was coming along well. Though the fire had caused some damage, it had actually made the demolition job easier. There were now fewer walls to knock down, which would hasten the speed of the project. Provided the plans were approved by the city council, he expected to be in a position to start working on the building by the end of the month.

During the meeting with Flynn, his cousin had volunteered that he was quietly confident that Grace's petition for unsupervised access would go well. The supportive report from the social worker, as well as Grace's newfound good health, stability and career prospects all boded well for a positive outcome.

And then there was his mother. She'd confided in him only a few nights ago that she approved of his choices—both leaving the seminary and Grace. It meant a lot to have his mother's support and knowing she was pleased with his decisions filled him with hope.

Filled with the anticipation of spending another evening with Grace, he half-jogged toward Joel's convertible. Callum had received another email from his brother the night before.

Joel was now in Paris and kicking up a storm. He'd sounded happy and relaxed and Callum was glad. Joel worked hard in his stressful job as a detective. He'd seen things no one should. And once seen, they were never forgotten. Callum stood in awe of the men and women who chose to serve and protect their people, often putting their own lives on the line. Though his life was headed in a different direction, he couldn't be prouder of his two brothers and his cousin who'd gone into law enforcement.

Unlocking the car, he opened the rear passenger side door and tossed the plans onto the back seat before climbing behind the wheel. Before he could start the ignition, his phone rang. He checked the screen.

Flynn.

"Hey, mate. How're you doing?"

"Good, Callum. I'm glad I caught you."

"What's going on?"

"Do you know where Grace is? I've been trying to call her. Her phone keeps going straight to voicemail."

Callum frowned. "No, I dropped her off at the soup kitchen straight after we left your office. She had some things to do. Then she was heading out to Richmond."

"Well, when you see her, can you ask her to look over her affidavit and give it the okay so we can finalize it? I emailed it to her a few hours ago but I haven't heard anything from her. I can't file her application without it."

"Yeah, sure," Callum replied.

"And Callum?" There was a note of caution in Flynn's voice. "Just make sure she keeps her nose clean. Don't give her in-laws even the slightest reason to argue she's not the well-adjusted, stable, loving mother we know her to be."

"Relax, Flynn. She's not that woman anymore. She's worked tremendously hard to get her life back, but she's done it and we ought to recognize her extraordinary achievement. I'm so proud of her."

"I agree, but we still need to be careful. These kids have lived with their grandparents for the past three years. That's a long time in a kid's life. I've told you before. The courts won't make changes without a good reason."

"Well, we have a good reason. The *mother* of those children is now well enough to have them back. They're *her* children."

"Hey! Don't shoot the messenger. I'm just trying to prepare you for how it might go down. I'll do my best, but sometimes these things don't go as planned…"

Callum sighed. His flash of temper receded. "I'm sorry, Flynn. I wasn't lashing out at you. It's just that Grace has worked so hard to get where she is, to be the kind of mom her children need. I just don't want it to go badly for her."

"You and me both," Flynn agreed. "Anyway, I need that signed affidavit."

"Yeah. I'll see if I can reach her."

"Thanks, mate."

"No worries. Talk soon."

Callum ended the call and immediately dialed Grace. It went straight through to voicemail.

"Hi, Grace. It's Callum. Call me as soon as you get this."

Tossing the phone on the seat beside him, he switched on the ignition and pulled out into the traffic. He was at the opposite end of the city from the soup kitchen, but he'd check for her there before driving the hour or so to Richmond. Perhaps she was on a busy train and couldn't hear her phone? Perhaps the battery had gone flat? She might have switched it to silent and forgotten to switch it back. There were a lot of reasons why she might have missed the calls. There was no need for panic.

Impatient to speak with her, he dialed her number again and when it too went unanswered, he called his mother.

"Have you seen Grace?" he asked without preamble.

"Not since she left here this morning."

"When do you expect her home?"

"Well I haven't spoken to her since breakfast. I guess I'll see her for dinner. She didn't say she wouldn't be here. Why?"

Callum debated about telling his mother, but then decided against it. "No reason. I'm just trying to get hold of her."

"Have you called her?"

He barely stopped himself from rolling his eyes. "Yes, Mom. I've called her. She's not answering."

"Her battery might be flat. Mine's always going flat."

This time Callum swallowed a groan. "That's only because you forget to put it on the charger."

"Yes, well, you're probably right."

"Anyway, Mom. I have to go. Let me know if Grace turns up there."

"Okay. Will you be here for dinner?"

"Yes. Of course."

There was a pause and then his mother said, "I'm so glad you and Grace found each other. She's a lovely girl. The two of you have my blessing."

Callum was touched by his mother's words. "Thanks, Mom. That means a lot to me."

"I mean it," she said simply. "Now, make sure you're not late for dinner. We're having your favorite: roast pork and a sundried tomato and feta couscous salad."

"Sounds delicious, Mom. I'll be sure to pass on the message to Grace."

As soon as I find her…

Callum swung into Grace's street and found a spot to park not far from the soup kitchen. With the lunch hour long over and lengthening shadows filling the yard, the place had a deserted air. He peered through the window into the kitchen, but the room was empty and dark. He went around the side to her apartment and knocked briskly on the door.

"Grace? Are you in there?"

There was no answer. He knocked again. Still no response, but he thought he heard the faint sound of whining. He tried her phone again and could hear it ringing. He pressed his ear against the door to confirm it.

She wouldn't have left without her phone. She must still be in there…

He tried the door handle and found it unlocked. Frowning, he let himself in. Grace was slumped across a tattered couch beside Bluey. Her eyes were closed. Faint snores came from her mouth. An empty bottle of whisky stood on the counter.

Callum rushed forward, his heart sinking in disbelief. Bluey had difficulty rising, but slowly got to his feet. He stared at Callum with an expression that almost looked like relief.

Callum shook Grace gently by the shoulder. "Grace? Are you okay? Grace?"

She came awake with a start. She blinked as if trying to clear her vision. "Callum? What are you doing here?"

He frowned. "What are *you* doing here? I thought you were heading back to Richmond. Mom's expecting us for dinner."

She blushed and scrambled to her feet. "Oh, heck. What time is it?" Her gaze cut to the window. Night had fallen. She looked back at Callum. "I must have fallen asleep."

He moved to switch on a lamp that looked like it had come from a yard sale. The sudden light was bright in the darkened room. He studied her closer. Her eyes were swollen and red. It looked like she'd been crying. His gaze flicked back to the whiskey. She followed the movement of his gaze and her eyes went wide.

"Oh, no, Callum! This isn't what it looks like! I promise."

He wanted to believe her, but the evidence to the contrary was right there on the counter.

"Where did it come from?" he asked, fighting to keep his tone even.

"You wouldn't believe what happened after you left. Daniel's parents arrived and started harassing me. They said some awful things. Then Phillip kicked Bluey. I… I think he's hurt. I checked him for broken bones and couldn't find any, but—"

"Grace. Why is there an empty bottle of whiskey in your kitchen?"

"That was a gift from your half-brother. Christopher Barrington."

Callum reeled back in shock. "Christopher? What the heck are you talking about?"

Grace's shoulders slumped on a heavy sigh. She sat down on the couch. Now that she'd had time to come fully awake, he could see her eyes were focused. She certainly didn't appear to be under the influence of alcohol. Feeling somewhat relieved, he joined her.

He reached for her hand. "Tell me what happened," he urged.

Grace recounted her run-in with her in-laws and then told him about the unexpected visit from Christopher. As she spoke, rage ignited in his belly. By the time she'd finished, his hands were clenched and his pulse raced.

"That son of a bitch! I'm gonna kill him!"

Grace gasped. Callum understood her reaction. The profanity alone was out of character. The anger that now consumed him was unrecognizable.

"I'm sorry, Grace. I… I shouldn't have said that."

She looked at him with eyes that were wide with concern. "I understand how you feel. He did a terrible thing. What I don't understand is, why? What have I ever done to him? I don't even know him!"

Callum sighed. "It probably has more to do with me than you." He explained about his father's will and how Christopher had been done over.

"That's terrible!" Grace exclaimed.

Callum nodded grimly. "Yeah. But it doesn't excuse his

behavior. He had no right taking his anger out on you. I'm going to find him and make darn sure he knows how upset I am over this and that you're off limits."

Grace frowned. "What are you going to do?"

"Don't worry. I'm not going to do anything stupid."

She looked relieved. He leaned over and gave her a kiss. "Are you okay?" he asked in a milder tone.

She nodded. "Yes. Seeing that bottle of whiskey... It brought back so many bad memories. I was determined not to go down that path again. I poured it all down the sink."

Callum's heart filled with tenderness. He kissed her again, softly, lingeringly, hoping she felt the love that billowed up inside him.

"I'm so proud of you, Grace," he whispered. "You're the strongest woman I know. I love you so much."

She twisted sideways and wound her arms around his neck, pulling him close. "I love you too and I thank God every day for bringing you into my life."

Their lips met again and they melded as one. The sweetness in her kiss overwhelmed him. Wanting to stay there forever, but knowing they should stop, he gently pulled away. She looked at him, her eyes wide with confusion.

"I need to speak to Christopher. Do you mind?"

"No, of course not."

Forcing himself to move away from her, Callum pulled out his phone. "Oh, I almost forgot. Flynn called. He needs you to approve the final affidavit. He said he emailed it to you."

"Darn. I've been so preoccupied with all that happened, I haven't given it another thought. I'll do it now."

She pulled out her phone and began tapping at the screen. Callum left the apartment, pulling the door closed behind him. Every time he thought of Christopher and what he'd attempted to do, his blood boiled. He didn't want Grace to overhear what might be said. A rumble of thunder made him look up and he noticed a storm was brewing. The air was tense with expectation. Almost as tense as he was.

Half expecting Christopher to ignore his call, he was surprised when his half-brother answered.

"Father Craigdon. To what do I owe this pleasure?"

Callum gritted his teeth at the fakeness in Christopher's tone. "Grace told me what you did," he stated without preamble. "You're despicable."

"Now, now, now, Father. Don't be like that. It was a joke!"

"A joke?" Callum spat in disgust, not even bothering to acknowledge Christopher's deliberate misuse of his title.

"Tut, tut, tut. You sound so…*angry*. I didn't realize the girl meant so much to you. Last I heard you were well on your way to the priesthood. What happened? Won't they take you?"

Callum clenched his jaw so tight it hurt. Even then, he could barely contain his anger. "You were unforgivably cruel."

Christopher's answering bark of laughter was devoid of humor. "Unforgivable? This from an up and coming priest? Shame on you, Father."

The effort it took Callum not to explode was almost beyond him. He clenched his jaw tight. "Stay away from her, Christopher. She's out of bounds."

With a vicious stab of his finger, Callum ended the call, not trusting himself to stay on the line a second longer. Sweat beaded his forehead. His breath came fast and his chest was tight, like he'd just run a marathon. He still couldn't believe how cruel Christopher had been to an innocent person. Grace had nothing to do with his beef against the Craigdon family. Callum would continue to make sure he knew that.

Doing his best to regain his equilibrium, he took a few moments to slow his breathing and swiped at the sweat on his brow. When he was satisfied his composure was almost back to normal, he returned to Grace's apartment. Another rumble of thunder was followed by a crack of lightning that lit up the evening sky. Before he reached the door, his phone rang again.

"Callum Craigdon."

"Mr Craigdon, it's Detective Anderson calling. I'm the officer in charge of the investigation involving the accident in Richmond."

Callum's breath caught. "Yes?"

"I'm calling to let you know we've finished our investigation. We've ruled the incident an accident. It's official: We won't be laying any charges."

Callum's breath *whooshed* out in a sigh of relief.

"We're willing to give you the identity of the victim if you still want to know who it was," the detective continued. "But I'd strongly advise you against making contact with the victim's family. This kind of case can be tough. Sometimes not everyone's happy with the outcome. They're often looking for someone to blame. Seeing as you were the one to hit the victim…" His voice drifted off.

"It's all right," Callum muttered. "I don't need to know who it was. It doesn't matter who I killed. I won't forget what happened for the rest of my life."

The officer was quick to reassure him. "It wasn't your fault, Mr Craigdon. Sometimes bad things happen and nobody is to blame. That's why they're called accidents."

"Yes. Anyway, thank you for your call, Detective. I really appreciate it." With that, he ended the call.

As if on cue, the heavens opened up and raindrops fell on his head. Dropping the phone back in his pocket, he opened the door to Grace's apartment and came to a sudden halt. Grace was on her knees, her back to him, cradling Bluey. He could tell from the shaking of her shoulders that she was crying…

Chapter Twenty Three

Grace heard Callum return, but couldn't bring herself to look at him. In her arms, Bluey drew his last breaths. It had been his tortured breathing that had first alerted her to his difficulties. Now she was filled with guilt that she hadn't taken him somewhere to have him properly checked over.

And then Callum was there beside her. He put his arm around her shoulder, pulling her against him. She leaned into him, drawing strength from his presence, all the while she stroked Bluey's shoulder and whispered words of comfort.

"What happened?" Callum murmured, his eyes full of sadness.

"He must have suffered some internal injuries when Phillip kicked him," she sobbed. "I thought he was okay, but he wasn't. I should have taken him to a vet. I should have done more to help him."

She was overcome with a fresh wave of tears. Her shoulders shook from the force of them. Callum stroked her arm and murmured unintelligible sounds against her hair.

And then Bluey gave a last huff of breath and lay still. Grace cried out in pain.

"Bluey! No! Please don't die! Please!"

She gathered him in her arms and held him as the tears coursed freely down her cheeks. She didn't know how long she sat there, but the next thing she became aware of was Callum easing her beloved pet from her arms.

"He's gone, honey."

Almost numb from grief, she rocked back on her heels and watched as Callum laid Bluey gently on the floor. He got a blanket from the couch and covered the poor dog's body. Grace sniffled. Bluey had been a connection to her children, a being who loved them like she did. And now he was gone…

With a cry, she flung herself against Callum. He took her in his arms and held her close. She clung to him, the man she loved with all her heart. Her rock, her safe harbor in the storm. A long time later, his arms loosened around her and he gently set her aside. The tenderness in his expression when he looked at her stole her breath.

"Are you all right?"

She sighed, but nodded. "I think so. I'm just so sad. Poor Bluey!"

"I should have taken him to Craigdon Manor, like I wanted to," Callum said.

"But your allergies! I thought he'd be fine here! I'm here every day!" She shook her head. This was all Phillip's fault!"

"We don't know that for sure, Grace. You said you checked him over after Phillip left and he seemed fine. Bluey was ten years old, honey. Not ancient, but not young, either. Perhaps his heart gave out?"

Grace instinctively opened her mouth to argue, but then closed it again. What did it matter how he died? Nothing was going to bring him back.

"How can I tell Seth and Alyssa? They're going to be devastated," she whispered hoarsely.

"Whatever you tell them, you won't have to do it alone. I'll be there beside you every step of the way."

He moved closer and tenderly reached out and cupped her cheek. His eyes were dark with emotion. Love sparkled in their depths.

As if of its own volition, her gaze zeroed in on his lips. Full and firm, the memory of them on hers pushed everything else aside. The air around them grew tense. It was like neither of them dared draw breath lest they break the spell that now surrounded them. And then she was in his arms and nothing else mattered.

His lips slanted across hers, seeking, tasting, tempting. She opened her mouth against the insistence of his tongue and gasped as it swept inside.

The kiss started out slow and gentle, but quickly erupted into a fiery battle of passion. Her arms went around his neck and she clung to him. His broad chest was a wall of muscle. He felt like a fortress, strong and safe and secure. On a groan of surrender, she kissed him with everything she had.

Her breath came fast. Desire ignited. Her nipples were taut with need. His erection pressed against her stomach. And then he lifted his mouth from hers and leaned his forehead against hers.

"We… We should stop," he gasped, reluctance in every word.

She nodded. "Yes. We should."

"You feel so good."

"So do you."

"I want our first time together to be special."

"Flowers and champagne?" she asked, giving him a wobbly smile.

"Whatever you want."

"I don't need flowers and champagne, Callum. All I want is you."

His eyes filled with emotion. "That means a lot to me, Grace."

"It's the truth."

And then he looked away and wouldn't meet her gaze.

She frowned. "What is it, Callum?"

"I… I've never been with a woman. You were once married. I'm afraid I might not…measure up."

His face flamed crimson. Grace's heart turned over with love. "Oh, Callum. If you had any idea what Daniel was like, and the emotion that was lacking, you'd never spend a moment worrying about that."

Hope flared in his eyes. "Really?"

She framed his face with her hands and kissed him tenderly on the lips. "Really."

"I love you, Grace. I love you with my heart, my soul, my everything."

The sweetest warmth rushed through her. "Oh, Callum! I love you, too!"

Their lips met and melded and passion once again overwhelmed them. Immediately, the mood between them changed. With hearts racing, they pulled away, staring at each other.

"I want to make love to you, Grace. Why don't I call Mom and explain we can't make dinner?" Callum rasped.

Desire flared higher inside her. "Yes. Let her know but be as quick as you can. Please, Callum. I want you too."

⌒

Callum stared at Grace and his heart beat so hard it felt like it might burst right out of his chest. Amidst the overwhelming desire to make love to her was a healthy amount of fear. Well, not fear exactly, but uncertainty, for sure. He was a thirty-year-old virgin and even though Grace was well aware of his inexperience, he was afraid he might disappoint.

What if I come too soon? Before she's satisfied? What if I fail to satisfy her at all? He worried that somehow his lack of experience might become a turn-off, a disadvantage as he fumbled his way through.

The questions and concerns built in his head until he was almost paralyzed with indecision. Seeming to sense his inner turmoil, Grace reached for his hand. Immediately some of his fears receded. Just the feel of her soft, warm hand in his was comforting. He instinctively tightened his hold.

She led him down a short corridor and into a tiny, cramped room. It was barely big enough to hold the single bed that was pushed up against one wall. A small chest of drawers was the only other furniture in the room. The room had an empty feeling and he guessed that was because she'd moved her personal property over to his mother's. At least there were linens on the bed.

Gently, Grace tugged him by the hand. He sat down beside her on the edge of the bed. He fought to get his nerves under control. Grace's smile was soft and tender.

"It's all right, Callum," she whispered. "Don't be scared. I'll show you how."

With that she cupped his cheek in her soft hand and drew his head down to hers. She kissed him softly, sweetly, slowly. Over and over, they kissed until Callum was once again burning with desire. His cock was rock-hard; his breath came fast; his heart raced like he'd run a marathon.

With infinite patience, Grace tugged the ends of his shirt out of his jeans and eased it up his chest. Her fingernails raked his skin. He sucked in his stomach like he'd been burned. She inched the shirt all the way up and pulled it over his head. She tossed it aside without looking, her gaze fixed firmly on his bare chest.

"You're so beautiful," she murmured.

She placed her hands flat on his pectorals, lightly massaging the muscles. She ran her fingers through the dark-blond hair that was scattered across his chest, pausing to pay particular attention to his nipples.

They hardened instantly and the contact tore a gasp from his throat. No one had touched him so intimately. The feel of her soft hands on his skin was mind-blowing.

Pushing him backwards, she followed him down and kissed her way from his sternum, across his ribs and down to his belly. As she dipped her tongue into his navel, his stomach muscles contracted. All the time, her hands were busy flicking at his nipples. The sensations she evoked in him drove him crazy.

"We're going to take this slowly, okay?" she murmured between kisses.

"Not too slowly, I hope," he choked as she began to suck on his nipples. "Oh, God! Grace! That feels so good!" He groaned.

As her tongue flicked over his turgid flesh, he buried his hands in her hair. She lapped at his nipples, sucked and pulled and finally lifted her head.

"You taste so good."

Her eyes were almost black with desire, her face was rosy and flushed. His cock throbbed behind the zipper of his jeans. He longed to feel her naked, skin to skin.

With that thought in mind, he reached for the buttons on her plain white blouse and fumbled his way down the openings. When at last he'd freed them all, he spread the shirt wide and stared.

Her full breasts spilled over a white, lacy bra. Her stomach was flat and taut. Unable to help himself, he trailed his fingers over her skin, tracing the outlines of her breasts through the fabric. Her breath hitched and beneath the lace he saw her nipples pucker.

All of a sudden he wanted to touch her without the barrier of her bra. Almost simultaneously, she reached around and undid the clasp and pulled the fabric free. He would have said something about her reading his mind, but all he could do was stare.

She was perfectly formed, two perfect breasts, full and round with dusty pink nipples. Unable to help himself, he reached for them and lifted their weight in his hands. Like she'd done to him, he bent his head and suckled each nipple into his mouth. She gasped and dropped her head back, giving him greater access.

Suddenly impatient for all of her and unsure how much longer he was going to last, he stood and tugged off his boots, shucked off his jeans and underwear and finally his socks. Naked and proud before her, he let her look her fill. She was the first woman to see him as a man, like that.

"Oh, Callum," she breathed.

The gleam of desire in her eyes gave him confidence. He reached out a hand toward her and drew her to her feet. In short order, he undid the button at her waistband and then pulled her skirt down over her hips. She wriggled it all the way down before stepping out of it and then stood there just in her panties.

"Touch me, Callum."

The husky command registered in his brain. Almost simultaneously, his cock rose. Already thick and hard, it jutted out like a rod. Slowly, he reached out and cupped her breast and then trailed his fingers down her chest. Inch by inch, he moved lower until he'd reached her mound.

Modestly covered in cotton panties, he slipped his hand beneath the waistband. Lower and lower his fingers searched until they came across her wetness. He slid one finger along her slit, reveling in her softness. She was silk and satin. She was all kinds of wonderful. She was more than he could ever hope. And then his finger slid lower and he slipped inside her and she groaned.

"Oh, Callum."

Her voice was thick with desire. She ground herself against his hand and he rewarded her with deeper stroking. One finger, then two slipped inside her, moving to her rhythm.

She's so soft, so silky, so wet...

Callum did his best to ignore the sensations rippling through his body. He wanted their first time to last forever. But as his body demanded attention, he was forced to face facts. Either they slowed things right down, right now, or he'd disgrace himself.

With that thought in mind, he withdrew his fingers. Grace made a soft murmur of disappointment. Callum merely took her by the hand and drew her back down on the bed. She followed him willingly and went into his arms, rolling over until he was on top.

"I'm sorry, Grace," he whispered. "I have to have you or I'm gonna die."

She smiled tenderly and reached for him. Her arms went around his neck and she pulled him close. His cock pressed against her entrance, seeking a way in. She spread her legs wider and lifted her hips in silent encouragement.

And then he was sliding into her wet heat and it was like nothing he'd ever known. Even his wildest fantasies hadn't come close to the way this felt.

"Oh, God. Grace," he gasped.

Just as he feared, it was over way too soon. Within moments of entering her, he climaxed, crying out in relief. He collapsed against her, breathing hard and then carefully lifted himself off her. Embarrassment heated his cheeks. He avoided her gaze.

And then she reached out and stroked his face and he looked at her. Her eyes were soft and filled with love. She kissed him tenderly on the mouth.

"That was beautiful," she whispered.

His face flamed. "But—"

She pressed a finger against his lips to silence him. "That was beautiful."

A rush of warmth and love for her overwhelmed him. He pulled her close and buried his face in her hair, breathing in her unique scent of vanilla and spice and honeysuckle.

"I'm sorry, Grace. I—"

Once again, she silenced him. "No apologies, Callum. It was your first time." And then she grinned. "Hopefully, the first of many."

He chuckled. Relief slid through him. "I forgot the flowers and champagne."

"And I told you all I need is you."

Oh, God, he loved her! How did he ever think he could go through life without this, without the woman of his dreams in his arms, loving him, supporting him, caring for him. A few days ago, he could never have imagined this and yet, here they were. The two of them. Together. In love. He wanted to shout it from the rooftops. And then another thought crashed into him.

"Oh, Grace! We didn't use protection! I'm so sorry! I didn't think! When I stopped by your place, this was the last thing on my mind. I wasn't prepared. I—"

"*Shh,*" she whispered, bringing a halt to his frantic ramblings. "It's all right, Callum. I wasn't prepared, either. So don't go taking all the blame. The chances of me falling pregnant on the very first time are rather slim." And then she looked at him fully. "Would it matter to you if I did?"

He looked at her in wonder. "Matter? Of course not! I want to have babies with you! I just thought… With all you have going on, you might not want to get married and start a family right away."

She blew out her breath on a soft sigh. "You're right. There's a lot going on. But you're important to me, too. I don't want you to think you don't matter."

"I love you, Grace. Nothing's going to change that. Our love is so new and so wonderful, I'm happy to take things slowly. There's no rush. All you need to know is that we can do this, Grace. Together we can do anything. I mean *anything*. Today you were confronted with an enormous temptation and at a time when you were under great stress. And yet you resisted that temptation. You kicked it to the fence!" He paused and then added, "I meant it when I said you deserve to have your children and I'll do anything I can to help make that happen."

She sighed quietly and pressed a trembling kiss on his mouth. Tears glimmered in her eyes. "I love you so much, Callum Craigdon."

He hugged her close. They held each other for a long time. In the stillness, Callum asked, "Have you ever thought about getting some professional help, like therapy, or maybe even going to rehab?"

"Of course I have. The thing is, I can't afford it. Attending an AA meeting comes for free."

He brushed a piece of hair out of her eyes. "You work for me now, remember? I happen to be a very generous boss. In lots of ways, but particularly when it comes to your salary. I think we should look into getting you into rehab, or at the very least a therapist who can help with all sorts of things, including helping you deal with what happened to Daniel, and everything that came after. What do you say?"

She slowly turned her head until she faced him. Fresh tears glittered in her eyes, but this time a wobbly smile accompanied them.

"I'd like that," she whispered.

As the storm raged outside, he looked at her and was filled with utmost peace and contentment. His heart swelled with love.

Chapter Twenty Four

After spending a glorious night together in her apartment and waking in Callum's arms, morning broke on a wave of sunshine and warmth. The storm clouds of the previous evening had blown out to sea and the sky was now clear and blue. There was a freshness in the air that lifted Grace's spirits. She'd never imagined she could feel such happiness. Even during the best times she'd had with Daniel, she'd never felt like this.

At Callum's suggestion, they agreed to bury Bluey in the gardens at Craigdon Manor. A quick phone call to his mother to obtain her consent to the plan and it was done. She met them at the bottom steps of her home and offered her sympathies for the loss of Grace's dog.

"Thank you. He was a much-loved pet," she murmured.

Elizabeth nodded. "I'm sure he'll rest easy here. You can visit him whenever you want. And your children, too. They're more than welcome, anytime,"

Grace was filled with warmth at Elizabeth's kind words. Over the weeks since she'd moved into the manor, the two of them had spent a deal of time together and were fast becoming friends.

"I'm so glad you and Callum found each other," Elizabeth confided.

Grace smiled and nodded. "So am I."

Elizabeth gave her a kiss on the cheek and pulled her in for a hug. "Welcome to the family, Grace."

The rich reds and golds and oranges of the autumn leaves were all around them, rising and falling and swirling in the gentle breeze that swept up from Circular Quay. Grace and Callum left the courtroom with Flynn not far behind. Every one of their team was smiling.

"I can't believe I've been given unsupervised access visits with my kids!" Grace cheered. "Finally we can spend time together without someone watching and listening in."

Callum grinned. "Isn't it fantastic? I guess Flynn was right when he said going for full custody straight off was unrealistic, but still, we gave it our best shot and this isn't the end, not by any stretch of the imagination."

"Of course not," Grace agreed, hugging him. "The judge said he'd review the orders in three months with a view to granting overnight visits. By then my kids will be so besotted by the two of us, they'll never want to leave."

Callum laughed. "Especially when they catch sight of the swimming pool, tennis court, nine-hole golf course, games room, spa and sauna at Mom's house."

The elation in Grace's voice slowly faded. She looked at Callum, the man she loved with all her heart. She still couldn't believe such a beautiful man had come into her life and complemented her so well.

"I can't wait for you to meet them," she said, her voice husky with emotion.

"Me, too. Though I never imagined I'd be a husband and father, I'm going to embrace both with everything that I am."

Grace smiled up at him, her heart swelling with love.

"I know you will." Their lips met in a tender kiss that quickly turned passionate.

Flynn came up behind them. "Okay, that's enough, you two lovebirds."

They guiltily moved apart. Flynn laughed. Callum put out his hand. "Thanks again for everything you did for us, Flynn."

"Callum's right," Grace added. "You were amazing."

"No thanks necessary," Flynn replied. "Besides, you were the one who did all the hard work, Grace. The way you stood up to that cross-examination… You were inspirational."

Grace blushed. "Thank you. I had a lot at stake."

"I'm sorry we weren't able to get you overnight access this time," Flynn said.

"It's all right," Grace assured him. "You did warn us there was only a slim chance the court would make such a drastic decision. We'll make it happen next time."

Flynn smiled. "You bet."

"Flynn Craigdon?"

Flynn turned at the sound of his name. A man in a plain dark suit and nondescript tie approached him. "Yes?"

"Are you Flynn Craigdon?" the man repeated.

"Yes."

The man thrust a large envelope into Flynn's hand. "You've been served." With that, the stranger repeated the performance with Callum before turning and striding away.

Flynn looked down at the envelope. "What the f—?" He shot an apologetic look at Grace. "Sorry, Grace," he mumbled.

"What is it?" Callum asked, turning over the envelope in his hand.

Flynn tore his open and pulled out a sheaf of papers. He scanned the first page. He cursed softly under his breath. "It's Christopher. He's suing your father's estate. We're the executors. That's why we've been served."

Callum groaned and shook his head. "I ran into him outside your office not that long ago. He told me that was his plan. Then he showed up uninvited to harass Grace. He and I shared a rather tense conversation. After all that's happened, I kind of hoped he'd given up on the idea. Still, I guess he has a right to feel angry," Callum added, feeling more generous toward Christopher now that Grace had won her case. "He was treated rather shabbily by Dad. If anything I feel sorry for him."

Flynn's expression hardened. "I sure as hell don't."

"So, what should we do to celebrate?" Callum asked as he and Grace walked arm in arm away from the courtroom. He refused to let Christopher's petition ruin their day.

She smiled up at him, a wicked gleam in her eyes. "I have one or two ideas."

He widened his eyes in mock innocence. "Really? What did you have in mind?"

Her hand crept under the lapel of his suit and slipped inside his crisp business shirt. Her fingers unerringly found his nipple and flicked at it. His body instantly hardened.

"I see," he managed, playing along. Stopping abruptly, he swung her around and pushed her up against the wall of a building. He framed her body with his arms and pressed his erection against her. Crowds of pedestrians passed them by, intent on reaching their destinations. Callum was oblivious to everything but the feel of her breasts and the sweet magic between her thighs that beckoned to him irresistibly.

As he ground his hips against hers, he was rewarded with a gasp. Her eyes darkened with pleasure.

"Is this what you had in mind?" he teased, nipping at her earlobes.

"Y-yes," she stammered, already breathless.

"Come with me." Just as quickly, he stepped away from

her and reached for her hand. He dragged her along with him, heading toward the Quay.

"Where are we going?" she asked, hurrying to keep up.

"Remember I told you I've been staying in Joel's apartment? Well, it's only a block from here."

Her eyes flared with excitement as the implications of what he'd said set in. In no time at all, they'd reached Joel's building and the elevator whisked them up to the fifth floor.

"Wow, this view is amazing," Grace breathed as she stepped inside Joel's home.

Callum nodded. "Almost as good as the view I have right here."

With that, he pulled off her jacket and tossed it to the floor. Her blouse and skirt and underwear quickly followed. At last she stood before him naked except for her high heels. The late afternoon sunshine gilded her from behind.

The sound of excited yapping brought a frown to her face. "What's that?"

He swallowed a groan. He'd forgotten all about his gift. "It's nothing," he mumbled.

The yapping came again. "What do you mean, it's nothing? It sounds like a dog." Her expression turned curious. "Does your brother own a dog?"

"No. Um. It was meant to be a surprise. The thing is, I bought you a puppy."

Her face lit up with excitement and disbelief. "You bought me a puppy? Callum!"

He squirmed under her amused regard. "Yes, well, after Bluey died, I thought it might be nice for you to have another dog. So I went to the shelter and picked one out. He's in a basket in Joel's laundry room."

Her laughter filled the room. At the same time, she grabbed him and planted a kiss on his mouth. Together, they headed for the laundry room and found the puppy.

"Oh, he's gorgeous!" Grace squealed in delight, cradling the labradoodle close. She buried her face against his soft coat. "Oh, Callum! I couldn't love you more for what you've done, but you're allergic! What are you going to do?"

He shrugged. "The vet at the shelter assured me he's hypoallergenic, so I should be okay. If not, maybe he'll be an outdoor pet. Would that be all right with you?"

Her eyes filled with love. "Of course it would."

With that, she reached for him and in no time at all had divested him of his clothes. He took her by the hand and led her down the hallway to Joel's bedroom. With its floor-to-ceiling glass wall that framed a magnificent view of the harbour, it was the best room in the place.

"Wow," Grace murmured for the second time.

"Yes, wow," Callum replied, nuzzling her shoulder, his voice muffled against her skin.

They fell onto Joel's king-sized bed and rolled over and over, giggling and laughing like teenagers. Staring into Grace's eyes, Callum's heart filled to bursting.

"I love you, Grace Gunning."

"I love you, too, Callum Craigdon."

The kiss started out sweet and tender, but quickly ignited a flame. Heat coursed through him, setting his nerve endings on fire. His cock throbbed with the need to be inside her, but this time he was taking it slow. He wanted to get to know every inch of her, bit by bit. With his tongue, his mouth, his fingers… He didn't care which. He just needed to touch her, to hold her, to possess her and marvel that she was his.

Pushing her gently back against the mattress, he took both of her hands in his and held them above her head. Kissing his way down her face, her lips, her neck, he eventually reached her breasts.

They were trembling from the force of her breathing and he suckled each one with his mouth. His tongue flicked over her nipples, first one then the other and he reveled in her moan of excitement.

And then he moved lower, kissing his way down her ribcage, her abdomen, the softness of her flat belly. She squirmed beneath him, but he held her fast and finally buried his face in her womanhood. His tongue probed between her wet folds, flicking and licking and kissing. Her hips bucked and she strained against his hold, but he refused to succumb to her pleading. This was all about her and he intended to make the most of it.

With rhythmic strokes he lapped until she was panting with need. Wrenching away her hands, she buried them in his hair. She held his head in place while he drove her to higher and higher ecstasy. And then she tensed and cried out and bucked her hips wildly. The wonder of her climax was like nothing he'd experienced. So beautiful.

His movements gentled. When she finally stopped shuddering, he stopped. He looked at her, all flushed and rosy and replete, and smiled.

"And that's just the beginning," he murmured.

She reached for him and dragged him up to where she could give him a searing kiss. Finding her slick entrance, he thrust hard into her and buried his cock to the hilt. The feel of her surrounded him, cradling him in her heat. He tried to slow the rhythm of his hips, but the effort was far too great. He thrust and stroked and plunged into her, over and over again. At last he threw back his head on a triumphant cry and emptied himself inside her.

He collapsed against her, exhausted and then slowly rolled to his side. Gathering her close against him, he fell asleep.

"What the hell?"

Callum came awake instantly and stared at Joel's amused visage. Scrambling to cover himself and Grace, he sat up in bed. "What are you doing here?"

"What the hell do you mean? I live here."

"But you're supposed to be in France, or Italy or… wherever," Callum spluttered. He glanced across at Grace who was thankfully still asleep. Easing himself out of the bed, he strode buck-naked from the room. Joel followed him, chuckling.

"Wow! I never thought I'd see the day when my brother, the priest-in-waiting was lying naked in bed with a woman."

Callum's face flamed. He found his pants in the living room and hurriedly pulled them on. He scowled at Joel. "I thought you were coming back next week?"

"I caught an earlier flight. I decided I'd had enough of gallivanting around Europe. There's only so many beautiful, bikini-clad women you can take." He winked at Callum. "Right, bro?"

Callum groaned.

Joel held his hands up in a sign of surrender. "Hey! What do you want me to say? When I left, you were headed for the priesthood. Now you're having sex with some woman. And what the hell is a puppy doing in my laundry room? I can't keep up."

Callum's scowl deepened. "She's not *some* woman. She's Grace. My Grace. And the pup belongs to her."

Joel's eyebrows rose. "*Your* Grace?"

"Yes. We're getting married."

Joel laughed. "Whoa! This is way too much for my jetlagged brain to handle." He looked at Callum and shook his head. "I've only been gone three months. What the hell happened?"

As quickly as it had surfaced, Callum's irritation faded. He gave Joel a sheepish smile. "I fell in love."

Once again, Joel shook his head. "Wow."

Callum grinned. "Yeah. It is kind of wow."

"Okay, you'd better fill me in."

"It's a long story."

"In that case, I might need to get a drink. Got any beer?"

"In the fridge where you left it."

Joel walked around the kitchen counter and opened the door to the fridge. He pulled out a beer and offered it to Callum.

In deference to Grace, he'd given up drinking. He hadn't told her yet. "No, thanks. I'm good."

"Suit yourself." Joel cracked the tab on the can and took a healthy swallow. "Ah, that tastes good. Nothing like a local brew."

"So you didn't like the beer in Europe?"

Joel grinned. "I didn't say I didn't like it. I sampled enough of it just to make sure. But there's nothing like coming back to something familiar. Like sleeping in your own bed." He paused and then added, "Oh, that's right. My bed's currently occupied by my brother's fiancé."

A fresh wave of embarrassment swept across Callum's face. Joel merely laughed.

"I'm only kidding, mate. I'm glad you treated this place as your own. That's what I wanted you to do. Now, pull up a chair and tell me what I missed."

Grace woke to the sound of male voices. For a moment, she didn't know where she was. Night had fallen and lights from the many boats that dotted Sydney Harbour twinkled like fireflies on the water. The room was dark. The space beside her was empty.

Gathering the sheet around her, she padded down the hall. From her vantage point, she spied Callum standing out on the balcony talking to a man who looked enough like him that he had to be his brother.

In a sudden panic, she froze. She was naked beneath the sheet. In another man's apartment. Her clothes were miles out of reach. She could see the edge of her bra on the floor of the living room.

Oh, dear God…

A wave of embarrassment washed over her. The men's conversation continued. She wondered how long they'd been out there. They hadn't yet noticed her. Perhaps she could sneak out and Callum's visitor would never know she'd been there…

But what about her clothes? She couldn't leave there naked. And her handbag. It was on the couch by the window. Another surge of panic went through her.

What am I going to do?

And then the decision was taken out of her hands when Callum looked up and saw her. He smiled. She lifted her hand and smiled weakly. And then he pushed open the glass sliding door and came toward her.

"Grace. You're awake." Framing her face between his palms, he kissed her softly on the mouth.

Keenly aware of their visitor who stood on the other side of the sliding glass door, Grace blushed. "Um…Callum. Could I…talk to you for a minute?"

"Sure." He remained standing where he was.

She gestured with her head toward the bedroom, becoming increasingly panicked. "In *there*."

Understanding dawned on his face. "Oh, of course."

She turned on her heel and padded as quickly as she could back to where she'd come. Callum walked into the bedroom behind her and pulled the door closed.

"That's my brother, Joel. He's home early from Europe."

Grace grimaced, still holding the sheet against her like a suit of armor. "Yes. I gathered. See, the thing is, I'm naked beneath this sheet. My clothes are *out there*. Where *he* is."

"No problem," Callum said easily. "I'll go and get them for you."

She relaxed the tiniest bit. "Great. Does he… Does he know I'm here?"

Callum grinned. "Of course he does. The bra and panties, skirt and blouse spread all over his living room were kind of a giveaway. It was only the puppy that confused him." He winked at her.

Embarrassment flamed across her face. She punched him lightly on the arm, outraged. "How can you be enjoying this? That's your brother! He knows nothing about me! What's he going to think?"

"It doesn't matter what he thinks. Besides, I already told him all about you. He knows you're the love of my life and that I'm the luckiest guy in the world that you feel the same. He knows about Seth and Alyssa and the soup kitchen and the puppy. He's cool with everything."

"Wow," she murmured. Some of her discomfort at the situation faded. She let him draw her into the circle of his arms.

"I'm dying to introduce you. Are you okay with that?"

She sighed. "I guess so. I'm going to have to meet him at some stage. It might as well be now."

Callum grinned and pressed a quick kiss to her lips. "Have I told you lately how much I love you?"

She melted against him. "I love you, too." She kissed him back. "Now, scoot out there and bring me my clothes. There's no way I'm meeting your brother wearing only a bedsheet."

Note to Readers

I do hope you have enjoyed reading Callum and Grace's story. If you've enjoyed this book, I would really appreciate it if you could leave a review at Goodreads and your favorite digital retailer. Every review increases visibility and helps other readers to find books they enjoy.

Receive a free book when you sign up for my newsletter if you like to receive news on upcoming stories, release dates, book launches and other snippets. I love to receive feedback from my readers. Please feel free to contact me at chris@christaylorauthor.com.au.

Joel is the next book in the Craigdon Family Dynasty series.

Keep reading for a sneak peek at Joel:

Chapter One

The throbbing tempo of the music was so loud in the densely populated nightclub it reverberated off Joel Craigdon's chest and hurt his ears, but he didn't mind. After the past week he'd endured, the pounding beat from the state of the art speakers in Sydney's illustrious Ivy Bar was a welcome distraction. He'd barely been home a week from his three-month European vacation, courtesy of a ten million dollar inheritance, but as far as work went, it felt like he'd never left.

Already he was knee-deep in a fraud investigation that involved a high profile company that also happened to be his late father's fiercest competitor. When it came to business, McClintock Property had a reputation for being ruthless. It seemed someone in their ranks also had a penchant for theft. As a senior detective with the New South Wales fraud squad, Joel had been given the job of determining who was behind the large scale transactions that were leaving McClintock accounts and heading offshore.

But it was Friday night in the city and he was hell bent on doing his best to forget about work for a few hours and have a good time. Already he had a buzz on. The drinks had been flowing freely between him and his mates. They were all work colleagues and were there by tacit agreement to let their hair down.

"Wanna another beer, James?" Joel shouted above the din. He lifted his empty glass toward Detective James Shepherd who'd been canoodling drunkenly with his wife. Sally-Ann looked at Joel and smiled.

"I think my husband's had enough," she replied.

James pulled a face, but then broke out into a grin. He pulled his wife close and planted a kiss on her mouth. "I think she's right." James winked at Joel. "We're going to get out of here." With that, James took Sally-Ann by the hand.

"Nice beard, by the way," Sally-Ann murmured as she passed him. "It suits you. Very European. Very chic."

Her husband merely rolled his eyes and turned away. With Sally-Ann in tow, James pushed his way through the crowd, headed for the exit.

Joel looked after them, feeling wistful. James was blissfully married to the woman of his dreams. Sally-Ann was part-Chinese/part Australian and was one of the up and coming lawyers at the reputable law firm, Sydney Legal. Joel had been working with James in homicide when he and Sally-Ann met and fell in love. Joel had never seen his friend looking so happy. Too bad Joel hadn't found the same thing with MJ. They'd sure tried hard enough to make it happen.

Joel grimaced. It was Friday night and The Ivy was going off. Determined to shake off his doldrums and the not-so-happy memories of his ex, he gazed around the club. Beautiful twenty-somethings, both guys and girls, were dancing to the throb of the music. Eyes closed, arms in the air, a press of bodies, heated flesh. Others were gathered near the bar. Conversation and laughter rang out over the din of the music. The general vibe was electric and tinged with a hint of desperation. It was as if the partygoers were determined to have the best time of their life...or collapse from trying in a sweaty, drunken heap.

Determine to recapture his party mood, Joel shouldered his way back to the bar and deposited his empty glass on the counter. Catching the eye of the good looking barman, he ordered another. With his arm casually propped against the bar, he turned to survey the crowd.

There were a rowdy group of young women screaming the words to the song being played by the DJ. One of the group wore a white veil. *A bachelorette party…* A bit further over were a couple with their tongues down each other's throat, pressed together, hips gyrating, as if oblivious to the fact they were in public. Or perhaps they just didn't care…

Joel's gaze drifted toward the place where tables and chairs were set up for those patrons who didn't wish to stand. His gaze landed on a stunning blond. She sat at a table of dark-suited men. Their ties had been loosened, top buttons undone, and much laughter was being shared. The blond smiled occasionally, but it was clear she wasn't absorbed in the conversation. Joel wondered which of the men she was with.

She sat closest to a man about Joel's age who looked like he could have just come from the set of a fashion shoot. It was late on a Friday night and the man didn't have a hair out of place. He looked vaguely familiar, but the beers Joel had consumed over the past few hours befuddled his mind and made it impossible to place him.

As if becoming aware of his scrutiny, the blond looked up and saw him. Their gazes locked. It was like something out of a sappy movie. Joel's heart pounded. His body instinctively hardened. She had the bluest eyes he'd ever seen. On top of that, she was gorgeous. Her long hair fell in waves over one shoulder. Her lips were full and red. The beguiling almond shape of her eyes had been emphasized with black eyeliner. The thick lashes were dark with mascara. And then she lifted a single arched eyebrow in silent query and he almost turned around to make sure there wasn't someone behind him…

Maintaining his cool, he calmly raised his glass in salute. Her eyes gleamed with amusement. She smiled, displaying perfect white teeth. She was every bit as glamorous as the man she sat beside. And then he bent his head and said something to her. She put her hand on his arm and nodded. The gesture was casual, familiar.

Jealousy stabbed Joel in the gut. He turned back toward the bar and drowned his disappointment in another drink. He might be known as a playboy among his circle of friends, but he drew the line at moving in on another man's woman.

Sheridan McClintock plastered a smile on her face and pretended she was enjoying herself. The conversation around the table had turned to football and she could barely suppress a groan. What is it about seemingly intelligent men who could almost come to fisticuffs over who would win the premiership? Watching football bored her to tears. It was even worse being forced to sit around with her brother and his mates and listen to the pros and cons of each team, the players who were injured and out for the season, others who were on report… Who cared?

Zane glanced at her. Bending close so she could hear him, he asked, "Having fun?"

It was all Sheridan could do not to roll her eyes. It wasn't her brother's fault. Zane had only been trying to cheer her up. After dumping her cheating boyfriend six months earlier, it seemed she still hadn't regained her former spirit. Zane was concerned for her. He urged her to go out, have fun.

"You're only twenty-seven, Sheridan. Hardly ancient. You're better off without that dickhead, anyway. I couldn't stand him from the start."

"His name is Neil and he wasn't always a dickhead," she protested. "And you didn't think so, either. After all, you were the one who hired him. We would never have crossed paths if you hadn't."

Zane growled. "So it's my fault, is it? I didn't tell you to fall in love with him. Now the asshole's broken your heart."

Sheridan compressed her lips and sighed. At the time she'd discovered Neil cheating she'd been furious and upset, but now she'd had time to come to terms with the demise of her relationship, she wasn't at all sure he'd broken her heart.

"Come out with me and the guys," Zane had urged. "We're going to the Ivy. Come and have some fun."

And so she'd pulled on a slinky black designer dress and matching black high heels. She'd carefully applied her makeup and put the straightener through her hair. To her annoyance, it still held a bit of a wave, but it was the best she could do. At least it wasn't curly, like it usually was.

She'd left for one of Sydney's most popular nightspots feeling good, determined to enjoy herself. And for awhile, she had. She'd known her brothers friends for a long time. They knew each other so well, they were almost family. A steady stream of drinks had flowed along with the laughter, but now the conversation had turned to football.

Feeling eyes upon her, Sheridan looked up toward the bar. Her gaze locked on the sexiest guy she'd ever seen. With hair so dark it was almost black and a neat black beard that caught the overhead lights, he seemed like something out of a dream. *Or a fantasy…*

Her heart skipped a beat and then pounded like she'd just run a marathon. He stared at her, his clear blue eyes full of challenge. And then his gaze dipped lower, over her breasts and lower still before returning to her face. There wasn't much of her he could see from her position at the table, but what he had seen was now tingling with awareness. Shocked at her boldness, she tilted her head and looked straight back at him, raising a single eyebrow as if daring him to come over.

And then Zane leaned toward her once again, a slight frown marring his expression. "We can leave, if you like."

She rested her hand on his forearm, grateful for his concern. "No, don't be silly. I'm a big girl. You're not responsible for whether I have a good time. In fact, I might go and get a drink."

"I can do that," Zane offered. "What would you like?"

"It's okay. I want to look over the cocktail menu. Have fun with the boys. Don't worry about me. I'll be fine."

With that, she scooted out of her chair. Collecting her evening bag, she slung it over her shoulder. Giving the men at her table a jaunty wave, she made her way over to where the handsome stranger now sat with his back to the room.

A whiff of expensive aftershave drifted toward her. All of a sudden, she was beset with a flurry of nerves. She'd never been the kind of girl who propositioned strangers. Hell, she'd never propositioned anyone, not even Neil. He'd pursued her for more than a year before she gave in and went out to dinner with him. They'd dated for three months before she slept with him.

And here she was, making plans in her head to flirt openly with a stranger.

What the hell am I thinking? Am I crazy? Maybe I should just turn and get out of here before he sees me…

And then he turned and smiled at her and all thoughts of leaving disappeared. He was even more good looking up close. His eyes were more cobalt than blue. His skin was tanned and healthy. His teeth gleamed white against the blackness of his beard. Her heart beat so fast she thought it might leap right out of her chest.

"Hi, I'm Joel," he said.

His voice was deep, confident, sexy. It matched his physical presence. He had an air of authority about him that was instantly appealing. So different from Neil who'd been almost groveling in his approach. In the beginning it had been flattering, but after awhile, it had become downright irritating.

The man in front of her didn't look like he'd grovel for anything.

She looked down at the hand he'd extended toward her and took it. "Sh-Sharon," she stammered, not at all sure why she'd chosen to give him a fake name.

His expression didn't reveal he had the slightest inkling of her deception. Instead, he said, "It's nice to meet you, Sharon. Can I buy you a drink?"

Recovering her aplomb, she took the empty seat beside him and pulled herself up to the bar.

"I'll have a vodka and tonic with a slice of lemon, please."

He smiled in acknowledgement. "One vodka and tonic with a slice of lemon it is," he murmured, his eyes alight with amusement. With that, he signaled the barman.

Sheridan watched the confident way he gave her order and then asked for another beer. He was a man used to taking control. She liked that. After being in a relationship with a man who always deferred to her, it was refreshing to spend time with someone who appeared confident in who he was and what he stood for.

"Are you sure your boyfriend won't mind you talking to me?"

The question was asked in a lazy tone, but Sheridan caught the watchfulness in his gaze. He must have seen her with Zane. She laughed and waved her hand, dismissing his concern.

"Oh, he's not my boyfriend. That's just my brother and his friends. He let me tag along." Realizing how pathetic that sounded, she pulled a face. "I'm sorry. I sound like a loser. A single, twenty-seven-year-old woman who has to rely on her brother for a date. Ugh!" And then realizing just how much she'd spilled about herself, embarrassment heated her cheeks.

"I-I'm sorry," she stammered. "I really should just shut my mouth. I mean, who tells a complete stranger something so personal? Jeez. I wouldn't blame you for eyeing off an escape route. In fact, the exit's right over there." She pointed through the crowd. "Quick, go while I'm not looking." She deliberately turned her back on him and silently wished the floor would open up and swallow her.

He threw back his head in a full-throated laugh. It was deep and rich and husky and sent shivers of desire pebbling across her skin. Her nipples puckered. When he reached out and gently turned her back around to face him, heat seared the bare skin of her upper arm where he'd touched her.

Ignoring her body's traitorous reaction, she kept her embarrassed gaze fixed on his shiny black boots. "Oh, great. Now you're laughing at me," she mumbled. "My humiliation is complete."

His laughter subsided. Out of the corner of her eye, she saw him reach out toward her. A long finger put gentle pressure on her chin and tilted her head up to face him. His cobalt eyes held lingering amusement, but it also held something else. Her breath caught as her brain registered what it was.

Desire.

She couldn't look away if she'd tried. Her heart thumped. Her mouth went dry. Her tongue darted out to wet her lips and his gaze zeroed in on her mouth. In fascination, she watched as his eyes darkened with emotion.

"God, you're erotic."

The words came out in a husky whisper. They wrapped around her, cocooning her in a sexual haze of attraction. She'd grown up knowing she was beautiful. Plenty of men had told her so. But no one had called her *erotic*. The very word was so…sexy. And so completely not her usual self.

Though she was pleased with the good genes she'd been blessed with, she'd never used her looks to get her way. It seemed so demeaning. Besides, she'd done nothing to achieve those good looks. She was far more interested in being judged on her wit and intelligence. Those she'd worked hard on.

But to have a man so gorgeous he could have stepped off a movie set calling her erotic... It was the sexiest thing she'd ever heard.

She made a slight movement toward him and her lips parted of their own volition. She heard his indrawn breath a moment before he kissed her. Shocked and excited by his forwardness, she took a few seconds to respond. He tasted of beer and spearmint toothpaste. It was an unusual combination... Exotic.

A voice in her head admonished her for being so easy, but another one, just as insistent urged her to take life by the hand. She was done with feeling despondent and discontent. It had been six months since she'd tossed Neil over. It was like Zane had said. It was time for her to let down her hair and have fun and Joel seemed like the perfect choice.

What could it hurt to have a night of passion with a stranger? It was the perfect way to get over a failed relationship. She'd never had a one night stand before, but plenty of people had. There was something about losing yourself in the arms of a stranger who found you so completely, desperately desirable...

With that thought in mind, she threw caution to the wind and relaxed into Joel's hard embrace. As one, they stood and came together. He pulled her in close. Her hands came up to rest on his shoulders. Thick muscles bunched beneath her fingers. He was tall and broad and muscular. In heels, she stood at six feet. He towered over her.

The kiss seemed to go on forever. They barely noticed when the bartender returned with their drinks. A few breathless moments later, Joel drew back from her slightly, his gaze dark and wild with need.

"Come home with me," he said, his voice husky and deep.

Sheridan nodded, once again shocked at her behavior. She glanced over to where Zane sat engrossed in conversation with his friends. She'd text him later and tell him she'd gone home. No need to bother him now.

Joel took her by the hand and they began wending their way through the crowd. As they neared the exit, Sheridan was filled with excitement and anticipation…and a sufficient degree of nerves.

They climbed into the back of a cab and after he gave the driver directions, he took her in his arms again. Instantly she was caught up in the heat of his kiss. Before she knew it, the cab had pulled over to the curb outside a block of inner city apartments.

"We're here," he said simply. Giving her another lingering kiss, he leaned forward and paid the fare.

Chapter Two

*J*oel's cock was so hard he was in physical pain. Though he'd sampled his fair share of the beautiful women while he'd gallivanted across Europe, it had been at least two or three weeks since he'd had sex. His balls were heavy and tight and with every flick of Sharon's tongue, he thought he'd shatter into pieces. And what an embarrassment that would be…

After indulging in another bout of heated petting in the elevator on the way up to his fifth-floor apartment, he fumbled with the key in the lock. They'd fallen into his apartment still wrapped in each other's arms. He couldn't believe she'd come home with him. She was obviously far more worldly than her passionate but rather inexpert kisses seemed to indicate. He wasn't sure what had cinched it for her, but from the moment she'd told him she was single, he'd wanted her for himself.

Not for forever, of course. Just like his ex-girlfriend, MJ had found out, he wasn't the marrying kind. But for right now, he burned for Sharon like he couldn't remember ever burning for a woman. And that's the very reason he needed to slow things down, give her a chance to change her mind. He might be rock-hard and desperate to be inside her, but he was still a gentleman.

Breaking off yet another scorching kiss, he pulled off his jacket and tossed it over the back of the couch. He loosened his tie and it soon went the same way. Sharon balanced her hand on the back of his couch and tugged off her stilettos.

"How the hell do you walk in those?" he quipped, grinning.

She shrugged, as if the idea of not being able to walk in them hadn't occurred to her.

"Would you like a drink?" he asked and went over to the bar he'd had installed within weeks of buying the place.

She nodded. He smiled. "Let me guess, a vodka and tonic with a slice of lime. Did I get that right?"

She grinned. "You have a good memory."

He poured her drink and collected a beer from the fridge and moved up close beside her. "I'm good at lots of things."

Her eyes flared wide and her lips parted on a silent intake of air. Blood thundered through his veins and once again centered in his groin. In an effort to distract himself, he handed her the glass.

She murmured her thanks and glanced down at it. Then that single eyebrow arched. "No lime?"

"Sorry." He shrugged, completely unapologetic. "I'm fresh out of lime."

She merely smiled and with her gaze still locked on his, brought the glass up to her mouth. He watched her sip and then swallow and all the time he wanted her. As if she was fully aware of the power she had over him, she lowered the glass and then with the tip of her tongue, she slowly traced the outline of her full lips.

Without taking his eyes off her, Joel set his beer down and then reached for her glass. He disposed of it in the same way he'd ridded himself of his drink. With heart thumping, he drew her toward him. His shirtfront brushed her dress and just like that, his control snapped and he pulled her in hard against him.

He fused his mouth to hers and the passion lying dormant immediately ignited again. She wrapped her arms around his neck and came up more fully against him. His cock throbbed. He cupped her ass and angled her hips so that she was flush against his erection. He swallowed her gasp.

In a flurry of movement, he tugged down her zipper and she stepped out of her dress. She reached for the buttons on his shirt and took way too long to release them. Impatient, he brushed her fingers aside and made short work of the task. His boots and pants and socks and underwear followed in quick succession.

He stood before her, naked and burning with need…and she was still in her underwear.

"You have too many clothes on," he muttered. "How about you let me help you with that."

She stood still, her gaze on his as he reached around and undid the clasp on her bra. The black lace dropped to the floor. And then she stepped out of the matching scrap of fabric that masqueraded as panties.

He took his time and looked his fill. Even without the heels, she was tall, with slender hips and thighs. But she was also curvy in the places that mattered. Unable to stand there a moment longer without touching her, with a muttered oath, he swung her into his arms and carried her down the hallway to his bedroom.

Sheridan's head spun with desire. Joel had been striking enough in his suit and tie. He was even more impressive naked. With his strong arms around her, he carried her effortlessly into his bedroom and deposited her on the biggest bed she'd ever seen. The curtains had yet to be drawn and she could see the twinkling lights of watercraft on the harbor. She didn't know who Joel was or what he did for a living, but it was obvious whatever it was paid well. And then he followed her down on the bed and the view was the last thing on her mind.

His body was hard and toned and muscular. They lay on their sides facing each other, exploring. Sheridan flicked his small nipples with her fingernails. They instantly tightened into hard little nubs. Her hand moved lower, scraping over the well-defined muscles that created a washboard across his stomach. Her finger dipped into the shallow indentation of his belly button and he sucked in a breath.

Not to be outdone, he lifted one of her breasts to his mouth and suckled. The exquisite sensations that rocked through her left her breathless. His erection was a heated, hard length pressing into her stomach. She squirmed against him, desperate for the feeling of him deep inside her. He lifted his head from her breast and captured her lips in another searing kiss. At the same time, he rolled with her until she was on her back.

Breaking off the kiss, he made his way back to her nipples and took each in turn in his hot mouth. She moaned and lifted her hips in silent, desperate need.

"Please," she urged.

But he was having none of it. Inching his way across her ribs he kissed he way over her stomach. At the same time, his hand delved into the heat between her legs. His finger stroked her slit before finding her opening and plunging inside.

"You're so wet," he murmured huskily.

She moved against his hand, urging him on. He slipped a second finger inside her and she gasped. He moved up to take her mouth in another sweltering kiss. All the time, his fingers worked their magic inside her.

"Please," she begged again, almost mindless with need.

His answering smile was lazy, unconcerned, but desire glittered like diamonds in the depths of his blue eyes.

"Please what?" he asked in that husky voice that was driving her even wilder.

"I want you… I want you inside me."

His fingers pressed even deeper into her moist heat. "Are you sure?"

"Yes!" She lifted her hips and ground herself against his hand.

He chuckled, but she saw the strain around his mouth. His erection remained a solid, warm brand against her belly.

"Do you want me to fuck you?"

His coarseness drew another shocked gasp. She'd never been spoken to like that. But her inner muscles tightened around his fingers as an arc of excitement flashed through her.

"Yes."

"Say the words," he demanded.

Embarrassment flamed across her cheeks. She could count the number of her sexual partners on one hand and none of them had treated her like this. His tongue flicked back and forth over her nipples. His fingers continued their relentless torment between her legs. Sheridan moaned and squirmed against him. She opened her eyes and stared at him. "I want you to fuck me," she said, shocking herself.

His expression filled with triumph, but it was quickly replaced by desire. The look he gave her was so hot she felt scorched. Quickly and efficiently, he reached into the bedside drawer and pulling out a condom, he sheathed himself. She watched in silent fascination. He was so comfortable with his body. There was no hesitation, no awkwardness. Just two consenting adults who wanted each other something fierce.

And then he was back between her thighs only this time his cock replaced his fingers. She felt him pressing against her entrance and a moment later, he plunged inside. They both groaned.

"Oh, fuck," he said on a sigh.

"Oh, my goodness!" She gasped at the feel of him inside her. He was so big. Too big. She felt herself stretching to accommodate him, filling her like no other had. And then he began moving, slowly at first, but as desire built inside her, he picked up his pace.

With her arms around his neck, she clung to him. As the need inside her grew more frantic, she dug her fingernails into his back. He pounded into her, his face a picture of tension and need. She closed her eyes and gave herself over to the incredible sensations he'd produced.

She climbed higher and higher, her breath coming fast. And then she was there, at the peak. She cried out on a gasp of ecstasy as she reached her climax. Moments later, he orgasmed on a shuddering sigh.

Their breathing was harsh in the silence. He rolled off her and lay on his back beside her, his hands stacked beneath his head. Suddenly shy, she reached for the bedsheet and tugged it up around them. He chuckled soflty, but didn't say anything, only turned on his side and drew her close. Within moments, he was asleep.

Sheridan eased herself out from under his arm and climbed out of the bed. Much as she'd like to spend the rest of the night in his arms, it would be foolhardy. She'd gone with him for a bit of fun, to lift her spirits and restore her self-esteem. There was nothing like being desired by an attractive man to soothe her battered ego. But that's all this was. A one night stand to help her get over her ex.

That was the reason she'd given him a fake name and given they lived in a city of nearly five million people, she needn't worry they might run into each other again. She'd had her fun. They'd had a great night, but this was where it ended. It was time to take stock of her life and get on with making the best of it.

As she eased out of Joel's bedroom, she sent one last wistful glance toward the bed. He slept with one arm thrown wide, his face relaxed in sleep. The sheet had slipped. Even asleep, he was gorgeous. She swallowed a sigh and left.

Joel woke with the sun pouring through the window. It beamed right onto his bed. He squinted against the brightness. He'd been too preoccupied with the gorgeous Sharon the evening before to bother with the curtains. Now as the sun burned a hole in his pupils, he covered his head with the pillow and groaned.

Of course, the bed beside him was empty which did nothing to improve his mood. He hadn't really expected to find her there in the morning. Neither of them had shared their phone number. They'd both been on the same page that this was a one night stand. Still, the sex had been amazing and he was willing to admit he'd ask her out if they ever ran into each other again.

Padding across the bedroom naked, he went into the bathroom. He caught a glimpse of himself in the mirror. The rumpled hair, the self-satisfied grin, the fingernail marks down his back…

He'd had a great time partying his way through Europe. With a ten-million-dollar inheritance courtesy of his father, the late Henry Craigdon, he'd managed to enjoy himself everywhere he went. There had been plenty of places to discover and to let down his hair and even more beautiful and willing women to help him celebrate. Even the memory of his difficult break-up with Mary-Jane Packham hadn't been able to dampen his mood.

Padding down the hallway, he smiled ruefully at the clothing that lay scattered across the floor of his living room. Of course, Sharon's clothes were no longer there. The little black dress that had fit her like a glove and the lacy black underwear… He grew hard at the thought of how he'd helped her out of her dress, sliding down the zipper, cupping her firm ass… What came afterwards still blew his mind.

Maybe it was best they hadn't exchanged numbers. In his experience, women lost some of their appeal over time. What had once been sexy soon became commonplace. In those early days of a new relationship, they were tearing each other's clothes off every second they could get, but a year or two down the track and it was a different story altogether. He and MJ were the perfect example.

He glanced at the pale mint green sofa that took pride of place before the huge wall of glass that overlooked the harbor. It had been MJ's favorite place to curl up in front of the TV. In the early days, they'd snuggled together and often ended up making love on the plush white rug. But looking back, it didn't seem all that long before the shine began to wear off.

Right from the beginning, MJ was angling for a ring and Joel had been just as adamant he wasn't interested in that kind of commitment. She persisted, somehow convincing herself that he'd change his mind. Five years on and right after the death of his father, they'd had an almighty row that had ended things for good. It was one of the reasons he'd hightailed it to Europe for three months. Joel could still hear the argument echoing off the walls of his living room.

"But we've been together for years! I've given you the best years of my life! We were going to get married!" MJ cried when he told her it was over.

He sighed wearily and shook his head. "No, MJ. We were never going to get married."

And then she got nasty. "Now you've inherited millions, you don't have time for me. What, you think you're too good for me anymore?"

He fought off a wave of irritation that she thought he could be so shallow. He did his best to reassure her. "No, MJ. Nothing like that."

"Bullshit. I don't believe you. I was good enough for you when you were a cop with a generous trust fund, but now you're a millionaire, I've been given the flick. You asshole! You promised me marriage!"

He bit his lip against a surge of impatience. "Now who's talking bullshit? We were never going to get married. Not now. Not ever. It has nothing to do with the money. You can't deny we fought more than we loved. I can't live my life like that. I told you. We're done. I want you to move your stuff out and don't call me again."

MJ's face filled with anger. There was a brittleness about her that shocked him. He couldn't believe he'd once found her beautiful. On the way out the door, she glared at him. "You're going to regret this, Joel Craigdon. You mark my words."

He'd been relieved she'd left without causing any damage to his apartment. He wouldn't have put it against her to throw stuff around the room and Joel had some nice stuff to destroy. He'd been fortunate to be the recipient of a generous trust fund set up by his mother and given to him when he'd turned eighteen. He'd spent the bulk of it buying the ritzy inner city apartment, but along with his detective pay, there was still enough to allow him to live a comfortable life.

And now there was an extra ten million dollars to add to his bank balance...

Though he'd mourned the loss of his father, Joel hadn't been as close to Henry as some of his children. Joel and Henry had locked horns early on Joel's career choice. Joel couldn't understand his father's opposition. After all, Joel's oldest brother, Jett had gone into policing.

But for some reason, Henry had other plans for his third son. Just like Henry had planned that his second son enter the priesthood, so Joel was meant to become a lawyer. In an effort to pacify his father, Joel had applied for and been accepted into law at Sydney University, but after a year of law school, he knew it wasn't for him. He'd braved his father's anger and had told him he was quitting. He'd already been accepted into the police force.

The row that erupted was savage in its intensity, but Joel wouldn't be deterred. He'd graduated the police academy with honors. He'd never once regretted his career choice. In fact, one of the reasons he'd decided to return to Australia after spending three months gallivanting around Europe was because he missed his job. He also missed his family and friends, but it was his work as a detective in the fraud squad that kept his adrenaline pumping.

He never knew what kind of investigation he'd be hit with next. He'd been instrumental in the convictions of several high profile criminals for money laundering. Drug money that ran into the millions. It seemed like there was an endless supply and the criminals were forced to come up with more and more creative ways of hiding it.

Fortunately for the police, there were still plenty of people willing to tip them off. Some of them were from anonymous sources. Others came from registered police informants. Of course, the informants always wanted something in return, be it a lighter sentence, an early release or preferential treatment. Occasionally an informant came from inside a competing drug ring, the only motivation being something as simple as revenge.

However it happened, Joel didn't care. What he did care about was making good on the information and locking up felons who carried on such illegal behavior. And it wasn't always the stereotypical criminal. Occasionally Joel was tipped off to some white collar crime that involved large sums of money. Like the case he was working on right now.

McClintock Property wasn't the usual kind of suspect on his radar, but right now it looked like someone inside the company was siphoning off large amounts of cash to an offshore account and none of it had been reported to the proper authorities. According to the anonymous tip they'd received, more than half a billion dollars had been transferred over the past three months.

He thought of his half-brother, Christopher Barrington. As head of contracts for McClintock Property, Christopher was in a position of trust. He was also disgruntled about being left out of their father's will. While some of the Craigdon siblings had inherited millions, Christopher had inherited nothing. He wasn't happy about it. In fact, upon Joel's return to Sydney, his older brother Callum had told him Christopher had filed a lawsuit against the estate. He was suing for more than a hundred million dollars.

Though Joel had some sympathy for the treatment his half-brother had suffered at the hands of their late father, he wished Christopher had first approached the family in an effort to settle the matter amicably before rushing off to the courts, but apparently that wasn't to be the case.

Joel couldn't help but wonder if Christopher was behind the large offshore transactions. Perhaps he was stockpiling his own inheritance…

Right now, all Joel had was a tipoff that the money was leaving the country. With the identity of the tipster unknown, he had no idea if the information was reliable or whether it was even true, but come Monday, he'd serve the CEO with a search warrant for access to the company's bank accounts and then the fun would begin…

JOEL is available for preorder at all of the digital retailers. It will be released on 27 September, 2020.

About the Author

Chris Taylor grew up on a farm in north-west New South Wales, Australia. She always had a thirst for stories and recalls writing her first book at the ripe old age of eight. Always a lover of romance and happily-ever-afters, a career in criminal law sparked her interest in intrigue and suspense. For Chris to be able to combine romance with suspense in her books is a dream come true.

Chris is married to Linden and is the mother of five children. If not behind her computer, you can find her doing the school run, taxiing children to swimming lessons, football, ballet and cricket. In her spare time, Chris loves to read her favorite authors who include Richard North Patterson, Sandra Brown, Kathleen E Woodiwiss and Jude Devereaux.

You can find out more about Chris and sign up for her newsletter at her website:

http://www.christaylorauthor.com.au

9 781925 119749